HUNTED

Also by K.F. Breene

Skyline Series (Contemporary Romance)

Building Trouble, Book 1

Uneven Foundation, Book 2

Solid Ground, Book 3

Jessica Brodie Diaries (Contemporary Romance)

Back in the Saddle, Book 1 – FREE

Hanging On, Book 2

A Wild Ride, Book 3

Growing Pains (Contemporary Romance)

Lost and Found, Book 1 – FREE

Overcoming Fear, Book 2

Butterflies in Honey, Book 3

Darkness Series (Paranormal Romance)

Into the Darkness, Novella 1 – FREE

Braving the Elements, Novella 2

On a Razor's Edge, Novella 3

Demons, Novella 4

The Council, Novella 5

Shadow Watcher, Novella 6

Jonas, Novella 7

Charles, Novella 8

Warrior Chronicles (Fantasy)

Chosen, Book 1

Hunted, Book 2

Shadow Lands, Book 3

HUNTED

BY K.F. BREENE

Contact info:
www.kfbreene.com
Facebook: www.facebook.com/authorKF
Twitter: @KFBreene

CHAPTER 1

FROM HIGH ON THE HILLSIDE Shanti surveyed what lay below. The sun had started to sink toward the horizon. The cool, soft breeze brushed her face as she lingered within the leafy trees. A valley bathed in soft, yellow sunshine stretched out below her. Shimmering grasses surrounded an encampment densely populated with tents and dotted with people.

The organization of the camp suggested this was one of the many planning headquarters cropping up all over the land. Information came and went, allowing the best and brightest to soak it up, consider it, plan the next steps, and then send out orders to the many smaller satellite camps. Seeing one of these camps this far east meant the Graygual were moving at alarming speeds. Xandre had an agenda, and Shanti bet his focus was on the man proclaiming himself the Chosen, a title her people had tried to give to her.

The only true Chosen would come out of the trials in the Shadow Lands, so it was possible neither of them had the right to the title that would command allegiance of the Shadow people, but Shanti had to admit that the scriptures had always said the Chosen would be a man, and this man would have a huge army. If she was honest with herself, he was better qualified for the role than she was.

So what did a girl do when things started unraveling around her? *Track down rumors, of course.*

After listening to a few drunken gossips in taverns, she'd tracked down the elusive Ghost; the man with light hair and eyes who haunted the Graygual's steps and picked off any stragglers. He was a phantom, a terror in the night, instilling fear in the lower tier of the Graygual army, and boosting hope in the oppressed townspeople. Often the word Ghost was uttered in the same sentence as the violet-eyed girl. They were both light of feature, both dangerous, and both unwilling to bow to the Being Supreme, Master Tyrant himself.

Shanti was almost positive the Ghost was actually her brother Rohnan, even though she had thought he died during the battle of her people to allow her to flee. There could be no one else, with a similar agenda to her own; not with features that came mostly from the northwest coastal area.

And only a fool would follow around after the Graygual. A fool, or someone with nothing left to lose.

Now that fool had been caught and imprisoned within the camp below.

"How does he get himself into these things? He evades for months only to finally get caught out in the open?" she whispered to herself.

The rumor was that the Ghost had wandered out into the open one day, hands out in front of him, asking to be captured.

"Why allow them to take you, Rohnan? What did you have planned?"

It was disconcerting when she asked questions that no one answered. That way lay madness. And yet, still she talked to the air. Things weren't looking good.

She glanced at the sun already halfway between midday and the horizon. She had some time before nightfall, when she would venture down into the camp and scout things out.

AS DAY BLED INTO DUSK, Shanti found herself on the edge of the Graygual camp crouched between a dirty wooden barrel and a canvas tent. The smell of horse wafted from a line of the tethered animals a few paces to her right. Murmured voices rumbled out of a tent across a walkway in front of her. The walls flickered with light, illuminating the shapes of three men bent over a table.

Shanti let her *Gift* cover the encampment like a light fog. Rohnan was being held no more than a little ways in front of her. He hadn't moved much all day and was exuding unconcerned patience. Six guards waited around his tent, all vigilant even though he was probably restrained.

Two more shapes ambled along the path in Shanti's direction. As they came into view, Shanti saw a man with his black uniform opened at the neck, exposing his hairy chest. His heavy arm draped across the shoulders of a woman with a pronounced bust. Her cleavage popped out of her gaping dress, with the sway of her hips and the unmistakable swagger of a whore who had found her mark.

Judging by the stagger of the man, and the lean on his ladylove, he'd had his fair share of alcohol. He would most likely be lowered into bed, fondled until he passed out, and then the woman would take his money and move on. This was great news. Shanti would be able to dart in, grab a uniform, and better disguise herself within the camp.

Shanti kept pace easily after they had passed, skirting between tents and hiding in the black shadows while the man made his way to his bed. Only once did the couple run into another person—a man in a crisp black uniform with the red circle etched across the breast slashed with three lines. A Graygual officer. He'd looked at the staggering man with a hard eye and straight face, but except for the thinning of his lips, made no comment on the man's drunken state. He didn't seem to notice the whore at all. She might as well have been invisible.

Shanti's intended choice of disguise changed instantly.

When the couple reached a small tent on the very edge of the encampment, Shanti crouched across in the shadows and waited. The woman led the man inside and then lit a candle. The flame flickered to life, the soft glow allowing Shanti to watch through the open flap of the tent as the whore begin the tedious labor of undressing him.

"Okay now, you get out of dem trousers, hmm?" the woman said in a husky voice loaded with a thick accent.

The man grunted then burped. He dug his hand into her top as she dropped his pants. A loud, wet fart ripped through the tent.

The woman rolled her eyes as her hand found his mostly limp manhood. Ignoring his fumbling hands, she worked him for a while, staring away from him with professional patience. "You go get to bed, hmm?" she purred.

"Mmmrr maa nuun." The man burped again and swayed on legs made of jelly. He nodded in an exaggerated way, his eyes drooping so low he looked asleep on his feet, before lunging toward his cot on the far side. Unfortunately, he misjudged the position of the small table in the middle of the space. His foot caught the table leg, throwing off his already impeded balance. Numbed hands groped for a brace that wasn't there before the man toppled over. He fell directly onto his face. Another fart flapped into the room.

"Oopsie," the woman said as she adjusted her top. She made no move to help him.

Acting quickly, Shanti tore off her hooded cloak, untucked her shirt, and ripped open her top until her breasts were mostly exposed. She stepped into the tent. "Can I help?"

The woman glanced up with a scowl. Hands on her hips, she turned toward Shanti with a haughty expression. She was twice her size in the waist, and three times her size in the bust.

"He be mine, honey." The woman raised her chin. She didn't bother to look behind her at the man struggling to pick himself off the ground.

"Yes, of course. I just meant, can I help pick him up? He looks too big for you to navigate."

Painted black eyebrows settled low over eyelids shadowed in pink. "Navigate, huh? Fancy word. I not seen you around." The woman's shrewd gaze traveled over Shanti's clothes, paused for a moment on her bust, then rested on her hair. "That hair not be naturally black. Not with light eyebrows. What you put in it? Coal?"

Yes. She had. She'd never claimed to be great at disguises, but usually men were too stupid to notice when a hint of breast peeked out. Whores, however, were extremely observant it seemed.

"Look," Shanti said in a placating tone. "I'll help you set that mark to rights. You'll never get him on the cot by yourself—he's just about to pass out. If he doesn't think he got something from you, he'll come for his money, and you'll be punished."

The woman glanced at the man lying limply on the ground. Gravity had been too much for him in his drunken state. He'd given up trying to stand and decided to sleep where he lay.

She looked back at Shanti with her hands still on her hips. "What you get out of it?"

"I want to trade clothes." Shanti rubbed the fabric of her cloak and then that of her shirt. "This is fine material. It'll fetch a nice price."

"You no whore, girl. You not from around here, neither. Where you from? You sound like them." The woman jerked her head at the man on the ground.

"What does it matter? You're doing what you need to, and I'm doing what I need to."

The woman considered for a moment before snorting. "Guess it don't matter. We all want somethin', that be true. But I got work to do. Your clothes be fine, but these *shelnas* be rich. I wear your clothes, I can't work. I lose out."

Shanti dug out two gold pieces, more than this woman would make in three nights. She tossed them on the table. The coins bounced twice on the stained wood before rolling to a stop.

The woman's eyes rounded before her gaze resettled on Shanti. "You rich girl, huh? Look like a scrap, though. You stole that money, that's what I bet. Up to no good, too. Lucky for you, I been with some of these fools before—not the officers. No, the grunts. They a mean, nasty bunch. Used me up bad. I no forget." The woman nodded decisively as a fierce light came into her eye. "I no forget."

The woman sauntered the two steps to the table and snatched up the coins. She placed them in her mouth, one after the other, biting down to judge the quality of the gold. Satisfied, she tucked them deep into her bodice. "Help me get this here trash up 'n we trade clothes. Good thing you wearin' sacks for clothes, neh? Otherwise, this no work. Skinny thing, you are. Still might not work."

Without delay, Shanti helped hoist the loudly snoring man to his bed. The woman took a small jar out of her large skirt pocket and dribbled a thick liquid onto the man's phallus. To Shanti she said, "They no question when they wake up in they own mess. Don't even notice it not the same stuff."

Sounded reasonable.

The woman turned and put the jar on the table. Without preamble, she stripped out of her clothes and held them out to Shanti. Shanti did likewise and exchanged.

"Binding the breasts, eh? Look at that muscle, girl. Goodness me, you isn't skinny, no way. You toned." The woman stepped into the pants—not nearly as roomy on her—and turned serious eyes to Shanti. "You cut a throat with this group and they track you down easy. They not like regular Graygual." She spat on the ground after saying the name. "You gotta be sneaky, hmm? Bide your time."

Shanti stepped into the skirt and tied the fabric in a knot at her middle. She slipped the shirt over her head. It looked like a blanket.

"Here." The woman reached for Shanti.

Hands coming at her made alarm bells sing. Shanti *swept* the woman's hands to the side with her forearm before stepping forward. Her palms slapped down on the woman's cheeks, ready to crack her neck before her brain caught up with her movements.

Shanti froze, letting the situation soak in. Immediately embarrassed, and hoping she hadn't scared this woman out of her willingness, she ripped her hands away and stepped back.

"Apologies. I startle easily." Shanti spread her hands

to the sides. "Sorry. Please. Fix whatever you like."

"Auuhh*wee!*" A haphazard smile crossed the woman's face. Fear was completely absent in her eyes, replaced by a hopeful sparkle. "*Oshawn* heard my prayer! He sent you. Get in close, He said. I did. Good and close—here I am. And He sent you!"

The woman's smile dwindled as she fixed Shanti's binding to show more cleavage. "There be a lot of us. A lot of women been done wrong. Not by these officers—they pigs, but the normal sort of pigs. No, the grunts. Young girls, old women, young boys—it no matter. Women and children being escorted through towns now. Men watching their womenfolk when these pigs around. We be quiet, okay, but we be ready to do our part. We ready to pay our vengeance. We ready to fight back!"

"I don't—" Shanti shook her head as the, now familiar, helplessness overcame her. She'd seen this plight across the land. She'd seen the bodies, bent and twisted, left in the streets as bait for flies. The young gave her the worst nightmares but she had no way of helping anymore. No army, no title to get an army—she was just another lost soul looking to right a wrong. She couldn't help the fallen when she could barely help herself.

As if hearing all these thoughts, the woman's gaze intensified. "You doubt. That okay. We all have doubt. But *Oshawn* sent you—he has a purpose for you, just as he has for me. You meant to find me, girl. My waiting is over. I'll spread the word, and when you ready, we ready. My name be Tauneya. You ask for me by name. You ask for me, someone find me, no matter where you are, hear? I been all over. People know me."

"I'm not the one—"

"Shhh." The women cut Shanti off and pushed her toward the flap of the tent. "This group be organized. You won't get two nights. You get your job done tonight, while they all drunk, and you get out. Go to Horse 'n Pony in town. Ask for Claude. Say Esme sent you—you need the map. That's all you be sayin'. Esme sent you and you need the map. Take horses from here if you be able. Get your job done quick and get out. When they sober tomorrow, they be on your trail quick."

Shanti snatched a well-worn tunic and a pair of matching pants from the ground where they had been cast aside. The woman had retreated to the other side of the tent—probably to get her money off her mark.

Without waiting another moment, Shanti worked the black uniform around her middle to hide it. She then adjusted the skirt and tied it off again. She now looked a little plump without the bust size to match, but she was still a woman, and available for business, so it probably wouldn't matter to someone looking for a little fun.

Stepping onto the main path, she adopted a sensual swagger to advertise her trade. Rohnan was still as calm and patient as before, but now he was in a different location—further north than he had been before. Was he on the move?

"Hey, babeee," a man slurred as he swerved in front of her. With half-closed eyes he glanced down at her chest and licked his lips. "I gotta need fer you."

A chorus of laughter rang from a bunch of shapes sitting inside a tent in flickering candle light. The crack of cards filled in the moments of silence.

"Whadda'r say?" His eyes were half-hooded and liquid wet his front. He reached out to cup a breast.

After the briefest of glances to make sure they were alone, Shanti batted his hand away and gave him a solid punch to the stomach. The breath left the man in a loud *whoosh.* He slumped over and started coughing. She walked him to the side of the path and eased him down to the ground. If anyone found him, they'd think he had fallen down drunk.

A moment later, she was cutting through the tents and heading in the direction of Rohnan. He was walking, but not quickly. She stayed to the shadows as much as she could before returning to the main path. Once there, she slunk down and jutted out a hip, having to adjust her sword to keep it hidden within the loose folds of fabric.

Only a few paces later she turned a corner and saw him.

Shuffling toward her with his hands tied in front of him and his ankles tied together with an arm span of rope, Rohnan held his head high and directed his eyes straight ahead. Each movement in his body in harmony, as fluid as a dancer's, he showed assurance and confidence. Muscles played delicately across his exposed arms and bulged within his snug-fitting pants. To a fellow fighter, every line in his body screamed *lethal!*

She'd trained him herself, working him every day, to be the best of their people besides herself. And now he showed it, like a prized horse among donkeys, gliding along the enemy tents with that killer's grace. Rohnan didn't even like to fight—he'd always said it was a necessary evil to protect his family—but he was exceptional, just like all of her people.

Shanti blew out a soft breath, eyes focused and intense, watching the brother she'd thought she'd lost. She knew she could rush forward and kill his captors easily. They were watchful, but not ready for an attack. She'd take them unawares.

The problem was, her deed would be found out quickly, and the enemy would be on her trail within an hour. This was an officer camp; they were the elite. They might be complacent in many ways, but at the first sign of trouble, their camp would be enraged like a hornet's nest. She couldn't take the chance.

Instead, she waited as the progression moved closer. When Rohnan got within the range of his receptive *Gift*, his eyes widened. His gaze swung unerringly towards her. Relief and intense longing colored his mental path as moisture filled his eyes and joy lined his face. He'd missed her as much as she him.

Revealing that would get her imprisoned right beside him, the fool!

She glanced at his captors before letting the desire for violence fill her. She could tell that it took only a heartbeat for him to feel her intent with his *Gift* and remember where he was. His face smoothed over as a tear leaked from his eye. He swung his gaze forward before giving the slightest shake of his head. *Not now.*

They were thinking along the same lines. She'd have to wait.

She hated waiting.

Slinking back in frustration, she watched her sibling walk by. When they were twenty paces ahead, she stepped out of her hiding place and adopted the sensual gait of her assumed profession once more. The progression disappeared around a bend ahead. Without needing to speed up, she sashayed along the path after them.

As she stepped around the same bend, Rohnan's party was disappearing around another bend up the path. In their wake stood ten men in a loose group, chatting with solemn faces. Two had rolled up papers tucked in their arms. Maps, she'd bet. Each had crisp, black uniforms with red slashes across the red circle on the upper breast. Her heart started to beat wildly when she counted one man with eight slashes!

What in Death's playground is a Superior Officer doing here?

Shanti's legs filled with fire as cold trickled down her spine. The urge to run was so great she couldn't stop the rigidity from overcoming her body.

A Superior Officer was a rare and coveted position, one step away from Xandre's inner circle. There were only a handful in the whole of the land. He would be a master at weaponry of all kinds, a skilled tactician, an excellent leader of men, and held the power to direct an army of thousands. In order to advance to guarding Xandre himself, a coveted position that came with vast rewards, he'd need an act of extreme valor, or to deliver a prize of war.

And here she was. The one person Xandre sought above all others stood fifteen small paces away, within a camp of hundreds. She was a gold coin to a beggar, and she was practically offering herself for capture.

She could take someone in Xandre's inner-circle—she'd proved that on a chance meeting while heading east. But she couldn't take a Superior Officer supported by others, and if she used her *Gift*, the whole camp would be roused by the Inkna residing there.

Her gaze scanned the men around him, officers all, many with four or five slashes, one with six. They were Death's Huddle. More importantly, they would be her captors if she didn't play this encounter perfectly.

Forcing herself to breath evenly, she pulled her top open a little to make sure her cleavage was on full display. Without changing her pace, and trying not to wipe her sweat laden forehead, she sashayed closer with hip and breast and sweaty palms.

Shadows licked her feet and crawled up her side. The urge to drift into those shadows tugged at her. If she did that, though, someone would notice. She was sure that these men already knew of her presence. To disappear suddenly would not be in keeping in character as a whore, which would raise suspicion.

Focusing on her breathing, and remembering to swing her hips, she sauntered closer. It didn't take long for a few of the officers to glance up from the map, taking in the various elements that marked her profession, before just as quickly going back to what they were doing. Like the sober Graygual she'd seen earlier, they paid no attention to whores if they could help it.

Her small and silent sigh of relief was short-lived.

As she drew closer, the Superior Officer tilted his head up purposefully and looked right at her. His gaze did a quick sweep of her from head to toe, before honing in on her breasts. A small crease worked between his brows.

In that moment she knew—he wasn't looking at her cleavage, he was looking at the binding containing it.

A crawling sensation worked up her spine in warning.

Cayan's artisans had created that binding, working off of her instructions. Their styling had merged with hers, representing both lands; the land that birthed the violet-eyed girl, and the one who took down an Inkna settlement a few months ago. What's more, it was made from material worth more than the rest of her outfit combined, intended for strength, durability, and comfort.

Her binding was the only physical thing showing on her body that hinted that she might not be what she seemed. And he'd found it right away.

A trickle of sweat ran down her temple, and the need to prepare for battle hindered the swing of her hips, straightening her walk into something too predatory for a normal woman. Something else he would surely see.

Terror ran through her. Not knowing what else to do other than kill him with her *Gift* and alert the whole camp to her presence, she veered into the middle of the path and trailed her hand down her chest, boldly presenting herself to him. Her fingers worked down her stomach and over her hips, back to their exaggerated sway. She tried desperately for a sultry smile, but only conjured up a stiff grimace. It would have to do. Hopefully the amount of sex she was oozing would overshadow her features.

The Superior Officer's gaze flicked toward her hand. Then toward her hips. His lips thinned and his eyebrows settled low over his eyes. He glanced at the men around him, stiffening as he noticed more than one set of eyes taking his measure. Responding to their unspoken judgment, he shifted, showing Shanti his back as she passed.

She was sure his curiosity had been piqued; a riddle had been posed. Shanti knew it was just a matter of time before he pooled all the little items about her that were out of place, and figured out who he had sharing his camp. At the very least, he'd want to ask questions.

The sand was pouring through the hourglass.

Barely daring to breathe, she continued on, noticing the two men standing beyond the officers dressed all in black. *Sarshers*, what the Inkna called their *Gifted*, stood guard.

She slammed her shields home so they wouldn't detect her *Gift* as she took the turn Rohnan had taken earlier. Being in that camp was suicide, and she needed to get out. *Now!*

TWO HOURS LATER SHANTI FOUND herself impatiently crouching next to the tent of a loudly snoring man. Opposite her hiding place stood Rohnan's guarded tent. Two guards stood at the front, staring straight ahead with tired, hooded eyes. She had every reason to believe those in back were also dead on their feet.

Their walk earlier had proved to be nothing more than a visit to the waste trench so Rohnan could evacuate his bowels. There had been one moment, shortly after she found them, that Rohnan had his hands free, his pants up, and within easy reach of a guard's sword. Together, with minimal effort, she and Rohnan could've killed them all, stashed them in the distant bushes, and been on their way.

Rohnan had shaken his head again at her intent. *Not now.*

Shanti's jaw clenched where she crouched, stuffing down her anger at the memory.

What was he waiting for?

She wiped the moisture from her face as the damp air, heavy with fog, shifted around her. The chill soaked through her skin and settled in her bones, making her long for the cloak she'd given away. The moon had worked its way across the sky, taking its light with it. Snoring ripped through the stillness of the night from a dozen nearby tents.

Like a flash of color, Rohnan's brain went from calm patience to agitated fear and warning bells erupted deep within Shanti. Her adrenaline kicked in and her fight reflex became active. It was his signal, a way to communicate with her through her *Gift—time to move!*

She only hoped it wasn't too late.

CHAPTER 2

She ran at the first guard, grabbing the sides of his face and jerking his head to one side. A crack rent the night as his neck snapped. His body fell limp at her feet.

Two more steps and her kick hit the next guard square in his jaw. His eyes popped open wide in surprise, but he was already falling. She stabbed down with her sword, piercing his chest. His dying scream muffled into her palm.

She ducked into the tent where Rohnan held out his hands. She cut the bindings around his wrists and ankles before hiking up the roomy skirt and yanking a second knife out of her leg brace. She handed it to her brother along with the Graygual uniform she'd kept around her middle. Making sure he knew to put it on, she ran from the tent and around to the men at the back.

The first was staring idly ahead, oblivious to the fact that two of his comrades had already been taken down. The snoring around them, along with their desire for sleep had masked her exploits, as she had hoped.

With quick hands she sheathed her sword, grabbed another knife, and approached him from the side. She snatched a handful of hair with one hand and slit his throat with the other. His gurgle brought the other guard's attention around.

"What did you—"

She stabbed him in the eye before he could finish his sentence, then clamped a hand over his mouth as she rammed the knife into his heart. His muffled scream was louder, and lasted longer, than the others, but no one close enough was awake to hear it.

Shanti dragged him toward the mouth of the tent where Rohnan had already moved the two guards from the front inside. Rohnan circled around and grabbed the last guard. The drag marks would not give them away until daylight, and by then it wouldn't matter.

"Okay, let's go," Shanti whispered with her hand on Rohnan's arm. He was so warm. Alive. So, so alive.

His smile at her emotion was short-lived. "We must get one more person." Rohnan grabbed her hand and yanked her to the right.

She took two steps before tugging back. In a fierce whisper, she said, "Rohnan, they have a Supreme Officer here. We don't have time for this!"

Rohnan turned to her with a gust of urgency. "I didn't get caught by accident, Chosen. You must know that. I needed to get closer to learn more—to *listen*. And

I am positive we need this man. He is paramount to the cause."

"There is no cause, Rohnan. A true Chosen has come forward. We need backup and—"

A steel edge crept into Rohnan's voice as he said, "The Supreme Officer is here because he is guarding this man. One of the selected elite is guarding a seemingly ordinary old man. What does that tell you? I passed right by him. Right by him! And I couldn't get any sort of reading off him. I had no idea what might be going through his mind. I couldn't even tell if he was happy or sad; his expression was of no more help. There's something different about him. We must have him."

Shanti stared at Rohnan's angelic face for a single beat before she was in action. Anyone a Superior Officer wanted was someone Xandre wanted. Xandre would want those who would fuel his war effort in some way. She knew that person needed to be on her side, or dead. There was no middle ground. Not when dealing with someone as smart and cunning as Xandre, the man who titled himself the Being Supreme. He could turn even the most devoted enemy to his side with his lies and manipulations.

Rohnan led the way through the paths of the camp, staying to the dark places and slinking further into the shadows when they encountered a guard or random wanderer. As they approached a large tent faintly lit with a flickering glow, Rohnan slowed and stepped into a pool of black beside a tent across the way. He crouched and stared at the nearest guard, a *Sarsher*.

"There are four guards—two on the outside, and two sit within. Sometimes there is a *Sarsher* with him. Like now." Rohnan let a knee fall to the ground to better stabilize himself.

Shanti squatted next to him. "Why only one *Sarsher*, I wonder? And he doesn't have much power. Are the other *Sarshers* in the camp stronger?"

"Most, yes, but his *Sarsher* guards don't have a lot of power, no more than half your former power. It seems your power is greater now, though..."

"My power found a mate. Long story, though no longer as shocking after hearing about the Chosen coming forward. My power increases greatly when I use it in tandem with his, and only has a small boost when I'm away from him. I don't know why the extra strength remains if he's not nearby, but... it does."

"It's a succinct mating. Only a few can ever find such a mate..."

"I hope you learned that on your travels, instead of keeping information like that from me." Shanti shifted, readying a knife. "But, now's not the time. The guards look half-asleep. This should be easy enough."

"Agreed. But, whenever there is a man on your

mind, you become violent. I want a weapon before this conversation."

"There is no man on my mind," she said. "Are we ready?"

"Yes, Chosen."

"I'm not the Chosen. I'll take the one on the far side."

"Yes, Chosen."

Shanti had time to scoff before reality smacked her. "Will this prisoner resist us?"

"I have no idea. I guess we'll find out."

"Let me compliment you on your preparedness, Rohnan. It really is awe-inspiring." Shanti straightened and started forward with quick but light feet. Rohnan was behind her a moment later, his knife twirling in his fingers.

It took two full seconds for the guards to realize someone was attacking. By then, Shanti had her knife in a guard's neck and her hand clamped over his mouth. Rohnan was just as fluid, sliding the knife between the man's ribs deadening the sound just as effectively. Both bodies dropped to the ground in a lifeless slide.

Rohnan ducked into the tent first. Shadow cascaded over him, and then swallowed him up. Shanti stepped in right behind. She heard a grunt to the right where Rohnan was dispatching a guard, and *felt* the mind of another guard to her left. Before the guard could raise his hand or shout, Shanti's knife found a home in his neck. Blood splattered her face.

"Ugh," she grunted, wiping her arm across her face as she turned.

Even though it was the middle of the night, an older man sat on his bed in the corner of the tent. A high and gaping tear in the tent let the moonlight spill over the side of his curly hair and across a shoulder. His hands rested in his lap with fingers laced together.

Despite having just witnessed the violent death of two of his guards he sat with a straight back and placid expression. In contrast, his mind was spinning with emotions, each flitting by so fast Shanti couldn't pick up any of them. They weren't his real feelings—it was clearly some sort of mental defense.

"Come." Rohnan said in a common Southern Region language. He held out his hand to the man. *"We friend."*

"You're terrible with languages, Rohnan." She stepped to the side of the tent directly opposite the man. In a calm and soothing voice, using the same language Rohnan had, she said, *"We do not wish to hurt you. We are freeing you."*

"A cage with no bars is still a cage," the man responded in a sing-song voice. *"But you know of cages, do you not? This is a dangerous place, for violet eyes."*

"How does he know that—he couldn't see it in this

light?" she asked Rohnan. Her stomach fluttered in unease.

"I don't know, Chosen, unless he assumes it. He's seen me in the camp—even in the moonlight he can see you're fair like me. It's not such a leap."

Yes, it was. But they didn't have time to discuss it. *"We need to leave,"* she said to the man.

The man brushed off his pants and stood. *"Then, please, let's change cages."*

"Well, at least he's being a good sport about it," Shanti muttered to Rohnan.

With her mind open, Shanti jogged to the mouth of the tent and peered out. Shadows loomed along empty, dirt paths. Canvas tents lined the way, quiet and still. The silence of the night was only interrupted by the lonely sound of a cricket hoping for a response.

"Let's go." She glanced back at the man. *"Can you ride bareback?"*

"We shall see," the man answered with a laugh in his voice.

That must be a "no". Lovely.

The dense equine minds waited both to the far east of the camp and to the north. She had every belief they were all excellent specimens and guessed most would be lenient with their riders. With half as many horses as riders, many were probably used for wagons carrying men and supplies. Prickly war horses only accustomed to one rider would be reserved for a select few. She hoped those were on the farther side of the compound.

Shanti pushed their pace as fast as she dared, knowing the older man wouldn't be able to keep up if she strode out too fast. He didn't need to be watched or coaxed, though; he seemed perfectly content to switch cages, as he said, but Shanti worried that he didn't question their motives. He was much too placid for Shanti's peace of mind.

"I've only seen him like this," Rohnan said in a whisper in their shared language as they neared the horses.

"Your *Gift* is like a shock to the system, Rohnan. I'd forgotten you could very nearly read minds." Shanti slowed as they neared the long, horizontal board around which the horses were tethered. Many slept, but some gazed at them with docile, unassuming eyes.

Ignoring her, Rohnan continued with, "I caught the tail-end of a whipping, once. It was only three hard slashes, but afterward, when they led him away, he smiled at me and winked. I could see the pain still in his eyes, but he seemed completely unconcerned."

"Does he understand us?"

The man stared at the far horse with an interested expression while he puffed wisps of white, out of breath.

Rohnan minutely shook his head. "I don't think so. The Graygual language is similar to ours but he never seemed to understand what they said. He took beatings for it before they realized."

"Berate first, get more information after. That's always the Graygual way when dealing with prisoners." Shanti began untying all the animals. "They didn't treat him softly, huh? He's a prize, but not a coveted prize?"

"No, he is coveted. This was before the Superior Officer arrived. Since then, he hasn't been physically harmed."

"You were in the camp all that time?"

"Not as a prisoner. I could come and go as I pleased before the Superior Officer and his team arrived. After that, it became harder to get around unnoticed. I don't have breasts."

"I don't either, but I do have the *suggestion* of breasts. Apparently that's enough for most men." Shanti hesitated near the last three horses. She glanced at the older man. *"Pick your ride."*

The man's eyes crinkled as he pointed to the farthest horse. *"He is here for me."*

Shanti quirked an eyebrow at Rohnan. That was a strange thing to say. She really hoped the man didn't have a touch of madness—she didn't need any more hindrances on the next leg of their journey.

"What about the horses on the other side?" Rohnan asked as he chose the highest mount.

"We'll have to run by and cut their leads," Shanti

answered. "I give it another few hours before this whole place is alive—the Superior Officer will have my riddle solved by then. Speed is everything."

Shanti took the last of the three horses. It seemed a little thinner than Rohnan's, just as shiny, and a touch impatient—it stomped at her as she approached. She stepped closer and reached for its bridle. The animal gave a sound that was so like a growl she had to look closer to make sure it was actually a horse. Her hand kept reaching until its head dipped down. Its teeth chomped at her shoulder, snatching fabric and giving her a nip.

Reacting, Shanti punched it in the face. Its head jerked back. It stomped again.

"This one is playing with fire," Shanti said in a fit of stubbornness. She threw a finger in the horse's face. "Try to bite me again, and I will castrate you. What do you think about that?"

"C'mon, Chosen, just choose a different mount. No sense bullying an animal," Rohnan prompted.

Shanti wasn't good with horses—they'd probably all react this way.

She grabbed the bridle with a firm hand and yanked it toward her. She stepped to its side, watching the animal dubiously for another bite. That strange equine-growl sounded again and the older man started to giggle.

"Great, a madman and a bastard of a horse," Shanti mumbled as the horse tried to dance away. "Hold still, you bloody bastard. I'm getting you out of here."

"Fear begets fear. Horsey, horsey, clomp, clomp, clomp." The older man smiled up at the sky.

"You've saddled us with a crazy captive, Rohnan. And that's the only thing we've got saddled. How am I going to stay on this dumb animal?" Shanti gritted her teeth and ran at the horse's side. It gave a disgruntled neigh as she jumped and climbed up onto its back.

"He's not crazy—I think he just acts like it to escape notice. He was always smiling at the sky in the camp. The first time he glimpsed me hiding, I expected him to sound an alarm or plead to be rescued, but he just smiled up at the sky. He's important to all of this, I can feel it." Rohnan walked his horse forward. The man followed.

Shanti's horse pranced in the opposite direction, completely ignoring her tug on its bridle. "He's right, though. Blasted horse! Go *forward!* If we ride around the camp, we're bound to draw notice by the sound of the hoofs. The lighter sleepers will hear it, and probably at least one of the guards will notice. There aren't many guards—obviously this camp has few fears—but there is one between here and the other horses."

"I'll go." Rohnan's horse pranced in place, waiting for Shanti, anxious to get going but still in perfect control.

Shanti's horse was still going sideways. Randomly. "Probably wise. I'll give their minds a shock when they're all free."

Rohnan came forward and reached. Shanti held out her sword as she spread out her mind throughout the camp. Only one *Sarsher* was awake, but he seemed… occupied. He must've found comfort for hire. He wouldn't notice her subtle mental working.

After the sword was passed over, Rohnan left, trotting his horse perfectly. His balance and ease on his animal, even sitting bareback, made it look like he'd been doing this all his life even though it must've been a more recently acquired skill. They hadn't ridden horses in their village; they'd been too expensive, and not needed.

Rohnan had always been a fast learner, though. There was very little he couldn't learn and master in a short time. Shanti had always thought she was the same, but the bloody animal beneath her was making a mockery of that idea.

"Okay, we'll head in the direction of the closest town." Shanti said to the man. She kicked the sides of her horse. It pawed at the ground, not moving.

"A leader is one who knows the way, goes the way, and shows the way." The man leaned forward slightly. His horse started trotting north. Her horse moved with

it, still ignoring her but apparently content to be heading out in company.

When they reached a small but well-traversed trail, they slowed to allow the horses to find their footing. She felt a blast of elation radiating from Rohnan. She grabbed the horses' minds around the camp and *wrenched.* A couple of horses screamed and the sound of hooves thundered in the distance.

"That is definitely going to wake someone," Shanti said as a new urgency filled her.

Rohnan was soon with them, pushing his horse as fast as he dared in the dark on the rough terrain. "I've set the horses loose before," he said. "It took the Graygual a while to properly investigate, and longer to collect them. They were in no real hurry."

"Was that before or after the Superior Officer settled in?"

"Before. We'll have to hope he's not as good as the rumors suggest. Can you identify him? Kill him now?"

"There's no point. I'd know the higher level officers by their sharp intellect, but I didn't map out the Superior Officer's mind. I wouldn't be able to tell which is his. I can't kill them all from this distance, either."

"Then we'd better hurry."

"Yes, Rohnan. Thank you," she said sarcastically. "That was the one part of my plan I had forgotten about—hurrying."

"Did this Mountain Region have many with the *Gift*?" Rohnan's emotions were colored with humor. "If not, how did you have any friends? A person taking you for face value, without the help of knowing your true feelings beneath, would surely want to beat you senseless."

Panic bled into Shanti. "How did you know about the Mountain Region?"

"The rumor was that the violet-eyed girl helped a place called the Westwood Lands liberate a city taken by a faction of Inkna. She—you—were believed to be with them. I understood that city to be somewhere in the Mountain Region—more of a remote location. Was that incorrect?"

"Then they are marked." Shanti's throat tightened as panic and anxiety dripped through her like acid. "If their name is known, in connection with me, Xandre will want them destroyed."

"Xandre will put them on the list, Chosen, but he'll be in no hurry to carry out the destruction. They're far to the north in the middle-land, are they not?"

"But if the rumor is that I'm still with them…"

"Speculation was that you were heading east, even in the taverns. Many think you will pit yourself against this newly proclaimed Chosen. Many believe that you are still alive. Some even claim you are a deity."

Shanti snorted, remembering what Tauneya had

said. "Madness."

"No, Chosen. Hope. In a land where women are ever becoming the victims, and men are dying to protect their families, it is a strange thing hearing of a lone woman causing this much trouble for a tyrannical leader. You are a beacon of hope, now. The violet-eyed girl who has not only avoided the Being Supreme's clutches, but also defeated a small army of Inkna? You have become a story, a legend. There are few heroes in this land anymore, and those that exist don't tend to last long. Yet here you are, rescuing the Ghost who has haunted the Graygual's steps. Hope, Chosen, is the most powerful weapon a person can yield. Hope creates miracles."

"Hope also gets people killed," Shanti said, feeling a weight settle in her gut. She barely had any left herself—had lost it more than a handful of times, if truth be told—she couldn't fathom being what Rohnan suggested. She didn't think she could live up to the expectation. Especially now that her title had been stripped from her.

A lone woman, indeed. What they didn't know was that she was also lost. Directionless. Running back to Cayan with her tail between her legs because she had no idea what else to do. Hope couldn't rest with her—it had to rest with him. Otherwise, the journey was over.

THEY ARRIVED AT THE Horse 'n Pony as light flared through the dawn sky in streaks of pink and gold. A pristine sign hung above the closed, green door with a thoroughbred-looking horse and a fat little pony beside it. Shanti thankfully slid from her horse's back and tossed the lead to Rohnan. The graying man sat straight and complacent, looking out over the cobblestone street as shopkeepers went about opening their stores down the lane.

"You might see if he has some decent clothes for you to wear. You don't fill those out," Rohnan taunted.

Despite the dirt and mussed, white-blond hair, Rohnan's face seemed just as fresh and youthful as she remembered. High-cheekbones and a straight, narrow nose set off a strong jaw. He could pass for a noble in most of the cities and towns she'd passed through. He would, and probably did, have women of all ages swooning as girls followed him around begging for his attention. Currently his shapely lips were half-curved into a sardonic smile, something he did often. Smile. And jest. Make light of the desperate situation in which they always found themselves.

"Did I teach you your charm, Rohnan? Because if so, I did a terrible job."

His mouth turned into a full smile showing even, white teeth. His mental tone was haunted, though, despite his glittering eyes. He was making the best of the situation, just as she was. "No, Chosen. I've had to learn to charm my way into women's beds, or else where would I sleep?"

"In the bushes and gutters, like me," she grumbled, turning toward the Inn.

The door opened on well-greased, maintained hinges. A tall, empty desk greeted her. To the right, a staircase led up to the second floor. Beyond the desk and out through an arched door the room opened up. She could make out a few tables on the shining wood floor. It was probably the common room where entertainment would come during busy times, where patrons ate, and where a thirsty traveler could find libation.

She wanted nothing more than to take a bath, drop down at a table, and drink until she couldn't remember her name. *Another life, Shanti. The next life, perhaps, the Elders willing.*

She passed the unoccupied desk and stepped through the archway. Two sleepy men sat at separate tables, eating bowls of porridge and sipping on mugs of something steaming. Each had a full leather sack strung over their chair-back, or resting at their side. One was newer than the other, but both identified the men as traders off to an early start. They probably had a long journey ahead of them.

One of them glanced up and caught her scrutiny. His muddy brown eyes took in her appearance before a scowl spread over his brow. She ignored him and continued to the bar where a portly man walked out with a clean, white apron. His gaze traveled a similar path as the traders' had a moment before. Disapproval radiated from his mind, but he didn't scowl. Instead, a seller's smile spread across his face. "Yes, ma'am. What can I do for you?"

He spoke in the language of the traders, a hacked-up common language, of sorts, spoken by travelers and wanderers, and ignored or unknown by the hierarchy. The language itself spoke of low class. Many of the more successful traders would use, instead, the language of the region they were in, speaking with richer patrons within their comfort zone, knowing all the major dialects as a business tool.

As Shanti was still dressed like a whore, and had fair skin denoting her foreign status, he'd obviously thought she resided at the lower end of society. A place she'd grown familiar with over the last year.

"I'm looking for Claude," Shanti said in an even voice as she kept her gaze lowered. The light wasn't bright, but it would be enough for him to make out the color of her eyes.

The man spread his arms to the sides in a welcoming sweep. "And you've found him. Welcome. How can I help?"

Shanti lowered her voice. "Esme sent me. I need the

map. And I'd love some clothes fit for a male traveler, if you have them."

Claude's smile turned brittle. Wariness crept into both his gaze and mind as his eyes flashed to the occupied tables. He turned to the shelf behind him and grabbed a mug before placing it on the counter and pouring steaming liquid from a clay pot. He leaned against the bar and brought up a pure white cloth to wipe down a pristine spot of wood in front of him. In a voice that carried, he said, "Well, ma'am, we don't have any rooms just at the moment. Maybe I can water your horses while I check to see when one might become available?" Caution and expectation lanced his thoughts, but not suspicion. Wariness lurked in his gaze.

"Yes, that would be fine," she said, playing along. "Though I am in need immediately. If you can't find anything, I will be on my way."

"Fine, fine. That's fine. I'll send my boy out of the barn to see to those horses while I check in with the Missus." His head jerked toward the archway.

"I'll wait outside, if you don't mind." Shanti turned without another word and made her way back through the room with a stiff back and high chin. She'd been refused lodging often in the past year. When a dirty, raggedy wanderer didn't have money, innkeepers didn't have patience. She knew what it was like to be rejected a warm meal or bed and forced back outside in the pouring rain. Her walk from the room could sell "down on one's luck" to even the most ardent disbeliever.

She emerged from the door and jerked a thumb to the side of the inn. "Barn."

Rohnan kicked his horse forward, leading Shanti's horse as he did so. The older man followed without prompting or complaint. They waited in silence as light crawled across the ground. The chill air began to warm up, welcoming the coming day. Impatience radiated from Rohnan, though his face remained passive.

Some minutes later, Claude appeared in his white apron with a hurried step and bundle of clothes. He wasted no time with pleasantries as he reached them. "Clothes will be big, but it's the best I could do. The map's in the middle. Get out of town before you open it."

"Thank you, Claude. Do you have saddles? I can pay for them," Shanti said quietly.

Claude couldn't help himself from gazing down at her clothes. He jerked his head away as embarrassment whirled in his mind. "No need. We help each other." He moved to the murky gray in the back of the barn. When he returned, a teenage boy was beside him. They each held a worn leather saddle. They waited only long enough for Rohnan and the old man to dismount before quickly saddling up the horses. To Shanti's surprise, her horse didn't growl or bite. It stood still with only a few stamps of a foot. The boy saddling the animal gave it furtive glances, as if knowing it was temperamental. Shanti couldn't blame the lad.

When they were finished, the man glanced out of the barn opening before wiping his hands on his apron. "Get gone, now. This town is always flooded with the Graygual army come mid-morning. That lot have gold—they keep the place clean and organized. Quite a change from the normal lot. But they police it, too. They'll stop you and ask about your business. They don't like outsiders around here—they have something of value in that camp down in the valley."

"Is that camp set up just for that purpose—protecting something?" Shanti asked as she stripped quickly and donned the fresh clothes. She handed Tauneya's clothes to Claude. "Can you see that Tauneya gets those back?"

"Tauneya—oh yes, of course. Then you're not a…" Claude rubbed his nose instead of finishing the question. Instead he said, "The word is, they'll be there for a while. Want to train up some snatchers or some such. Inkna. Those mind-weapons the Graygual have. That's what I hear. Men come and go all the time from there—up here to drink sometimes. They don't say much, but I listen as best I can. They might act right, but they are policing matters they shouldn't be troubled with. They think they run this place—tell me how to run my business, send performers away for being too coarse, tell me what's what." He shook his head and glanced back out the barn door. His gaze refocused on Shanti. "Watch yourself. If you're running, you'd better run fast, because they'll kill you if they catch you."

"They'll do much worse than that," Shanti mumbled, opening her satchel. She took out a handful of gold and forced it into his hand. "Thank you for the help."

"Oh my—oh no, m'lady. No, indeed. This is too much. Even if I were to charge—which I'm not, mind. I'm—"

"I have it to give. Help someone else with it if you won't keep it."

Claude bowed, clutching the money between his aging hands. "Thank you. Thank you, m'lady. Tauneya said she'd find someone to help if she was patient—thank you. I didn't believe her. You understand—her god isn't even real. But—thank you! I'll make sure this goes to those who need it most."

"That's all you can do."

Shanti tucked the map in her belt and covered it with the front of her shirt. She rolled her hair into a bun and stuffed it under the cap Claude provided. She looked him directly in the eye for the first time. "Keep yourself safe, Claude. Don't get noticed."

Claude's eyes rounded. The breath rushed out of his

mouth. He glanced up at Rohnan and started to shake. "It's true. My word—it's true! I thought his hair seemed awfully light for these parts. The Ghost and the Violet-eyed girl! It's true! Oh my, yes. Yes, I'll keep my head down. But I am here to help. We all are—there are a lot of us. We aren't warriors, but we aren't useless, m'lady."

"Of course not." Shanti walked back and stepped up into the stirrup. The horse pranced sideways. "Blasted animal!" She hopped after the horse, losing the dynamic mounting she'd intended. *Legend, indeed.*

"He knows you're uncomfortable with him, m'lady. Horses are like women—they can sense true intention," Claude helped.

It wasn't helpful. Rohnan snickered.

She pointed her finger in the horse's face. It must've sensed it'd get punched again because it stopped moving. She hoisted herself up and swung a leg over the saddle. When she was settled, a little out of breath, she once again looked down at Claude. "After a week, you can say you saw me ride by with the Ghost. You can say we escaped the Graygual."

"Not just the Graygual, Miss," Claude said as he picked his nail in nervousness. "The Hunter. He's the one at that camp down there. You best ride on. It's said that when he's on someone's trail, he doesn't stop until he catches his prey."

"The Hunter? Is that what you're calling the Superior Officer?" Shanti asked.

Claude nodded with serious eyes. "Yes, m'lady. I heard he's trying to get into the Being Supreme's guard. You don't want him knowing where you've gone."

"Great." Shanti fixed Rohnan with a blistering stare. "Of all the camps you could've walked into, Rohnan."

She gazed back down at Claude. "Thank you for the help, Claude. Stay safe."

"Yes, Miss. Of course, Miss. I will, Miss, yes."

A piercing stab of mental power ripped across Shanti's consciousness. She slammed her shields into place as Rohnan started and looked behind him with wild eyes.

"They're already here," Shanti said in a low tone. She looked at Rohnan. "We're going to have to fight our way out."

CHAPTER 3

"YOU REVEALED YOURSELF," ROHNAN SAID as he turned his horse.

Blessedly, Shanti's horse followed. The old man, for the first time, sat straight in his saddle with a tense back and serious face. She still couldn't get any sort of reading on him, though. She didn't even know his name! If he decided to use this opportunity to betray them, she wouldn't be able to do anything about it. All she had was trust and Rohnan's word, and from what she'd seen and heard, Rohnan knew as little as she did.

"I need to be seen here and for the rumor to spread. I need them to know I'm not with Cayan." Shanti winced as spikes accosted her mentally, the strength of power nearly matching her own. The *Sarshers* were close, and there was more than a few of them.

Her heart started to pound as she thought of their escape. The Hunter was probably already closing off the city, building his forces to overwhelm her small party.

"Cayan—that's the man who steals all your thoughts?"

"He doesn't steal anything. Can we trust this old man, Rohnan?"

"We have to."

Shanti gritted her teeth as another scorching attack slapped her shields, trying to break through. "We need to look at the map," she shouted, grappling with the onslaught.

Rohnan jerked his horse down an alley as Shanti opened up again and tried to block the constant barrage of minds. Fighting it, she felt along their merge until she found the pinnacle user and *struck.* Her sharp mental blade sliced into the opposing mind with all the force she could muster. She felt their pain well up before they withdrew behind blocks. She slammed her shields home again, only to realize they were in front of an empty store.

"What in Death's bad humor are you doing, Rohnan?" Shanti demanded as Rohnan sprung from his horse. "We don't have—"

Shanti cut off as the clattering of hooves came around a corner down the small lane. A villager dropped an armful of bread and dived out of the way as three horses fought for position between the shops. All wore black uniforms with the red at the breast. Swords gleamed in the early morning sun.

"Save your mental strength! Stay on your horse," Rohnan shouted. The window of the storefront shattered. Rohnan jumped through.

"Have you lost your mind?" Shanti asked as she pulled her sword from its sheath, staring at the oncoming riders. "They're almost on us and we're just sitting here!"

She kicked her horse, willing it forward to meet the challenge. Rohnan's horse was in the way, though, blocking her attempt.

"Hurry!" she screamed at Rohnan, watching the three riders descend in a thunder of hooves.

Rohnan emerged from the shop at a jog with a long staff equipped with two small blades on each end. He took a running leap with the grace of a dancer and pulled himself into his saddle. His staff whirled, each knife at the ends sparkling in the sun.

The first rider reached Rohnan just as he was settling on his horse. Shanti chanced opening her mind, ready to lash out, only to immediately feel the attack from the waiting *Sarshers.* She ground her teeth, striking back before forcing her shields down again. The first strike fell toward Rohnan. He batted it away expertly before bringing his staff across the enemy's body. The wood portion battered the first Graygual in the stomach, bending him over, before the blade sliced through and opened him up. His insides tumbled over his saddle. His body slumped and fell, sliding down between the two horses.

Rohnan urged his horse forward, knocking the now-rider less horse. The loose animal squealed and backed away in panic. It bumped into the third Graygual, forcing the man to maneuver his animal to get into the action.

The second man's blade swung at Shanti. She blocked with her sword as a knife on the edge of Rohnan's staff swiped the back of the Graygual's neck. He arched with the pain. Shanti thrust forward and stuck her blade through his stomach, clutching onto her horse's mane to keep her balance. Amazingly, the animal didn't seem to object. Instead, it shifted to the side, shielding them behind the dying Graygual to keep the last enemy out of striking range.

The mental assault battered at her shields as Rohnan yelled, "I have him!" He worked his horse in the small space to get behind the remaining Graygual. The other man turned in his saddle, trying to see behind him. Rohnan reached forward with his long staff and jabbed the back of the man. The blade sank in halfway, no more than a knife strike.

The Graygual reached behind him in reflex, screaming with the pain. Shanti slapped the horse in her way, but by the time the animal moved, Rohnan had closed in. He raked his weapon across the Graygual's throat. The man dropped to the ground.

"I can't fight on these accursed animals," Shanti

growled in frustration, kicking her horse's sides to get him to move. "How did you learn such skill, Rohnan?"

"I stole a horse early and traded up as often as I could. Riding a horse is faster, and less tiresome, than walking."

Shanti wasn't convinced about the latter.

"Toss them some of your wealth to pay for what I've done," Rohnan said, motioning toward the broken shop window. "If we can afford to give it, we should."

Shanti tossed a couple gold pieces through the broken window before they turned their animals west. Shanti opened her mind again, ready for a mental attack without the interruption from a physical one. None came—the *Sarshars* were probably regrouping, or getting into a different position. She didn't dare *search* them out, though. They would be forced to attack if they felt her presence, and she needed to save her mental resources for whatever might be to come. Instead, she made a mental map of the area surrounding them, making sure no Graygual lay in wait. All she found was the sleepy minds of townspeople going about their morning routine. No *Gifted* and no Graygual. For now.

"The Superior Officer is behind this," Shanti said as they raced down the empty, residential street. People pressed their faces against windows or stood in open doorways, half-dressed, with fear and shock on their faces. Most watched them pass. Only a few ducked back into their houses to hide.

Shanti spread her mind wider, lightening her touch. To the east, beyond the awakening minds of the town, coiled a cluster of anxious and eager individuals. There she felt the *Sarshers*, but her readiness was not called on. If they felt her lightly brush against their shields, they made no sign, gave no reaction.

"There are too many *Sarshers* for me to break their blocks, and even if I did, I would expend all my energy if I tried to take down that many. They're getting ready for something, though. They think we are going that way, I'd bet. Or waiting for instructions."

Rohnan turned into an alley and reined in. Shanti's horse mimicked the action, once again ignoring her attempts at control. The old man stopped beside them, his expectant gaze trained on her. If he was looking to leave, it wasn't to get back to the Graygual. He'd had his opportunity to run, but he'd remained out of the action, weaponless, waiting for Shanti and Rohnan to deal with the attackers. It wasn't much of an assurance, but it would have to be enough.

Shanti yanked out the map and opened it. Three loose sheets of paper tried to slide off the top. "Rohnan, look at this."

Each map detailed a portion of the land. Each section contained detailed plans of cities and towns and the wilds surrounding. Within the wilds were routes marked in blue, red and yellow. Red circles appeared in various places, black "X's" often next to those, or in isolation, and orange circles randomly spread out throughout the land, most often in the wilds, but with at least one in every city.

A gnarled pointer finger stretched toward the corner and touched a small key at the bottom right of the map. Shanti glanced at the old man, who was looking intently at the map. She looked at the spot and spoke in a language they could all understand. *"Blue indicates an often-traveled route, red is an often-traveled Graygual route, and yellow is the 'Thieves Highway'. So we'll be away from honest people and Graygual, but subject to bandits."* Shanti pursed her lips. *"Could be worse, I suppose. Red circles are known Graygual camps—yes, there's one where we just came from. Black 'X's' are Sarsher camps—it'd behoove us to burn them all to the ground if we could. The orange are people dedicated to the cause."*

"That is an extremely dangerous map for the orange circles." Rohnan's thumb wiped a spot of blood from the wooden shaft of his weapon.

"And the thieves, yes," Shanti agreed.

"He handed it over pretty easily." Suspicion rolled from Rohnan's mind.

"Esme has to be a code name. I bet they change it

often. Remember what I looked like—a whore that didn't do much business. He'd hardly think I worked for the Graygual or their spies."

"Crimson flies in violet skies."

Rohnan and Shanti stared at the old man as he smiled knowingly for a moment. Shanti turned back to the map without comment. Switching back to her and Rohnan's shared language, she said, "Okay, so we need to get to—"

"That map would lead us west. We'd backtrack." Rohnan looked up with calculating eyes. "You are using the wrong map…"

Shanti met his gaze with a stubborn set to her jaw. "We need backup, Rohnan. Two of us and an old man against a large army of fighters and mind-workers? Even if we were to get to the sea, we'd be spotted along the way. They'd be waiting for us. If the Graygual are already this far east, and if the real Chosen is—"

"*You* are the real Chosen," Rohnan interrupted with a warning in his eyes.

"—working toward the sea as well, equipped with a large army and packing as much power as I have, then we won't get to the Shadow Lands. Even if we do, we'll be killed once we land. We need someone at our back. This journey is suicide without help, Rohnan. We must head west."

"Who is this man Cayan, in the Mountain Region?

Every time you take a piece of gold the guilt eats away at you, but if you mention going back the eagerness drowns out other emotions. Is this love or is this duty? Can you tell anymore?"

"Rohnan—" Shanti ground her teeth in frustration. "We don't have time for this! The *Sarshers* are working our direction. The guards are spreading out around the town. The Superior Officer is nowhere on my mental map, which means he and his men are waiting for us outside my range. The longer we stay here, the more time they have to organize."

Rohnan stared deep into her eyes as his *Gift* was surely reading her urgency. She sighed and said, "I have to go west, Rohnan." She didn't prevent the pleading from soaking into her voice. "There are a million logical reasons why it is the right thing to do, but I am thinking with my heart. It isn't romantic love, but I care for that city and the people in it. I won't deny it. I have to go there."

A wry grin tickled Rohnan's lips. "Thinking with your heart, huh? I'm amazed you could find that blackened, shriveled thing, as small as it is."

"This is the right thing to do, Rohnan." She placed her hand on his. She had one moment to stare into his green eyes to sell the gravity of the situation before her horse shifted, almost dumping her onto the ground.

"Do you *see?*" she scoffed as she clutched onto the

saddle. The maps crinkled in her lap. "The animal has something against me."

"If we make it through the next few hours, we will have a long talk, you and I." Rohnan tapped the sides of his horse with his heels. "I seem to have missed some important milestones in your life."

Like nearly dying? You won't love hearing about that after what you sacrificed for me.

"I have a few questions of my own," she said, folding the maps to keep their chosen route on top. "Like what did you plan to do once you were a prisoner in a camp with a Superior Officer? How could that possibly seem like the best way to get information…?"

Humor colored Rohnan's mind. "Yes. A long chat."

People were milling through the streets, starting their day. Horses pulling carts clogged the road but Rohnan didn't let that hinder his progress. Twirling his staff at his side and yelling, "Heyah!" at his horse, he forced his way through, making people jog or yank their animals out of the way.

"The *Sarshers* here are trained," she yelled to Rohnan. "I'm better—at least when I'm on my own feet—but these are the best trained *Sarshers* I've come across."

"We'll kill them if we can."

"Yes, Rohnan. Thank you for, again, stating the obvious. What did I do without you all this year?"

"You certainly weren't riding a horse," he yelled as he expertly steered his animal around a child.

"Ohhh... bloody... *Apologies!*" A mother stood in Shanti's wake screaming and shaking her fist. The child had thankfully been pulled to the side in time.

The dwellings thinned as they approached the edge of the town. The road veered around a short fence encircling a small vegetable garden. Instead of following it around, Rohnan cut through. He jumped his horse over the fence and continued on. Before Shanti could even react, her horse followed suit, nearly bucking her off in the process.

"Bloody—" Shanti clung onto the horse's mane as the horse's landing jarred her forward. Its neck tasted like soot, hay and manure. "—bastard," she finished as Rohnan increased his speed. She took one last jiggling assessment of the map, made sure the old man hadn't fallen off his horse, then grimaced when she realized she was the worst rider of the three. She leaned forward into the run, telling the horse to go faster.

It was the first time the stubborn animal listened to her not-so-subtle cues.

It lurched forward with a burst of speed she wasn't expecting. Her body yanked back with the change in pace. "Bloody—" She pushed forward to get her bearings as her horse shot past Rohnan.

The animal raced up and over a hillside. The tree

line loomed closer. A tiny little path cut through the dense foliage away to the left. A larger route cut through the right.

When Shanti saw what waited near the larger road, her heart started to pound and she yanked back on the reins without thinking. The horse skidded and bounced to a stop, breathing hard. Shanti stared with a churning mind, also breathing hard. Rohnan's horse pranced to a halt beside her, warning and fear radiating from him. The old man was there a moment later, smiling at the sky.

A large group of black clad men blocked a hasty escape. Twelve Graygual, ten on foot and two on horseback. Shanti couldn't see the stripes on their tunics, but none of them had the intellect of a higher-level officer. The Hunter wasn't one of those twelve.

A group of *Sarshers* stood in two neat rows, five in each on the grass at the side. One wore white—a master executioner, an expert at attacking with his *Gift*.

"The Superior Officer thought we'd go east. Toward the Shadow Lands." Shanti analyzed the minds ahead. The officers on horse were keen and level-headed, probably skilled with a sword, but hopefully not excellent; they lacked a cunning that most advanced swordsmen had. The others were lower ranks and wouldn't pose too much of a problem for her and Rohnan. It was the addition of the *Sarshers*, though, that gave her cause for concern.

She wasn't as good a fighter when she was engaged in mental warfare at a distance. Fighting with a sword and her *Gift* simultaneously was something she'd trained for all her life, but fighting one person with a sword, and another with her mind, was like patting one's head while also rubbing one's stomach. It took great concentration and slowed her down. With ten of them, all reasonably powerful, her odds did not look good.

"They are too many, Rohnan," Shanti admitted. "We have no chance. It'll take everything I have to fight off the mental attack, even with your help through a power merge. You can't take on twelve Graygual, not with two of them being good swordsmen."

"Can we race them to the route we mean to take?" Rohnan asked with a desperate edge to his voice.

"Then what? We'll have to walk the horses even if I manage to find it quickly. The Graygual will just pour in after us, mentally fighting the whole way. I can feel them already, gathering power. We don't have much time."

Rohnan looked over at the old man. He was staring into the distance with sparkling eyes. "If we're killed, or taken, he'll be taken as well. I don't know what he's capable of, but he's important or they wouldn't have organized this quickly. We can't let them have him."

She knew what Rohnan was saying. *Kill him—we can't risk Xandre with him.*

Shanti looked at the old man. He sat so peaceful. So placid. He was waiting patiently in his own world as two powers fought over him. He didn't seem worried, or afraid of what might come. With the prospect of death, or capture by a people that had whipped and beat him, that seemed odd. Maybe he *was* mad.

She thought back to when she had first realized Cayan had a powerful *Gift*. She remembered thinking she had to kill him—she'd even tried. She was so thankful she had failed.

Shanti hung her head as the Graygual began to walk in their direction, readying for battle. "No, Rohnan. I know this was the way we always agreed we'd handle this situation. We'd kill our own people, we'd kill ourselves, and we'd kill any human weapons before Xandre could use them for his own devices. It seems logical, I guess. And so far I've followed the wishes of our people. I killed our friends and family when they were captured. I attempted to kill Cayan…"

She swallowed through the lump in her throat and watched the collection of black uniforms draw closer. The path she had to follow seemed so obvious. It was also the opposite of her instinct this far on the journey.

"Chosen or no, at some point I have to think for myself," she said, coming to a decision. "At some point,

I have to trust the Elders. I have to *believe* that I am on the right path. This is that moment, Rohnan. You found this man. I found you. And we will all go and join with Cayan. That feels right. So I will trust in it."

She barely heard Rohnan's sigh.

A somber voice said, *"You are in a prison of your own devising. Only when you allow yourself freedom of thought can you obtain freedom of mind. The path is before you, you just have to push through your fears to traverse it."*

"And I'm positive he can understand us," Shanti said, tucking her map deep into her binding to make sure it stayed. If she failed, she'd betray the only other uprising she knew of. She couldn't fail.

The weight of the gold was light in her hand as she pulled away the satchel and tossed it to the old man. *"Hold this for me, please. I'll collect it later if I'm still alive."* She swung her foot over her horse's back and jumped down.

"You are harder to kill on horseback," Rohnan said as he twirled his staff.

"Think before you speak, Rohnan."

He smirked. "True. All they'd have to do is blow in your direction and you'd fall off, land on your head, and be killed by a rock. I'll take the riders, you take everyone else."

"Sounds fair," Shanti said in a dry tone.

The sword glinted with a dangerous light as she freed it from the scabbard. Her knives hugged her thigh in comfort. The sun continued its slow rise, shining down on their battlefield as if Death wasn't present in every moment. Shanti closed her eyes and felt the trees swaying in the light breeze, infusing her with strength. The grasses gently tapped her legs, grounding her. The minds of animals moved deep in the dense foliage way ahead of them. Shanti and her party would be joining them. She *felt* it. The Elders were guiding her feet this day. They would not let her fail.

She brushed Rohnan's mind and was immediately merged with family. Shanti glanced at the old man, who was squinting at the Graygual. She waited until he caught her stare with intense, calculating eyes before she said, "*You don't want to be captured—both for your benefit and ours. You might've been treated reasonably well so far, but that won't last. If we start to lose, you had best run. Freedom is more than a state of mind.*"

He nodded, almost imperceptibly. Then, in her and Rohnan's language, said, "You are a rare creature, and the loyalty you inspire is legendary. I am seeing but tiny glimpses of the fruits of your labor, but it is enough to nod to the Divine Leader—or the Elders, in your case. They've chosen correctly. But you are a long way from your journey's end, and you have yet to balance with the Left Hand. An exciting prospect—I am eager to meet the prophecy." He put his hand to his chest. "I have been selected to guide you, Wanderer. I have waited long for my path to intersect with yours, and now that it has, we have much planning to do. So please, continue. I will ensure we move forward."

Shanti couldn't help the gaping stare.

"Here they come, Chosen," Rohnan said as he kicked his horse to a trot.

Shanti ripped her gaze away from the old man. There were questions that needed answers, but first there was a battle to win.

"Told you he wasn't mad," Rohnan yelled over his shoulder as his horse carried him away. "I'm right, admit it. I know everything."

Shanti started to run. "You still got captured with no hope of escape. Being right doesn't mean you're not stupid."

She heard Rohnan's snort, but felt his mirth drip away. The Graygual on the ground started to run, too, their feet thundering on the dirt as they increased their pace. The horses trotted behind them, but Rohnan was closing the distance. They'd go faster soon.

The *Sarshers* stayed where they were, no doubt waiting until she was good and close before unleashing their nasty tricks. She didn't wait. With a sharp blast of power, she aimed for the *Sarsher* in the white shirt. Her mind slammed against a tight block, sending the man a step back into one of his comrades.

Didn't expect that much power, huh?

The first Graygual fighter met her, then. She slashed down with her sword. He raised his weapon for a block. Her arm vibrated from the clash. Without losing speed, she stepped to the side and stabbed with her other hand. The blade of her knife jammed in his eye. She pushed him back with her forearm and yanked her blade free. Tossing it up, she caught the tip and threw it at a Graygual with a face ruined by a wicked scar. His throat blossomed around the hilt and blood poured down his neck.

She threw another sharp mental jab at the Master Executioner. Her power smashed into his mental block, again. She sent another pulse, battering at him. Trying to break down his shield. Weakening his defenses.

A sword whipped by her head. A quick feint and rapid feet had her at the Graygual's back, deftly stepping over the dead bodies from moments before. She stabbed through the center of him and whirled to three oncoming figures. She slammed down her mental shields, knowing this was the perfect time for the *Sarshers* to attack.

She blocked a sword strike from a thin man while dancing left. She kicked high, catching one of the three in the face. His jaw cracked. She snatched a knife as she spun. The blade sliced across a vulnerable throat. The follow-through had her arm even with the thin man's neck. She stabbed, only to catch air. He'd ducked.

She took two fast steps and struck, her sword slashing through the stomach of the fighter with a broken jaw. The thin man's sword came down, barely missing her head.

He was getting irritating.

She turned to him, only to find herself squaring off against two more. Metal rang somewhere behind them. *Hurry Rohnan, I'm about to be overrun!*

Knife in one hand, sword in the other, she feinted one way then the other and waited for someone to bite. A sword came, as expected. She danced out of reach then stepped back, cleaving a huge man through the gut. He staggered, cutting off an advance from the thin man.

"Hurry Rohnan!" she shouted.

She swung and thrust, dodging one swing and blocking another. Another man joined the foray as the thin man darted behind her. She spun toward the little bastard.

"Bloody die!" she yelled in frustration, striking. His sword swung as a grin lit up his face. Another man was closing in to her side. Things were getting dicey.

Then she realized that the mental attack had not come.

In a rush, she peeled back the block from her *Gift*,

wondering if they were waiting for another attack from her before engaging. Instead, she met nothingness. It was as if no one in the clearing had mental powers.

She blocked the quick man's sword and jerked forward with her knife. The blade cut through fabric but only entered a shallow amount of skin. Taking a lesson from Sanders, Cayan's army Commander, she kicked upwards as hard as she could. Her foot connected with the apex of the quick man's legs. She heard the second crack of the battle, but this one elicited a higher pitched scream.

She mentally stabbed again, intending to blast through the block and snatch up anything that came at her. Her *thrust* met soft, squishy tissue. Like a hot knife directly into an exposed brain, her power sliced right through, killing the Master Executioner in an instant.

A sword appeared above her. The sun glinted off its clean blade as the death blow raced toward her. In a moment of panic, she stepped to the side and *slashed* with her *Gift*. The man howled in agony. He contorted backward. One hand clutched his head, the other dropped the sword and tried to reach behind him to claw at his back.

Without a moment to lose, Shanti turned with sword, ready to meet the next attacker as she prepared a killing sweep of the *Sarshers*. A staff with a wicked, curved blade swung down. Rohnan had finally arrived.

She let loose a blanket of mental pain, aiming for the *Sarshers.* They were staring at the dead Master Executioner or looking confused and wild-eyed. But why weren't they using their powers?

Not about to question the help of the Elders, she *raked* through their exposed and fragile minds, completely vulnerable without blocks or attacks. They each clutched at their heads and screamed as she stepped forward and slashed through the body of a Graygual.

Seeing Rohnan advancing on the remaining Graygual with a killing strike at the ready, Shanti threw the blade. The knife struck the middle of the red circle on the Graygual's breast. Deep crimson stained his front as his shaking hands groped for the hilt. Rohnan pulled back his staff as the horse ran by. He glanced off toward the *Sarshers*, who had all sunk to their knees and fallen where they knelt.

He slowed his horse to a walk as his incredulous gaze came to rest on hers. "How—"

"I don't know," she said, checking to make sure everyone was dead.

"We should search them." Disgust lanced Rohnan's voice.

Shanti nodded as her gut twisted. Swallowing back bile at the most loathsome part of killing on the run, she bent to the first dead and bloodied body and searched his clothing, pulling out money and weapons, but leaving personal artifacts.

"I hate this part, too, but it's necessary." Rohnan slid off the horse and followed her example.

"We haven't much time before someone comes to check in," Shanti murmured, patting down the next man. She glanced again at the downed *Sarshers*. "They never engaged. It was like they suddenly lost their mental power."

She moved to the next Graygual as two horses trotted up. The old man led Shanti's horse by the lead. He said, "We all have different gifts. It is how we use those gifts in unison that will determine the eventual outcome."

Shanti wiped her hands on a clean part of an enemy tunic before she straightened up. She used her palm to block the rays of the sun as she looked up at the old man. His mind was as unreadable as ever. "You can block mental power. Is that what you mean? That is your *Gift*?"

"We have much to discuss, but not now. Let us look at that map and get out of harm's way."

"There is no getting out of harm's way," Shanti responded, pulling out the map. "The Hunter will find our trail and track us. The best we can hope for is to outrun him."

Finding the trail on the map, Shanti pointed in the right direction before mounting up and heading out. As they moved, she couldn't help but think about what the old man had said before. "What did you call me earlier?"

"The Wanderer." The man grinned. In a somber and flat voice, he started speaking like he was reciting something from a book. "Women who have suffered, no matter how afraid, hold out their hands in aid to help others. To create a loyalty like no other—as strong as an oak, as enduring as a mountain, and as brutal as Time—look no further than a female who has risen from the ashes. The Wanderer must be rightfully welcomed into a network of mothers and warriors both. With one hand she will nurture, and with the other she will strike out against evil. The Wanderer will be a woman from great suffering. She will unite the lost, the forlorn, and the survivors, and she will form the bond of the ages. Aid her!"

Shanti shook her head as the weight settled in her stomach again. She didn't understand what he was talking about, and understood her journey even less. She was lost, drifting. She hoped Cayan had some ideas.

"Do me a favor," she said to the old man as they neared the path. "When you speak madness, do it in the other language. It's less confusing that way."

Rohnan huffed out a laugh as they entered the trees.

CHAPTER 4

MARC HUNCHED OVER THE PALE man lying on the ground who had his eyes squeezed shut with his breath coming in fast pants. One arm lay at his side, clutching at leaves and dirt. The other was delicately held over his stomach for Marc's inspection.

Wiping sweat from his eyes, Marc looked over his shoulder to see the crazy eyes of Commander Sanders. The commander didn't say anything, but the set of his jaw and his flexed muscles screamed *impatience*.

Marc turned back like a man who didn't want to acknowledge a ghost at his back and stared at the sentry in obvious pain. Taking a big breath to steady himself, he reached out with trembling hands to gingerly touch the hurt man's forearm. His action was met with a slight moan immediately cut off in an act of sheer will.

He cleared his throat and said, "It's, ah… it's broken, sir. I think."

"You *think*?" Commander Sanders moved around until he could look down at Marc's face. "The man can't move the thing without complaining, it's hot to the touch, and you *think* it's broken? Try again."

He summoned all his courage, trying to pretend it was the patient and understanding S'am looking down on him. *Shanti*, he reminded himself. Calling her S'am meant she had a leadership role, and leaders just didn't wander away in the middle of the night when their men needed them.

Marc hunched, trying to hide the redness he knew colored his face. Then he bowed even more, *feeling* the gaze of the toughest, meanest, most impatient man in the entire army boring into the top of his head.

"We—well, sir," Marc stammered, trying to get the ordeal over with. His brain churned, but all he could think of was that intense stare and the grisly scar down the left side of Sanders' face. Or maybe it was the fact that Sanders got that scar while killing four Mugdock with nothing but a small knife and a bad attitude.

He cleared his throat, seeing that the lines of the arm were true and there weren't any obvious signs of bones out of place. The man had fallen out of the tree—his post for sentry duty—and landed badly. Kids did it all the time. Plus, Sanders knew it was broken, so what was Marc needed for? Take the man to get a brace, tell him to be more careful, and be done with it.

Although…

Marc looked up at the branches and then to the body sprawled out on the ground with his head facing the trunk. A trickle of blood seeped from a spot of matted crimson hair. It was not a deep gash, but the sentry had definitely hit his head.

He leaned forward and delicately touched the skull. The sentry winced. Marc gently opened the sentry's right eye and noticed the dilated pupil. The sentry had probably hit his head when he hit the ground. His body broke most of the fall, but his head definitely bounced. The trauma hadn't killed him, but he had a concussion. He'd need treatment for the arm, and the head wound would have to be monitored.

"He doesn't do well when you smother him while he works." Xavier marched up, a note held out for Sanders. He was a large kid for fifteen, with broad shoulders, a wide chest, and already stacked muscle. He wasn't quite as big as the Captain, but Xavier wasn't done growing, either. Too bad all the ambition had gone out of him when Shanti hadn't returned. Almost all of the Honor Guard—the faction of five that were set to spy on, then get trained by, the strange foreign woman they'd found in the dead lands—had the same problem. Her practices had been fun, if also terrifying. Standing around in the practice yard while someone yelled at them just didn't compare.

Sanders glared at Xavier as he took the note. He read it before looking back at Marc. "Your dense friend thinks I'm smothering you somehow. Is this correct?"

Marc's eyes rounded before he stared at the ground. "No, sir."

"What is his ailment?" Sanders pushed.

"He probably has a concussion. He needs to go to the hospital to have his arm set and get watched for his head," Marc rattled out.

He sighed in relief when Sanders said, "Stenson, get yourself to the hospital and do as the boy says."

"Yes, sir." The sentry painfully rose to his feet.

"You might, uh, go with him, sir," Marc muttered with his hands in his pockets. "Just so he doesn't get dizzy or lost. Head wounds can do strange things."

After a tense beat, Sanders said, "C'mon, Stenson. I'm going that way, anyway. These boys need all the time they can get in the practice yard."

"Yes, sir," Stenson wheezed while clutching his arm.

"Get gone," Sanders barked at Xavier and Marc.

The two boys took off as fast as possible without actually running. It wasn't a great idea to hang around when Sanders was in a mood like this. A guy might find himself getting thrown through a tree that way.

After they'd put some distance between themselves and the prickly Commander, Xavier said, "Took a long time on that diagnosis, huh? Was it Sanders breathing down your neck, or did you really not know what was wrong with Stenson?"

"Sanders jumbles all my thoughts," Marc admitted.

"But... I don't really think I'm living up to Shanti's expectations..."

Xavier kicked at a rock. "Yeah, well, she had impossible expectations in the first place. Then she left. So..."

"I just feel like things are unfinished, you know? There's still a ton of danger out there—I saw what the Inkna did to that city. And they have a bunch of mind-thrower people. We can't stand up to that."

"We have the Captain. He's as strong as Shanti."

"Except he doesn't know what he's doing. And who's he going to train with? He could just as easily kill with that mind thing as do nothing with it. And Shanti was the best—"

"So she said," Xavier interrupted with spite.

"Okay, well, she was way better than any of those Inkna, and she's better than the Captain. If she's not the best, then we're all in trouble. She wasn't afraid of the Inkna, and didn't mind running straight into battle, but the Graygual made her go pale. If they come calling, we're screwed."

"The Captain is forming alliances. He's got a bunch already on our side. We've got help."

"Xavier!" Marc shoved the larger guy. "Will you wake up? She left, and that sucks. I hate her for it, too, but if you pulled your head out of your ass, you'd see the bigger picture. Alliances are all well and good, but the Graygual are still bigger. They are *breeding* people like Shanti. We need more than a few old farts from prosperous cities merging with us."

They turned a corner at the last house before they reached the large, dusty training grounds.

"Well, the Captain is the best at what he does, and he's working it out," Xavier said. "He—"

Someone rushed out of the shadows.

Xavier reacted hard and fast. He grabbed the man and threw in one smooth, precise movement.

Hands windmilled as a body flew through the air. Before it hit the ground, they heard Leilius utter, "Why?" He landed in a tumble of limbs.

Xavier turned to Marc with a grin. "Did you just *scream?*"

"Did I?" Marc put his hand to his chest, out of breath. His heart pounded against his rib cage. Images of the Inkna battle had flashed through his mind, making him think someone was attacking with a sword or knife.

Xavier doubled over in laughter. "You screamed like a girl!"

"*Well?* He jumped from out of nowhere!" Marc defended.

"What'd you do that for?" Leilius asked as he picked himself up off the ground, dusting off his plain gray clothes.

Lanky and average looking, Leilius was the only one

of them that was still as good with his skills as when Shanti left. He loved slinking around the town, randomly waiting in various places and watching people, waiting to see if they would notice him. He was the only one among them that had absolute faith—absolute, unequivocal faith—that Shanti would return.

The problem was, the army didn't acknowledge silent loitering as a quantifiable trait. Of what the army did recognize as necessary skills, Leilius was only good at working with a knife at close range. Sanders often threatened to send him to work in the mines.

"What if you had been a Mugdock and I didn't react?" Xavier asked Leilius as they continued on.

"How would a Mugdock get into the city without the sentries knowing?" Leilius said with a put-upon expression. He wiped at a small cut on his cheek. When his fingers came away with a smear of blood, he held it up with an incredulous expression. "You made me bleed!"

Xavier ignored the accusation. "You've gotten past the sentries without being noticed…"

"But then I got in trouble by the Captain for wandering around outside the walls when I was supposed to be cleaning out the horse stalls. *He* knew where I was. You think he wouldn't notice a Mugdock sneaking in?"

"What if you'd been an Inkna? They can hide their minds." Xavier hesitated as they neared the edge of the practice yard. Men of all ages and abilities congregated there to practice with swords, or to work in the pit throwing knives. There were even long-range archery targets set up into the trees beyond the perimeter of the city.

"Not really," Marc cut into the argument, spotting Rachie and Gracas, the other two members of their old Honor Guard. The two guys were standing on the periphery of the crowd of cadets waiting for their Training Captain. "If the Captain was paying attention, he'd know they were there. They wouldn't be hidden."

"You said yourself," Xavier pushed. "He's not great with his power. Someone might slip past."

"Oh, now he's not great with his power? Desperate to be right, as always, huh, Xavier?" Marc rolled his eyes.

"All I'm saying is," Xavier said to Leilius, "You can't pop out and not expect me to react."

"Well, next time I'll pop out and avoid the throw. That's something to work on. And you can work on not letting me avoid the throw. S'am would give us that homework."

Xavier sighed in defeat. Leilius never took the hint that Xavier didn't want Shanti's name mentioned in a favorable light around him. "Whatever. C'mon, let's go. Maybe we'll do something interesting today."

"Doubtful." Leilius' body slumped as he and Marc

followed Xavier into the training grounds.

CAYAN SAT AT HIS DESK in his private office; a place few knew about, much less visited. For official business or meetings, he used the space that was more like a hall than working quarters. These days he spent little time there, though. Things were starting to heat up and he didn't have a firm handle on the direction of their future as a city, or more importantly, as a people.

The door opened, letting in the brisk fall chill. Commander Sanders marched in with Cayan's note clutched in his hand and expectation etched in his features. He gave Cayan a nod before coming to stand directly in front of the desk. "You wanted to see me, sir?"

Cayan sat back and prevented himself from rubbing his eyes. Sleep was a luxury he no longer indulged in. "Yes. I've received a letter from the Duke of the Southern Peninsula. He is the last, and most important, ally. He's agreed to help for the time being and indirectly join our cause." He was also a pompous fool who thought more of himself than he ought. Still, the man was great at managing his assets, and had some equally great commanders. Cayan needed him.

"Yes, sir. Has anyone turned you down?"

Cayan glanced at the papers on this desk. "I was late

to the party, actually. Krekonna from the west was already accumulating help. I joined *their* alliance, if truth be told. I then extended the request to a few nations closer to me, and of course, the Duke's. Those further west have already seen the effects of the Graygual armies. Refugees have flocked to Krekonna and surrounding cities in droves. Women have disappeared, many turning up dead. Men have been killed in the street. It's utter lawlessness. Their army is sick with power and unimpeded. They do whatever they desire."

"Fear mongering." Sanders clasped his hands behind his back. "Thieves do it all the time on our routes. They pick off some of the weak travelers and leave them to be found as an example of their brutality. Then, when the thieves approach softly and with a smile, people are so thankful not to be run-through with a sword, or their wives abused, they dump out their pockets quietly and obediently. Foul play, that. But it speeds up the process—so I've heard. They know better than to try that with my men, of course."

A ghost of a smile passed Cayan's lips. "I bet. Well, their plans are working. Krekonna is terrified of a Graygual invasion. He looks around him and sees the eventual death and destruction of his people. Unlike some, however, he doesn't plan to surrender quietly. Or at all."

"Does he have any in his city with mind power?"

Cayan couldn't help another smile, this time with an underlying of sarcasm. "He's seeking the violet-eyed girl. He wants to appeal for her aid."

Sanders snorted and walked a few paces to the window. His muscles flexed. "I'd love to be in a locked room with that foreign woman." He turned back to Cayan, regret and uneasiness warring on his face. "Don't get me wrong, sir, I'm thankful for what she did. Not happy to admit it—*I* should be saving the damsel, not the other way around. But how she left… that wasn't right. Took off like a fart in the wind. Cowardly, that's what it was. She's got her own agenda, the other nations that need her help be damned."

Without warning, rage welled up within Cayan. Power boiled and bubbled before blasting the room. He wrestled with his control, quelling his *Gift*, but not before Sanders' back straightened and his expression went blank, a sure sign that the commander was in pain.

Forcing his *Gift* down, Cayan took a deep breath and entwined his fingers, hiding his shaking hands. "I'm going to be frank." He kept his voice level and tone somber, trying to hide the conflict within. "I'm sending you to the Duke with gifts—I have every belief he wants to be included in our new alliance, but he wanted us to beg. So I begged, promising him gifts." Sanders nodded without comment. "And once we have him secured, I'll be leading an expedition to go after Shanti. I will want you with me."

A hard, brown gaze hit Cayan. Incredulity fought with rage in Sanders' expression. "She takes off, leaves us in the lurch, and now you want to go after her like she's some runaway child? Excuse the blunt speech, sir, but that is madness. We have no idea where she went, what she's up to, nor what her grand plans are—she's a ghost. And you want to leave this city without its Captain to go traipsing after her?"

"You've heard of the emergence of the Chosen on your trade routes." Cayan waited for the nod. He ignored the corresponding clenched jaw. "And you know that they weren't talking about Shanti."

"Some Inkna was named Chosen. She lied about her title."

Cayan's fingers turned white with tension as he clamped down on that raging inferno within.

Willing calm, Cayan maintained a steady voice by sheer will. "Her people thought she was the Chosen. She was on the way to merge with her distant kin to continue the war effort. Being called Chosen was a burden to her. Nothing but a weight to hold her down. The actions she took to fulfill that duty were… unspeakable. Yet, she thought she had no choice. No, she didn't lie. And I'll bet she wasn't thinking when she left. The title of Chosen was leading her around by the nose. I should've realized it then and used a different approach in speaking with her. But what's done is done."

Sanders' lips thinned. He obviously didn't agree, but he didn't have half the facts. Nor had he heard a quarter of the rumors.

"She has a full dose of power. As do I. As does the Inkna claiming he's the Chosen," Cayan continued. "I don't know anything about the rightful Chosen, or even how such a person is defined. I also don't know the myth behind the person called the Wanderer. Both are rumors, as far as I can tell. But I do know that many are stationing themselves throughout the land, trying to intercept this person called the Wanderer. They say she is a woman, and the key to our salvation from the Graygual. Rumors don't help me, and they aren't the basis for my decision. Here is what I am sure of..."

Cayan sat forward and pinned Sanders with his stare. "A power that mates with one of its kind multiplies in strength. Two full doses of power, both rare by themselves, mated, becomes an anomaly. Shanti and I, together, create that anomaly. I also know that Xandre, the pinnacle of this land, the one holding all the power, still ardently seeks her. Chosen or no, he wants her badly. Maybe he just wants her power to mate with the Inkna, I don't know. But she is important, and she and I together, are essential. *That* is what I know. I am sure of it. I need her on my side, Sanders. I need her power to mate with mine. It is the key. Without her power, we might as well just sit with our hands out, waiting to be tied and taken. Without my power, she might as well wait for the same. Together, we have a chance. Perhaps our only chance."

Sanders shifted. His gaze dropped to the floor, his brow knotted in consternation. Cayan could feel the uncertainty radiating from the battle-hardened commander. "And how do you plan to find her? She's long gone by now," Sanders asked in a gruff tone.

"She's headed to the same place as the other Chosen—the Shadow Lands."

Sanders' head snapped up. Wariness crouched in his expression. "The *Shadow Lands?* Sir, forgive me, but knocking on the door of a bunch of devil-worshipping, black-magic users is a little extreme, even for that woman. I know you were told the same things I was as a kid—eat your vegetables or I'll whisper your name to the Shadow people. Don't bite your brother, Sanders, or I'll ship you off to the Land of the Mist where they'll cook you up and eat you..."

Cayan let a smirk quirk his lips. "Afraid of children's tales at your age, Sanders?"

"Half of that is hearsay, sure, but legends often come from truth. There's not one person who doesn't fear what they call the Shadow People. Why else would they be banished from the mainland to a small island only reached through a treacherous journey across the sea? Location doesn't lie, sir."

"People fear what they do not understand. My power could be called dark magic. Shanti is as violent and destructive as they come. As are you, I might add, and you still bite. Banished might really just mean relocated to a more fertile land. That's how this city started in the early days. But yes, that's where she was headed. That's where this Inkna is headed. *That* is why there has been a pause in the raids and attacks—I won't say stopped. The Graygual focus is now away east. In their effort to secure these Shadow People, they are unwittingly giving the rest of us time to get organized."

"Xandre seems smarter than that, if what you say is true. Why would he allow us to organize?"

Cayan stood. "He's one man with a lot of pursuits, and we are small cities, however prosperous. He thinks we'll be here when he's ready. And he's right. A few of us combined still don't equal his might, especially with the number of Inkna and power he has. We need Shanti to get those Shadow People, and we need her to unite with us. I've thought long on this—her help is the only way. Krekonna thinks the same thing. He urged me to go after her. He was thinking of sending a battle commander of his who spent some time with her—"

Without warning, a blast of power surged, consuming Cayan, locking his jaw. It boiled his blood, blasted through his control, and gushed into the room. He staggered against the desk, fighting with everything he had. With the effort equal to wrestling a wild boar to the ground, he sucked it back in and shoved it deep, down within himself. Still, his mind swam and dizziness clouded his vision.

When the haze cleared, Sanders was leaning against the wall with a pained expression. "Sore subject, ay sir?" Sanders wheezed. "Don't like mentioning that pain in the ass in the same sentence as other men, looks like. That makes you crazy, you realize that?" Sanders rolled his shoulders and shook out his arms as the power subsided. "Thank Satan's butt those Inkna didn't have your power in that torture chamber, or I might've broken."

Cayan leaned over the desk as he huffed out a laugh. "No, you would've died quicker, and then you wouldn't have to live with being saved by a girl."

Sanders huffed. "True."

Cayan rolled his head to loosen the sudden tightness in his neck. "She has a way of getting under a man's skin."

Sanders stiffly pushed away from the wall. "Yeah. Well. I plan to get her alone and beat some sense into her. Don't think I'll take it easy on her just because you want to see what's under her skirt."

"She's going to beat *you* senseless, Commander. Which you know. Still wanting that fight makes *you* crazy, do you realize that?"

"Nah. I'm used to fighting battles I can't win. Hell, I don't think I've won an argument since I got married. I'll just need to get another dame to save me from her."

Cayan smiled and took a deep breath. "Anyway, I need you gone within two days." Cayan shrugged into his jacket. "I have men waiting for you, and a wagon of goods to take to the Duke. Once you have his support, you'll come back, get a day or two rest, and then we leave again."

"Junice won't be pleased," Sanders mumbled.

"She knows what she married. She'll probably be happy to see the back of you by now."

Sanders snorted. "Got that right. She's stopped asking what I want for dinner. She just makes what she wants and allows me to eat it."

"Honeymoon is over."

"Long over." Sanders followed Cayan toward the door. "One thing—who's going to guard the city when half the army is gone?"

Cayan raised his eyebrows a fraction.

Sanders nodded and rocked back on his heels. "The Duke's men, right. The only leader with men to spare. He doesn't think he needs them—and he might not for a while. He's too far south at the moment, with no foreign woman to call attention to him. So you're going to pay him for some manpower, then?"

"You're not as dumb as the men say you are." Cayan laughed as he swung open the door and waited for Sanders to stalk through. The man looked like he was in a hurry even when he had nowhere to be. "I've organized for the most disciplined of men to go with you—this journey is about speed. When you get back, we'll get the Duke's men in place, and then we leave. If we're not in this battle, then we'll be ground under by it. I will not let that happen to my people."

They walked through the town without speaking. Townspeople smiled at Cayan as he passed. Many greeted them and more than a few young and available women batted their eyelashes and stuck out their chests. He let himself look, but that's as far as the desire went. He could have them for a night, or maybe a few, but his attention would inevitably wander, as it always did.

"How do you plan to make her join our cause?" Sanders said, breaking the silence as they neared the practice yard. If he wondered why Cayan was escorting him there, he didn't ask.

"Dangle her Honor Guard in front of her. Her interest in them was genuine. Through them, she had a way of fitting in to this city. She has pride in them. I plan to leverage that."

Sanders looked at him sideways. His lips tweaked upwards at the corner. "I wondered why you left them with the cadets, especially Xavier. They're bored, they're flagging, but you're two steps ahead. How long have you been planning this?"

"Her leaving was never an option. I'd hoped she'd return on her own. She hasn't. I don't like not getting my way."

Sanders barked out a laugh. A group of scarred warriors on the edge of the yard turned to look. When they saw Cayan and Sanders, the humor from their expression drained away. Their group broke up almost immediately. Some walked toward the sword fighting area, while others headed towards the town.

"You're a buzz kill," Sanders said as they stopped within the practice yard.

"You're the one they're terrified of." Cayan didn't let the smile touch his lips. "There's a rumor you bit someone's nose off."

"I'm not the only one they're terrified of. You blast the whole city with that curse of yours. They don't know what it is, but it hurts, and they know it comes from you."

"I'm going to be the first one carted away if the Graygual come calling."

"No. You'll be the reason they come in the first place."

Cayan felt all elation drip away at the gravity of that statement. He was the best hope his people had of staying in one piece, but he was also their biggest danger.

His mind invariably went to Shanti as he nodded at Sanders and made his way to the large park within the city limits. She'd always been balancing on that sword's blade—her people's best hope, but their inevitable downfall. She'd carried that unimaginable burden since she was five years old. Shouldered it like a weight, knowing her duty would lead to the deaths of everyone she loved, and everything she knew.

Not only that, but Cayan was positive she'd saved some from the last battle. She'd been forced to choose who would live—who would be the biggest help in her continued war effort—and who would die. She sent her own people to get cut down, watched it happen, before being forced to flee… alone.

How could she stand it? How had the guilt, and remorse, not eaten her alive?

How would he be able to stand it, if he ended up having to do the same thing?

Cayan took a deep breath as he wandered into the trees, letting the healing touch of nature rejuvenate his *Gift*. It soaked into his body and smoothed out the ache and fatigue of training and stress. He sank down next to a large tree, closed his eyes, and let his *Gift* unfurl, trying to keep up the practice until he met her again.

CHAPTER 5

THE FIRE CRACKLED WITHIN THE clearing. Sparks danced and swirled into the air, barely dodging branches reaching overhead. A brook, weaving in and out of rocks, gurgled as it wound down the gentle slope.

She and Rohnan sat beside the fire, watching the dancing flames as they curled around dried timber. The light flashed across Rohnan's handsome face, highlighting the straight lines and perfect features. The sun and wind had put an unnatural reddish hue on his cheeks, and made his once-porcelain skin just a little ruddy, but despite the year of travel his health shone through. His long, blond hair was glossy and light. His muscle made him lithe and agile, his movements refining his overall appearance.

"You're prettier than me," Shanti said with a smile, hating to look away from him in case she woke up to realize this had all been a dream, that meeting him again wasn't real. If she did wake up, and find him gone, plunging her back into the bleak loneliness she'd been living, she had no idea how she'd cope.

"Always was." Rohnan glanced at her out of the corner of his eye. She could feel his soft humor.

"Yes, true. But this last year has been harder on my appearance. You still look…fresh. How is that possible?"

Rohnan shrugged. A smile worked at his lips. "Women in some of these foreign lands try to sell their chastity as a virtue. But what they're really after is secrecy. They have the same urges as our people, they just live a double-standard where they're not supposed to indulge sexually like the men. When I realized that, and made it clear I didn't believe in that double-standard, I had no problem finding beds whenever I chose. And I chose often. Loneliness has never suited me like it does you."

"It doesn't suit me, Rohnan. It plagues me," Shanti said quietly, looking back at the fire.

Rohnan's smile fell. She felt the comforting pressure of his hand on her forearm. "I am sorry about Romie. I didn't know he had put himself up for Sacrifice, but he was a good man. One of the best. There were better people to watch over the children—he wanted to help in any way he could. He gave his life for our future."

Shanti took a shuddering breath. The memory of those earth-brown eyes rimmed with blood flashed through her mind. She wiped a tear from her cheek. "He could've told me."

"You wouldn't have acted sensibly—he probably knew that. You didn't understand each other. You didn't have anything in common."

"I loved him."

"Forgive me." Rohnan ran his fingers through her hair. "You had love in common. A deep, soul-clutching, first love. But aside from that, you didn't line up in any other way. You wouldn't have understood his choice because you didn't understand his calling, and he didn't understand yours. You wanted to fight as often as you made love. He was too sweet for you—he just wanted to hug you and make you happy. He never understood your temperament."

"You make me sound like a villain." Shanti slapped his hand away.

Rohnan waited a moment, and then resumed his gentle stroking. "You're a warrior. You need to fight, to dominate, and to be dominated. Your life is a permanent struggle, and you need that in your intimacy or you can't completely respect your partner. How often did you beat on me when we were kids?"

"You deserved it."

Laughter rumbled in Rohnan's chest. "Very rarely. The difference between Romie and me was that I understood the warrior mentality since I was training in it. It wasn't my calling, either, but it became my duty. Then you gave me the rare privilege of being your

Chance. That distinction built up my ego, something I have always needed help with. You made me tough, and your guidance made me better."

"If only it improved your jokes…"

Rohnan chuckled quietly and looked back at the flame. The crackling of the fire permeated the otherwise peaceful night. After a few moments, Rohnan said, "Cayan."

That was it. He just said the name. Even so, Shanti went on the defense immediately, and she had no idea why. Rohnan could probably figure it out with his horribly potent *Gift*, but she wasn't sure she wanted to know.

Feeling her reaction, Rohnan smiled. He poked at the fire. The flame rose and whirled into the air, sending sparks up toward the reaching branches overhead. "Your power found a mate. We didn't think one would exist for you."

Shanti shifted her gaze from the orange flame to focus on Rohnan's face, mostly blank but for the knowing smile.

"How long have you known my power could have a mate?" she asked.

"Since before you started east."

"And you didn't mention it…"

Rohnan sighed. "I overheard your grandfather talking. He asked that I keep it to myself. Obviously I wouldn't have. My duty as Chance is to tell you everything, but when I found you, you were sitting with Romie under your favorite tree. Even if I couldn't feel your love for him, I could see it in your eyes. Our future was uncertain, your desire to mate him was more than false hope, and we didn't think you could ever have a power-mate, anyway. I couldn't fathom the point in depressing you further. So I didn't mention it."

Shanti dug at the ground with a twig, hating and loving that memory of Romie at the same time. Bittersweet. "I can't fault you. From what we knew at the time, the information wouldn't have mattered. But it might have helped avoid some awkward situations on my journey…"

"We will witness fireworks. Bright, powerful fireworks that will change the world," the older man, who'd revealed his name was Burson, said in a soft voice. He barely moved within his place in the shadows from where he had been staring at the stars and muttering to himself.

Shanti rolled her eyes. "What did I tell you about talking crazy in this language, Burson? Forbidden, remember?"

"It is a wonderful journey on which I find myself. Full of surprise and humor. I did not expect that. But then, we were only given milestones—we were not given personalities."

"I think it's about time you told us more about this Wanderer. And about your *Gift*. Are there others like you?" Shanti asked.

Burson rose and slowly moved closer to the fire. He sat opposite Shanti and stared at the flames. "I do not like to repeat myself. There are many journeys we will take. I'll tell you more about myself and my mission when the two halves..." Burson paused and switched languages. He glanced back up at the sky with a smile. *"When the two halves finally unite and blast power into the sky."*

"The two halves?" Rohnan asked.

"The creator needed two hands to mold the world—one for stability, one for flair, and both, together, to hold it tight to his breast and keep it safe."

Shanti glanced up at the sky. A blanket of twinkling stars were stitched into the velvety black. "I think we should at least hear why humor makes you look upwards like a madman, Burson. Are you hearing voices?"

Rohnan huffed out a laugh as he followed her gaze. "Chosen, you went from traveling alone—or should I say running away alone...?"

"I'm almost over that villainous comment, Rohnan, and not far from beating you senseless."

Rohnan's laughter echoed through the trees. "Traveling alone, then. You went from traveling alone to traveling with family and a mysterious madman. It could be worse."

Shanti sighed and stretched out beside the warmth of the fire. She braced her head on her hand, still staring at the flame. "It could be, I suppose. I don't know how, but it could be."

After a beat in which smiles around the fire flickered like the flames, Shanti said, "When did you hear about the other Chosen, Rohnan?"

She barely saw his shrug as the shadows played across his expanse of shoulder. "Along the way. A woman said something of it while we lay in bed. She liked to gossip—she was a barmaid. I found all I needed from her, but still sampled the rumors in other taverns just to be sure."

"What did you think?"

Rohnan hunched forward. "Until then, I wasn't sure you were still alive. I feared the worst. When I first heard about the new Chosen, I was happy and terrified at the same time. I thought it was you. That you were alive. Scared, of course, because the Chosen was rumored to be part of an organized army. You didn't have that, so I thought you had been taken. Then it turned out to be an Inkna. As I happened in taverns for more information, I heard about the violet-eyed girl. Sightings. They said you helped a great Captain take down a city of Inkna..."

"Yes."

Rohnan studied the flames. "I am eager to meet this great Captain of men. He is rumored to be eight feet tall and as big as a forest."

"As big as a forest?" Shanti laughed. "My goodness, that is certainly large. Even being as big as a tree would be a feat."

The smile didn't reach Rohnan's eyes. "You were right when you said this has become bigger than us, Chosen. All of this. I hunted down Burson because I didn't know what else to do. I didn't know how to find you and no idea how to combat this upstart-Chosen. They wanted Burson, so I figured I should get him. We couldn't have possibly prepared for all of this."

"No, we couldn't have," Shanti said quietly. "Which is why we are going to get help."

"But you are still the Chosen. That much I am sure." Rohnan's lips thinned—him at his most stubborn. "The Chosen must reunite her distant kin. That was clear. The Shadow People are our distant kin. The Inkna are not."

Shanti was about to retort when something tickled the very ends of her awareness. The wide-reaching net of her *Gift* picked up a mind she recognized.

She sat up in a rush. "He's coming. Death's playground," she cursed, "He's on our trail! Coming slowly, but he's got our trail."

"The Hunter?" Rohnan asked, standing. "You're

sure it's not just another band of thieves?"

Shanti gave Rohnan a level stare as she felt the intruder's mind. Two *Gifted* crouched around him, watchful. They waited for an attack. Other, less intelligent but no less dangerous men traveled with him. Eight of them in all.

"The distance is too great to attack with the *Gifted* blocking his mind. I'd just alert them that they are gaining." Shanti swore and kicked dirt onto the fire to smother the flame. "Burson, can you deaden their *Gifts*?"

"Not at this distance. I don't have anywhere near your range. But neither do they, so they have no reason to push any faster. Although, they are already moving faster than we are." He helped Shanti put out the flame as Rohnan packed up their sleeping sacks. Cunning intelligence burned in Burson's gaze, a look Shanti realized was locked with survival and his insistence on being her guide. "That particular officer is extremely ruthless. He will drive those with him to death without compunction. You may be determined, but he is obsessed. We need to get off this trail and cover our tracks."

"He wants into Xandre's inner circle, and he is on the trail of the violet-eyed girl and a man who can prevent the use of the *Gift*—two finds of the greatest importance to Xandre. I don't think *obsessed* really covers it," Rohnan said as he jogged to the horses. "We can move faster on this trail if we leave the animals behind..."

"No!" Burson finished with the fire and walked toward his horse. "These horses play a part. We must keep them."

"I was hoping you'd say that," Shanti said as she lowered her head and approached her horse. It jerked its snout up, something Shanti now recognized as annoyance. "My bloody bastard of an animal is temperamental, but I would hate to leave him behind when I am winning this battle of wills."

"You are well-matched with your animal," Burson said in complete seriousness.

Rohnan guffawed despite the danger.

They hurried to get everything packed and headed out, traveling as fast as they dared on the rough path in the darkness. A horse breaking his fetlock now, or worse, a human, would mean definite capture. They couldn't risk it.

TWO DAYS PASSED IN A desperate plight, pushing themselves to the point of exhaustion. No matter how fast they went, or how reckless in their escape, the Hunter still gained on them. Slowly, methodically, that mind worked his way closer, ever persistent on their capture.

Two of his men had dropped, near-death, and had been left behind.

"I don't understand how he can do it," Shanti huffed as she made her way groggily. "No human can keep this pace."

Her foot slipped off the side of a rock and sent her balance way to one side. She clutched her horse's reins to keep herself from stumbling into the small stream. A toe left a deep imprint in the mud on the bank. Mouth dry, legs aching, she forced herself forward, sparing only a tiny glance back to make sure Rohnan was still following. He looked just as haggard as she felt, and she had every belief Burson was just as weary.

"He wants rewards more than life, it seems," Rohnan said in something close to a groan. He stumbled, falling against his horse.

"He is without horses," Burson called, his voice tight with strain. "He can move faster, but when we reach the larger road, he will have no chance. He is short-sighted."

"I didn't think Superior Officers were short-sighted." Shanti closed her eyes for a moment, stumbling blindly.

"He *is* human, and he has not yet come up against someone with your skill. I have a feeling he will not enjoy the lesson."

"The trail is wider here. Can't we ride?" Shanti

asked.

"The horses are slipping just as much as we are with only the weight of our packs. If we add our weight, one of them is bound to step wrong and break a leg." Rohnan answered.

Shanti shook her head and dug out her map. Her foot slipped again, tilting her away left. This time her horse jerked its head upwards. The reins slipped from her hand and she fell in a heap into the middle of a prickly bush.

"I am going to cook and eat that blasted animal, never mind setting it free!" Shanti growled. Jagged branches cut into her back and arms.

Rohnan stepped forward, graceful despite his fatigue, and offered a hand. She grasped it with her own and accepted the pull. Once on her feet, she brought the map up. A tiny portion of the trail carried on until it branched to the left. To the right lay a larger thoroughfare. They were almost there.

Shanti tucked the map away and grabbed the bridle with a rough hand. Her horse huffed, but let her. "Exactly. You're bigger, but I'm meaner—"

Shanti's voice hitched as strangers entered her awareness. She groaned and slumped as she walked. "We've got thieves coming and I don't have enough energy to scare them away mentally."

"Save it for danger," Rohnan agreed as they kept

moving. "We can offer them gold, like the others. That usually seems sufficient."

"These aren't normal thieves," Shanti said in a low voice as she felt the watchful minds coming her way. Intelligent and sly, she could sense them, but not hear them. They had some skill sneaking around, which meant they'd had some training.

"Graygual?" Rohnan asked, warning coming into his voice.

"I don't know. They don't have the brain power of an upper-level officer, but other than that, I can't tell."

Shanti staggered forward as she sensed a surge of adrenaline within a pack of four males and one female. They were drawing near, quickening their pace through the trees and rough landscape. The female's mind started to soothe, then become tranquil. Shanti could feel the single-minded concentration of an excellent shot.

"*Flak!* Archer!" Shanti attempted to dive to the side, but her legs gave way beneath her. She dropped and rolled, tucking herself into the foliage.

Rohnan stepped behind his horse with his staff at the ready. Burson was hidden back behind the animals, his colorful mind disappearing entirely.

"Did Burson get hit?" she yelled, grabbing all five minds in a steel grip, ready to defend if it came to it.

"No. He's behind his horse," Rohnan yelled.

"His mind vanished," Shanti explained, monitoring the movement of the five. The woman stood still, hiding within the trees. The other four spread out, one in front of them, one behind, and the other two about to burst out onto the path.

Definitely trained. They'd surrounded Shanti's small party and were moving closer in a coordinated effort.

Shanti did not have the energy for this. She barely had the energy to keep walking.

"That is my *Gift*. It has many facets," Burson called.

A man stepped out on to the path in front of her as Burson yelled, "I have one down here. What do I do?"

"We're surrounded," Rohnan said, looking over his horse at the man who stepped into an open space between the trees.

"We have money for you," Shanti said in an elevated voice as she faced the bearded man walking on balanced feet up the path. She used the local language to appeal to them. They didn't walk with halting steps or nearly cry at what could only be food in the packs on the horses. This band had the intent to kill seeping out of their awareness.

Shanti changed her strategy. *"I have been granted access to this path. I also have the ability to kill you where you stand. As a truce, we will impart you with more wealth than you'd make in a moon's cycle."*

"I, too, have the ability to kill you where you stand." The man smiled through his thick, black beard. Piercing black eyes looked out of a ruddy face. An intricate hilt peeked out of a scabbard at his side. *"We don't take kindly to strangers in these parts. Dangerous people are about."*

"The woman is preparing to shoot," Rohnan warned.

Shanti let her power whip out. She locked onto the woman's mind and immediately used a trick to siphon off the woman's energy supply, trapping her within Shanti's hold. Brief shock and panic flooded the woman's awareness. Her fingers began to release the string of the bow as Shanti *twisted*, draining the last of her resources. The woman jerked. The arrow *zinged* away to the right as a scream split the afternoon.

"She's one of them nasty froons!" another man said in a terrified shout.

"Inkna don't allow women to use mind-power. They're more valuable as breeders," the bearded man said, a throwing knife in his hand. He crouched down and drifted to the side of the path. Judging by his body language, he'd dive into the trees in an instant if an attack came.

"I'm not a Sarsher, *if that's what you're worried about."* Shanti brought a knife out of her leg pouch.

"A man is preparing to throw a knife, Chosen,"

Rohnan said in their home language as he held his staff.

"Chulan?" The man with the beard edged up. His gaze hit Rohnan over the body of the horse. *"You called her* Chulan?"

Those piercing black eyes swung toward Shanti. His knife lowered a fraction.

"You might also know her as the Wanderer. She is the violet-eyed girl, and with her travels the Ghost." Burson's voice rang high above the horses.

The bearded man's knife lowered further. He tucked it into his belt. *"Quite a few titles..."*

"You have no idea..." Shanti couldn't help a loud sigh.

"Please. Pass. You are always welcome here," the man said.

Shanti hunched against her horse, shaking from exhaustion. She'd used valuable resources on the woman, and now had virtually nothing left. *"Thank you. We're on the run, though. A Graygual Superior Office chases us."*

Shanti tossed him a pouch of gold. He snatched it out of the air and tucked it into a pocket, all without looking away from her eyes.

"This Superior Officer knows who he is chasing?"

"Yes."

"Then he will not rest until he has you. We'll slow him down if we can."

Shanti started forward, leaning heavily on her horse. *"Thank you, but be careful. He's one of the best. It might be safer if you steered clear to the side. He won't bother you, then."*

"It was said you were coming. We follow the scriptures. When you command, we will be ready to follow." The man put his fist to his chest. *"We are the keepers of the Thieves Highway, and we stand ready. We'll do what we can."*

Shanti shook her head, too tired to argue. A sweep of pain lanced her mind. Sharp needles cut into her eyes and stabbed at her ears. The *Sarshers* were in range.

She lashed out with a *jab*, slicing through the mind of the strongest of her attackers. She didn't have anything behind the attack, though, there was no energy left. She slammed up her shields as the returned assault fell away. Burson had sheltered her.

"Great find, Rohnan. Really great find," she muttered in a hollow voice. Her legs shook and her balance wavered. "I get rid of one title only to pick up another. It's like a bad joke," she murmured, barely holding onto consciousness as her adrenaline ebbed.

"Go Chosen. You must keep going," Rohnan urged.

Those words called up memories of a grisly battle long past. She saw her grandfather hacked down with a giant, curved blade. Blood spattered as a deep gash split down his back. Kallon, her First Fighter, fled, followed by the dozens she'd chosen to live, to hide until she sent word from the Shadow Lands. Hundreds fell, crumpling to the ground in pools of blood as the enemy ran them through.

"Too many, Rohnan," she whispered, overcome by the memories and succumbing to exhaustion. "We don't have a chance." Her eyes grew heavy as her body sagged. The memories crowded her drowsy consciousness, like a walking nightmare.

"Keep going, Chosen. You need to push through this. We're almost there, and then you can ride. Then you can rest."

Shanti took a deep breath and staggered forward. She felt a large, blunt nose hit the middle of her back. Her blasted horse was shoving her on.

"What is wrong with her?" she heard through a fog of fatigue.

Burson's voice drifted up as that blunt nose pushed her again. *"Stand ready, my friend. Stand ready. The journey has begun."*

CHAPTER 6

SANDERS RODE AT THE HEAD of a long progression of soldiers. He'd spent only one night in the Duke's city, showered with food, drink and attention from dancing girls with heaving bosoms. When he was younger, one night would certainly have turned into a great many, but now, with a wife at home and a gut constantly threatening him, he just wanted to get the job done and move on.

"Hurry up, you lot. Dragging your ass only makes the journey longer," Sanders yelled at the men behind him.

He let his eyes glaze as he stared straight ahead. They traveled a common road with wide, easy to navigate lanes. It was a large, barren thoroughfare that cut through the land from the west to the east. Traders and travelers both, wanting to save time and travel quickly, used this route regularly, often employing hired swordsmen, or like Sanders, military men, to protect them against rough folk looking to make an easy few pieces of gold. There were always those who didn't think they needed protection, though, assuming that with a heavily traveled route someone would come to their aid if a bandit tried to stop them. They turned out to be easy pickings—only the best bandits and thieves worked this road, appearing as traders themselves until they were in a position to seize their treasures quickly and brutally, often stealing horses in the process.

Sanders had stopped a couple of robberies in progress, but mostly he just saw the aftereffects—men on foot without a bronze penny to their name, walking to the nearest town. Skimping on guards created broke men; he'd seen the proof.

He leaned forward and braced his elbow on the pommel of the saddle, letting his gaze drift out to the side. Sparse trees dotted dusty, flat land. Mountain ranges lined the horizon away to the right, and rolling hills away to the left, but through the middle there wasn't much but boredom, occasionally broken by people-watching, scratching and farting.

"I don't like the look of that crowd." Jerrol, a good rider and decent swordsmen, trotted up beside Sanders. He pointed ahead to a small group of riders.

Sanders squinted into the glare of the afternoon sun. Three slight figures rode with two larger ones. The breadth of their shoulders, even those with thinner frames, suggested men, but you never could tell in this part of the world. He'd seen some big women thundering through.

"What's the problem?" Sanders asked, glancing at the younger man.

"Well, for one, they're trotting. Their horses look shiny, like they've been trotting for a while. This is a long road—a trot in this area is a sprint between two close towns."

"Okay, they're in a hurry. What problem is that of ours?"

"They've got swords, too. Two of them do, anyway. Those are good horses—I'd bet they're army."

Sanders squinted into the sun again, straining his eyes at the waists of the incoming group. He shook his head with his blurry vision—his eyesight wasn't what it used to be. "Most people along this route have swords, Jerrol. Have you always been this jumpy? We've got four times the number of men they have."

Jerrol gave Sanders an incredulous look. "I would've thought you, of all people, would be leery of men in black uniforms."

Cold washed through Sanders. Adrenaline spiking, he squinted into the glare again, focusing on those uniforms. Three of them wore long sleeved, high necked, black tunics. The uniforms of the larger men were of a different style, but also black.

"What color is the Graygual uniform?" Sanders asked. Heat worked into his body as his temper rose.

Memories of the torture sessions at the hands of the Inkna burned into his mind. He could only think one thing: *Vengeance!*

"Black, sir. I remember the Captain saying their uniforms were black with a red circle on the front. Two of those approaching have the red circle, with slashes through them."

"I'll take your word for it." Sanders gritted his teeth, reining in the fire shooting through his limbs, begging for immediate action. "The Graygual own the Inkna, and the whole lot of them are our enemies."

"What do we do, sir?"

The intense rage fueled a manic grin on Sanders' face. "Kill them all. I will not let one Inkna walk this land if I can help it. And Shanti would thank me for taking out the Graygual. Let's clean up this road."

"But what about their power? We have no defense…"

Sanders could hear the fear in Jerrol's voice. If Sanders was in any way sane, he'd have felt that same fear pinging around his body. They'd both seen, firsthand, what that mind power could do. And they'd get a full blast without Shanti or the Captain's protection.

But Sanders was past fear where the Inkna were concerned. He'd extinguished all his fear in those torture sessions. They'd put him through the fires of hell, and he'd come out burnt and laughing. He would be damned if he'd bend his knee now.

"Act as if nothing is amiss. We'll just walk along, calmly, letting them draw near. When they're close, we'll spring. Hopefully we'll kill the Inkna before they have a chance to use their power. I want to capture one of those Graygual, though. We need to know their plans. Take that back and let the men know."

"Yes, sir." Jerrol didn't hesitate to move back into the line. Sanders could hear the murmuring begin behind him as the message spread. Leather creaked and metal sounded, each man preparing for a confrontation.

Sanders didn't want to tell Jerrol, but this skirmish would be important for the Duke's men to witness. They hadn't had any interaction with mind power, and they'd never seen a Graygual—not as far south as they were. Not yet. He wanted them to know, firsthand, what it felt like when invisible sandpaper raked over their eyeballs. The Duke's men needed to know what they might be up against—the type of people that might come calling when the Captain was away.

As the group of five trotted closer, Sanders saw that Jerrol was right. Those horses were under pressure and close to exhaustion. They were in a hurry, and had been for a while. They didn't care about obviously expensive thoroughbreds, which meant they were rushing to catch up with something infinitely more valuable.

Sanders wondered what that might be as he let his gaze drift to the side. Staring was the wrong way to make friends. He had to be patient. He had to act as if nothing was wrong. For a surprise to work, the other party couldn't have any suspicion. When it came to the Inkna, the element of surprise, or having Shanti at one's back, was the only way to play it.

Yes, the very best of friends. After his days in the dungeon, he could say that he was on intimate terms with the Inkna. They were such welcoming hosts, switching from one torturer to the other, taking turns hurting him as acutely as possible. Great bedside manner.

Sanders felt a grimace twisting his lips. Rage welled up, hot and heavy. His fingers itched to take his sword and run screaming at that group of disgusting people—they *trained* to be torturers. That was their trade. That was their sole purpose.

The grimace twisted Sanders' mouth further. That foreign woman had turned his life upside down, but he'd break his back to help her put this land to rights. To scrape out all the filth like the Inkna and burn the vermin that put them in positions of power. He owed his future children justice. He owed the downtrodden his help—every able-bodied warrior did.

"They're slowing Commander!" Jerrol hissed from behind. "They're looking straight at you."

"Shit." Sanders turned his head slowly, the grimace still twisting his lips into a crazed sort of smile. He could see the approaching group clearly now. Three *Sarshers*, and two Graygual, one with four slashes on his chest and the other with three. He had no idea what rank that made them, but based on how they sat their horses, and their movements, they were certainly higher than an average foot soldier. Their swords were pretty, too. New leather on the grip and polished where the metal peeked out of the sheath. Not used often, which meant they were probably trained men who had been given a post, rather than warriors who had been elevated out of the dredges.

He'd long ago learned the differences in fighting style between those two types of men. And he'd once slapped the Captain on the back for making his army work for their positions.

"Play it easy, Jerrol," Sanders said in a low tone, leaning over the pommel of his saddle in faux relaxation. "The Inkna that tortured me weren't great at reading emotion or intent. They specialize in pain. The only emotion they recognize is suffering."

"We're wearing our uniforms, though..."

Sanders couldn't help glancing down at his crinkled blue uniform. He gave a quick look back and saw most of the uniforms to the front of the progression were also blue. He shrugged. "Blue isn't an unusual color. Just keep your body language relaxed."

"Most of these guys were at that battle, sir. Hard to be relaxed when you know what kind of pain they can inflict."

Sanders ground his teeth in frustration as one of the Graygual took out his sword. The other followed suit a moment before an intense, searing pain cut out Sanders' thoughts. It felt like hot coals were dumped into his head while claws raked across his throat. Searing heat pierced his gut and churned his stomach.

"Push through the pain and take them down. That's the only way to end this!" Tears of agony trailed down Sanders' face. He kicked the sides of his horse. The animal burst forward into a gallop, heading straight for the enemy. Hooves sounded off behind him as the men followed, not to be deterred by the mind power.

His eyes were attacked next, like hot needles pricked into his pupils. He squinted, trying to block out the pain. He leaned forward to increase the horse's speed. His horse screamed. It reared, throwing him back. He clutched the reins and squeezed with his knees, barely holding on.

The horse screamed again, bucking wildly. Sanders' body ripped to the side. His weight carried him as the horse bucked again, throwing him completely. His eyes snapped open in time to see the ground rushing toward his face. The torrent of pain cut off for a moment, giving him time to feel the full effect of his cheek smashing against the hard dirt. His head bounced, dizzying his thoughts.

More horses screamed. Face on fire but his body fine, Sanders bounced up and ripped out his sword. Only one man managed to hang on to the back of his animal. The rest were on the ground, scrambling up just like him. Then the second attack came.

Pain lanced his body, buckling his legs and stabbing his head. Bursts of light flashed behind his eyes. Claws raked down his chest. He staggered forward, falling, sword out, desperately trying to keep going. Trying to get at those Inkna. He couldn't get off his knees, though. He couldn't fight whatever they were doing to him enough to get to his feet.

A shiny, black boot crunched the dirt and stones in front of him. Another joined it. Sanders looked up through tear-drowned eyes. A black uniform with a red circle and four red slashes stared back at him. An immaculate sword came up, reflecting the late afternoon light in its polished blade.

"We have heard about you. Westwood Lands, yes? The man with scar. Big brave man. Your head will make the perfect warning for this Cap-a-tan I have heard about. And perhaps the Being Supreme will give me a nod for doing what the Inkna failed to do and kill you." The tip of the sword came up. The flat of the blade touched the underside of Sanders' chin and applied pressure. Sanders kept his head down, resisting the unspoken command to look up.

"Ah. Proud. There are ways around this, of course." The blade tilted until the sharp bite of metal cut into his soft flesh.

Sanders sucked in a breath, but did not raise his head. They were going to kill him anyway, what was the point in going quietly? To that end, he said, "You know, I really hate your accent. It sounds like you're chewing shit when you speak. And it's *Captain*. Cap-tain."

The pain keeping him grounded surged, stabbing through his body and knocking him forward onto his hands.

"You see? There are ways to make you obey," the Graygual said.

"You're not making me obey, your minions are. Doesn't count. You're still a pansy with your shiny boots and stupid, swirly sword. I'd call you a girl, but I know a girl who could kick your ass..."

The Graygual's boots scraped on the ground as the man shifted. The blade bit deeper into the underside of Sander's chin and a trickle of blood dribbled down his neck. "Just know that your Cap-a-tan has been noticed by the Being Supreme," the Graygual hissed. "Once he is done with his business in the east, he will burn your city to the ground, rape your women, and skin your men alive. Those that survive will be sold as slaves. Your Cap-a-tan will be put on display as an example of what happens when a nation defies our rule."

"Promises, promises," Sanders growled, gritting his teeth against the pain.

The grating laugh above him made his blood boil. The sword came away and swung upward. Sanders closed his eyes and took what came in silence.

SHANTI WIPED THE DROOL FROM the side of her mouth. She blinked into the late afternoon sun right before a sparse tree branch *thwapped* her in the face. Ducking to the side to avoid the next branch, she strained against a tight rope looped around her torso and the neck of her horse. Rohnan traveled in front of her, one arm pushing the branches out of his way without regard to their swinging back and hitting the person behind him. That person being her, obviously.

"What's with the rope?" Shanti asked in a groggy voice. She fingered the coarse material, tracing it until she found the knot at her side. *A slip knot.* A quick tug and the rope came loose. The horse gave a nondescript whinny.

Rohnan glanced back. The soft light highlighted his features and set off his vivid green eyes. "How much do you remember?"

Shanti's mind shuddered to a start. Hazy images of battles and blood seeped through her memories. The horror was sliced with the feeling of rocks tripping her feet and the sound of running water. Piercing black eyes and a matted black and gray beard swam into focus. She remembered mounting her horse in a daze of bloody memories.

"Ah. I passed out shortly after we hit the main trail, then." Shanti coiled the rope and stuffed it into one of her saddle bags. The movement had her shoulder screaming. She swung it in a circle, trying to release some of the stiffness, only for the pain to intensify.

She pulled down the neck of her tunic. The skin on her shoulder and upper arm had started to turn a frightening shade of blotchy red. Soon the blood would pool and the area would transform into a fantastic bruise. Since they hadn't seen an enemy, and Rohnan wasn't in the habit of kicking women who were passed out…

"Yes, you fell off your horse, which is why we tied you on."

"We've talked about that, Rohnan. It's more gratifying when I get to figure these things out for myself. Using your *Gift* to read me is cheating."

Shanti glanced around. They traveled amongst sparse trees within dry and brittle grasses. Two hundred strides or so from where they rode ran a wide and tightly packed dirt lane. Judging by the desolate land, and the barren area alongside the road, that path was the Cross-Land Travelway.

"Rohnan, could you have chosen a more visible road to travel?" She let her *Gift* blossom and spread, reaching behind them as far as she could. Small animals and a few men and women dotted the area, but she couldn't feel her pursuers.

"We rode hard for a while to get away from that small mountain path," Rohnan explained. He pushed a branch out of his way. When he let go, it swished back at her, barely missing her face. "That's when you fell off. Have we lost them?"

"Yes. Why this road, though?" She leaned to the left, spying Burson leading the way in front of Rohnan. "Ah. He's in charge."

"He said we had to come this way. I would've chosen the smaller trade route, but…"

"For a man we don't know, we are certainly giving him free rein."

Rohnan shrugged. "He seems to be using some inner compass based on ancient texts and knowledge. In our blind spot, he has vision. When the tables turn, he is quiet until he is needed. He fits. I trust him to lead when we cannot."

"You're starting to sound like him." Shanti let her mind reach out in front, focusing her *Gift's* strength and coverage on the road to come. No animals brushed her consciousness this time. With as many humans as traveled this route, critters found somewhere else to be, or they found themselves over an open fire. As her reach stretched, an alarming sensation tickled her awareness. The edges of consciousness, nearly out of reach, blasted out fear and pain.

"Something is happening," she said, pulling on the reins. The horse didn't slow. "There is a battle ahead."

"Yes. We must hurry," came Burson's voice ahead of them.

"*Hurry?* We need to find another—" Shanti's body jerked backward as her horse lurched forward. Rohnan's horse had already begun to run.

"This is madness!" she yelled, tugging on the reins again in a futile effort. She grabbed the horses' minds, trying to figure out how to get them to stop running without spooking them into throwing their riders. "We don't have the manpower or energy to—"

Shanti cut off again as a mind she instantly recognized drifted into her consciousness. Determination and steadfast stubbornness colored intelligence, currently braced against something that made him wince inside. Sparks of fear burning through his aggression made her heart thump. He'd only be afraid for those he loved, and as he was away from home, it meant he was afraid that his death would leave his family defenseless.

Sanders was in grave peril.

She leaned forward in sudden desperation. Her horse gave another jolt of speed, faster and more agile than the other two horses. She passed Rohnan easily. Burson was next. Huffing and beginning to pant, the horse pushed harder. It ran faster, another burst of speed that had Shanti's cheeks rippling and adrenaline coursing through her blood.

Speed is fantastic. Balancing on this animal at this speed is terrifying. And exhilarating.

She felt the pulsing of power, focused and intent. *Sarshers* made the pain rain on Sanders' men, keeping them on the ground, but not having enough power to kill them. She found two smug and superior minds that weren't buckled down in pain. Graygual, she'd bet, and one of them was right next to Sanders, anticipating some sort of action.

Probably a killing blow.

Shanti blasted out with a cutting strike, aiming for the *Sarshers* but sparing a *slice* for the man standing over Sanders. Her substantial power cut into the enemy minds, catching them unprotected and unaware. A new brand of pain welled up, one flared higher by fear. She felt them falter, writhing in the pain searing their minds.

Her horse drew closer, bearing down on an army in the road slowly realizing they were free from agony.

Three *Sarshers* lay beyond them, sprawled on the ground, clutching their heads. One Graygual paused in his advance of the army with his sword drawn. The other Graygual had his sword in the air, one hand braced on his forehead, frozen in pain.

"C'mon!" Shanti yelled at her horse. She pulled her sword from its sheath and flung a leg over the saddle so that she stood in just one stirrup, a move surprisingly easy at this speed. She cut off the power and yanked at the reins. For once the horse responded, and slowed enough for her to jump off.

WITHOUT WARNING, THE PAIN BLINKED out of Sanders' mind. Without wasting one moment, he leapt up as his vision cleared. The Graygual in front of him staggered back, one hand on his forehead, the other hanging at his side, still holding his sword. Like a phantom, a woman thundered into their midst standing on the side of her horse. Barely slowing, she jumped off her mount, hit the ground and rolled before rising, sword bared and a hard look of steely determination on her all-too-familiar face. The *Sarshers* were starting to pick themselves off the ground when she was upon them.

"Damn it! I was supposed to save *her* the next time!" Sanders snatched his sword off the ground as the Graygual shook his head. He looked at Sanders with hard, brown eyes.

"That's the lady that can kick your ass, by the way." Sanders advanced with a slow, balanced step. The Graygual bent at the knees and crouched into a 'ready' position. Balanced and poised, his sword work would be exactly as his teacher taught him, but that didn't make him battle-ready.

"You have to know when to make threats." Sanders circled the Graygual, seeing how his body moved. Seeing if he was the kind of guy to make the first advance, or to wait for a mistake. "I've got the backing of the most powerful mind-fucker in the land. You've got dead friends. See the difference?"

Sanders let his empty hand come out to grapple as another phantom, this one with streaming white-blond hair down to his shoulders and wielding a spinning staff, thundered through. "Oh. And she has a friend."

"You talk a lot for a fighting man. Is this because you are scared?" the Graygual taunted.

"Nah. Just bored." Sanders didn't lunge, as the Graygual expected. He charged. Hand out, sword ready to stab, he barreled toward the other man with wide eyes and a maniacal grin. Fear was a powerful weapon, and an unpredictable madman accomplished that much more quickly than a poised swordsman with excellent technique.

Sanders dodged the strike he knew would come,

batting the sword to the side with his own, and punched the Graygual in the face. The man's nose cracked. His eyes blinked, then started to water. His sword lashed out in a precise arc.

"I'll bet you were the pride of your teacher." Sanders blocked, circled, and blocked again. "I hated guys like you."

He batted the sword away for the third time and grabbed the man's forearm. He slashed down with his sword, catching the wrist and severing the sword hand. The immaculate and shiny sword fell to the ground in a shower of blood.

The man didn't so much as grunt. With a face immediately draining of color, the man clutched at Sanders tunic with his good hand and ripped to the left, then the right. His nose gushed blood down his lips. The man was beaten, but he wasn't giving up.

"Hell's turnips, you had brutal training, didn't you?" Sanders said with a somber tone as he stepped away. Still the man followed him with his maimed arm pressed tightly to his chest.

The second phantom appeared behind the Graygual with a graceful glide on deathly silent feet. He swung his black staff that ended in curving blades at the head of the Graygual. The wood hit the enemy's head with a solid *crack*. The man's eyes rolled back in his head before his body went limp.

The blond man looked up at Sanders with cutting, green eyes. Sanders' grip on his sword tightened.

Sanders had seen death and emotional scarring in the eyes of a few. The people the Inkna had conquered looked at the world through a hollowed-out funnel of misery, but Sanders had never seen such turmoil and raw pain bleeding through the eyes of an emotionally desecrated soul. This man had clearly seen some shit, and it had torn his world out from under him. He wasn't an empty shell; he hadn't shut off to hide from the agony of his past. He'd hardened it, sharpened it, and filed it down into a vicious killing edge that would slice right through an enemy three times his might.

Sanders glanced over to see Shanti helping someone to his feet.

For the first time, he realized that he *had* seen this look before, but he had been too wrapped up in the idea of someone dangerous having a pair of tits to notice. Both of these had not only seen Hell, but had run out of it on fire. Within the green eyes staring at him, he could see that fire still burning, fueling his vengeance while eating him from the inside out.

The worst realization of all was that the shit Shanti and this man had been through was rolling downhill, toward the Captain and all his people. The Captain had been right—they didn't have any time to lose.

The man spoke in a voice that sounded more like a

song than speech but the words weren't something Sanders recognized.

"Huh?" Sanders asked dumbly, fingering his knife.

The man turned to Shanti, who stepped over the other Graygual's body to affectionately hug Jerrol. More singing erupted from the stranger. She glanced over, winked at Sanders, and answered in the same foreign language.

"Oh good, it's going to be a club of two," Sanders said in a dry voice as the blond man turned back to him.

"You bandage hand." He nodded to the Graygual. "Keep alive."

"Where the hell did you two come from?" Sanders demanded, moving to the rest of his men, making sure that no one was dead or seriously wounded. Most men had pale faces, trying to hide their shaking limbs, but everyone was alive. The dead Graygual hadn't had a chance to slice off any heads.

"Rugger," Sanders barked. A wide-eyed man with dark hair looked his way. He stepped forward on uncertain legs, trying to look everywhere at once, including the trees behind him. This had been his first fight with mental weapons and it wasn't sitting well.

Sanders knew how he felt.

"Y-yes, sir. Yes," Rugger answered with a waver in his voice.

"You'd best get used to that style of fighting, son.

You're going to see and feel a whole lot more of that before this is through. If you make it that long."

"Yes, sir." Rugger gulped and glanced at the tree line.

"Make sure that Graygual lives. We need information." Sanders stepped out of the line of sight so Rugger could notice the enemy behind him.

Rugger's eyebrows sank low in determination. "Yes, sir."

The Duke had sent their field doctor-in-training. The kid was supposed to be quick to react and fearless in battle when someone fell. From what Sanders had observed, he also said stupid things and didn't have a real quick wit. But then, Marc was supposedly a genius, and he was not responding well. Sanders would take quick action and idiocy over intelligent stuttering any day.

Putting away his weapons, he swallowed his pride and marched toward the woman who had turned his life upside down. She stood with a couple of his men, peering in eyes and asking questions, but when Sanders got close, she stepped away.

Sanders found the affirmation in those violet eyes of what he'd just seen in the green; a deep, haunting sadness creating an edge that whispered of death and burning bodies. The way she stood, graceful and lithe, spoke of beauty and dancing, but the sleek, predatory quality of her movements screamed danger. Her sword work was every bit as smooth and precise as the Graygual warrior Sanders had just fought, but within those practiced movements was a harsh brutality learned through desolate travels and cruel survival.

"When we truly open our eyes, we can finally *see*." A squat man with graying hair plodded into their midst. He smiled at Shanti. "You have learned to trust again. By discarding the burden, you have allowed your mind to blossom and allowed your allies into your world. Only now can you fulfill your destiny."

"I liked when you spoke in the Southern Region's speech better," Shanti said to the older man.

"Yes, but we are breaching a smaller sphere, now. We are walking into the lands of the once-protected. They speak only that which they were taught." The man looked at the sky and smiled. "A man who charges and breaks noses against the finest quality Graygual training in this land. What a treat. And look who was the victor! Xandre will not be pleased, and these warrior-men will not be safe. What a lovely new facet. I do so enjoy watching the Wanderer's journey unfold. I am lucky to have been chosen to lead the way."

"Here we go with that title again. I'm sick of hearing about titles," Sanders spat. He glared at Jerrol, who was staring at Shanti with stars in his eyes. "What are you looking at, Staff Officer? Go get those horses."

Jerrol started. His gaze cleared as he met Sanders' eyes. "Sorry, sir. Yes, sir."

The blond man said something in his sing-song voice.

Shanti replied, "Yes, he's a real treat. But if you mention it, he'll try to kick you in the balls."

"Don't talk about me when I can't understand you," Sanders snapped. "Now, where did you find your twin, who's this older man, and why are you suddenly coming to my aid after I haven't seen your ass for months?"

"I answered Rohnan in your language, dummy," Shanti replied easily.

The blond man smirked before saying something else and taking off at a graceful lope toward his horse.

"Where's he going?" Sanders asked as he squinted after Rohnan. The sun was a bastard for being in the way today.

"He's my brother and my Chance. He's going to round up the horses. The men in red are still on edge; they will only succeed in scaring the horses further." Shanti nodded at the older man, who was watching everyone with a crooked smile. "And he's sometimes extremely intelligent, sometimes half-cracked, as Rachie would say, and always mysterious. We need him, for his *Gift* at least. You can thank him for saving your life. If he hadn't been leading, we would not have come this way."

Sanders couldn't help a moment of relief. He didn't want to owe her any more than he already did. She smirked, probably reading him with that weird mind-thing she had. Thankfully she didn't say anything. She knew he wasn't above punching a smartass woman in the mouth—as long as she wasn't looking and he could get the jump on her.

"The Captain has begun gathering people to his side?" Shanti asked in a level, even voice.

The unusual decorum from the woman had Sanders squinting into her face, trying to read through her blank expression. The old man started to chuckle.

"Yes," Sanders answered slowly. "This was the last holdout. Krekonna had already started bringing together like-minded cities and towns before the Captain contacted him. He's seen the most Graygual influence."

"Krekonna..." Shanti's violet gaze shifted for a moment, probably trying to place that name. A smile came over her face. "Yes. I stopped in his city. Tachon is his Battle First, the leader of their army. I dined with him a few times—a gentleman."

"That's him. We have a decent-sized army if everyone pulls together. At least in theory." Sanders shielded his face from the glare of the sun.

"In theory... meaning, now it will take organization and power-struggles to determine who will lead this larger army." Shanti nodded and glanced after her twin. "Yes, that will certainly be an issue, but not a pressing one. Not yet. Your army won't be enough if we don't also have *Gifted*."

"Yeah. We know. Are you coming back with us?" Sanders tried to remain nonchalant. If she said no, he'd be following her like a ghost until he found someone who could send a raven to the Captain. No sense in letting her get away and having to start the search from scratch.

But if she did come back, she'd bring her circus with her. She'd been hard to manage before—with a twin and this crazy old man, she might prove to be a nuisance.

"I need to speak with Cayan." She cleared her throat. "With the Captain. So, for now, yes. We can travel behind if you don't want us riding amongst you."

Sanders squinted at her face as her twin rode up. He jumped off his horse and stalked in that strangely elegant stride to reach her side. He said a few words that made her straighten up.

Sanders knew that look.

"You hurt?" he asked.

"We have some very scary Graygual on our tail," the old man said, walking toward his horse. "They are probably on the wrong road at present, but they will come. They will come, and when they do, they will cause the uniting. We had best hurry. There is a lot of journey between now and then. A lot of stones to throw."

The twin stared at Shanti as he said, "She is near deplete. We need tie her to her horse."

"I'm fine, Rohnan." Shanti waved him away.

Sanders rolled his eyes. "Same old bullshit. Let's get moving. And I'll help you tie her. Would a gag be out of the question?"

"I missed you, too, you ass," Shanti said in a dry voice.

"We wait until she fall off. Reward for stubborn," the blond—Rohnan she had called him—said.

"Even better." Sanders stalked toward his horse to hide his smile.

She was a pain in the ass and caused him nothing but hassle. And yes, she gave him headaches constantly, messed up his training yard, and had his men looking at her with either suspicion or stars in their eyes. But he couldn't deny he'd missed having the distraction. Whatever she was, she knew her stuff, and was never boring. Never, ever boring. In the months to come, that might be a prerequisite for survival.

As he climbed up into his saddle, Sanders couldn't help another smile, brighter than the first. The fireworks she and the Captain would create when they inevitably butted heads would light up the sky. He couldn't wait for the battle of wills.

CHAPTER 7

CAYAN SAT IN THE PARK with his legs crossed and forearms resting over his knees. The cool of the night blanketed his face as he let his power bubble up and blossom out. He let out a sigh as his mind drifted. Tonight he didn't want to play leader and protector—he just wanted to relax.

He'd spent the last couple of days in a storm of activity. The crew he wanted to take with him to find Shanti was organized, the routes mapped out. Even Daniels had agreed that the trip was the best course of action. The older Commander didn't like the strange foreign women, as Daniels called her, but they had no other choice; not if they wanted to have a fighting chance against the Graygual.

Cayan let the stress and fatigue melt away. He rolled his neck to loosen sore muscles, then did the same thing with his arms and shoulders.

He'd trained with Lucius earlier that day, his Lieutenant and oldest friend. While Lucius was a skilled and capable fighter, he wasn't as good as Cayan. No one in the city was. Sanders often made up for it by bringing his own vicious and brutal edge to the fight, but Cayan's people didn't have the inherent viciousness that could hone a warrior's skills to a sharp edge. In his experience, only Shanti had had that. Since fighting her, no one else had been able to compare.

Cayan let his mind flit through the town briefly, ensuring that nothing was out of the ordinary. A few people blasted out the sting of rage, but he knew who those were, and if they weren't fighting with their spouse they wouldn't know what to do with themselves. Soon the anger would turn to another emotion just as intense, and it wasn't one Cayan wanted to spy on.

He drifted out past the gates and checked on the sentries. All were alert and watchful, probably knowing Sanders would be home in the next couple of days and not wanting to be caught unawares.

He pushed out farther, testing his ability. Soon, though, he felt the first traces of minds, slowly making their way toward the city.

Cayan sat forward, focusing in on each mind, realizing immediately that they were his own men returning, with a few foreign minds scattered in. The Duke's men. Sanders was back early.

Good, that'd give him more time to prep for their journey.

He sampled the emotions radiating from the group

as they came further into his range. Most were tired and sore, but Cayan also felt wariness and intense relief, as though supremely glad to be home. He searched for those he recognized, before stuttering on a female. A jolt of electricity blasted through his body.

Shanti.

She'd returned!

Cayan hurried to his feet, everything in his being tugging on him to hurry to the gate. Plans and actions whirled in his mind, thoughts of what they could accomplish now that she was here, and how they would prepare for the next steps.

Then his thoughts started to slow, and reality seeped in. He sat back down slowly.

Why had she come back?

She wasn't like other people. She could be stubborn right down to her core, and she had flat-out denied him. It would take something big to bring her running back, and if he didn't play it just right, she'd make his life hell while walking all over him. Her soft vulnerability coupled with her cutting insight and strength were a lethal combination—one he had a hard time combating even with a level head. He would need to have his wits about him to maintain a firm hand, and a firm hand was the only way to deal with that woman.

He felt her mind notice him. Their *Gifts* mingled. Warmth infused his body as a unique type of strength straightened his back. Energy surged in his blood and fueled his tired body. Adrenaline kicked up, reminding him of battles won and promising of enemies yet to feel his wrath. His fingers tingled, itching for his sword.

He felt her embarrassment for the briefest of moments before she lashed out in a playful mood. She must've been talking to the man coloring with humor beside her, but Cayan didn't recognize him. The interaction seemed comfortable but not sensual. Loving but not romantically so.

Before he could consider this further, his breath left his body as her *Gift* mingled with his. Without warning, his power answered in a growl. It bubbled, growing, and then surging higher. Their *Gifts* circled then entwined, boosting their individual powers into a combined might exponentially higher and stronger than he remembered. Then came that spicy quality that simmered deep in his gut. It flowered until he could almost smell it, spicy-sweet.

It took everything he had to push away the urge to meet her, and instead, sit exactly where he was and let her come to him. This meeting was on his terms—she saw to that by being the first to cave. By returning, she'd handed him the power, and he wouldn't let her steal back the sweet victory of the upper hand without a fight. The battle for control had begun.

SHANTI ABSENTLY WIPED AT HER stomach as butterflies invaded. Her chest felt tight and her head swam with the surge of power she'd felt when her *Gift* had flirted, then merged, with Cayan's.

"You are nervous," Rohnan said in their language. Thankfully he realized now wasn't the time to embarrass her, not with Cayan's army in earshot.

"Yes. I answered his plea for help by stealing his gold and running in the middle of the night. He has every right to deny me access to his city."

"But, you are happy. You merged with him—I felt the huge boost in power. He must not want you out too badly."

"He's fickle. He probably doesn't clearly remember what I'm like."

She didn't mention that, being a man, he was probably remembering that last kiss, and how she fell against his chest like a love-starved fool. His ability to charm women into bed was no secret, and Shanti believed that ability extended to charming women to get whatever else he wanted. With a heavy dose of attractiveness, a stellar physical frame, and all his other… assets, the man had a swinging door with all the women coming and going. Throw in a pair of mouthwatering dimples and the man should just be avoided altogether. It was the safest route to take.

"You've stolen things all your life. It's always been

sport—why is this different?" Rohnan inquired. *"Judging by the horses, their clothing and their various weaponry, the land has riches. I doubt he missed it. So why the guilt?"*

"Because he saved my life and then invited me to share his home—his city. He gave me a sort of family when I had nobody. He had the chance to trade me to the Graygual, and instead he let me stay. Do you hear what I'm telling you? He found out that the most dangerous man in the land is looking for me, making his city a target, and he was prepared to shield me anyway. All he asked was time to settle things, and then let him accompany me on my journey. After all that he'd done for me, it was such a small request. My response? Cowardice. Running away like a frightened little girl. What would be the punishment for that with our people, Rohnan? For that utter lack of loyalty when he'd earned my allegiance..."

Rohnan's lips thinned. *"Being that we need you, pain so acute it would make you pass out. Otherwise, probably death, depending on the mood of the prickly yet enigmatic leader. Or don't you remember administering such punishments yourself?"*

"I really wish you knew when questions were rhetorical..." Shanti felt that heavy weight of guilt settle onto her. *"I have disgraced myself. And I need to atone for it."*

"Is he the sort of leader who will punish you as he

ought?"

Shanti scoffed. *"These people fight well. They are brutal at times, but they are not hard. They have no reason to be. They're pampered in wealth and luxury. What little strife they know is with a nation close by who are dirty and disheveled. They pose no real threat. No, he will not punish me. In fact, when he fights me, his thoughts often turn sexual. He humiliates me to avoid having to strike me. He will not harm a woman if he can help it."*

"You are aroused, but yet, you've not bedded him?"

"Would you stop using your Gift*? It's irritating! Some things are private."*

Rohnan laughed. *"You have a prudish nature hiding behind that bold mouth. You gave yourself to Romie without a mating ritual—very rare. And now you are... what? Shy?"* Rohnan laughed again. *"Who is this girl I grew up with? She's not the woman she tries to be."*

Shanti's face heated with embarrassment. *"This man is cunning. I would've been happy with Jerrol if he had defied his precious Captain. But Cayan is not someone to tamper with."*

Rohan glanced at Jerrol, the man who had entranced Shanti with his beautiful, earth-brown eyes that reminded her so closely of Romie. When he turned back, his smile had dwindled. *"I can see why. It's in the eyes."*

"Yes," Shanti said simply.

"But Jerrol will not make the pain go away. It will probably only intensify it. Only time and loving anew will diminish that pain to a dull ache."

"Thank you, Master All-Knowing. Wait until we get to the town; you can use needlepoint to put those words on a pillow."

Rohnan's voice took on a wispy quality. *"I would have given myself solely to one person if I had loved. My* Gift *makes me feel harder, though. I may only be able to love once in my life."*

"Better once than not at all."

"More words for this pillow. But what is needle-point?"

Shanti laughed as they worked closer to the large wooden gates at the front of Cayan's city. *"You'd probably like it. I'll have Junice, Sanders' wife, show you."*

After a quiet moment, Rohnan asked, *"Can this Captain fight?"*

"Physically, he can outmatch me. He is a large man but extremely quick. His style is ever-changing, as well. He adapts to each new enemy, almost instantly. I've never seen his equal."

"That is good. Hopefully the Graygual haven't, either. And his Gift?*"*

"A little stronger than mine, but all brute force. He can only blast with a heavy hand. Maybe it's just a lack

of knowledge, or maybe his Gift *is different than mine, I can't be sure. I need to train him, though. I showed him enough to make him dangerous, and then I walked away."*

"You will need to right that wrong, Chosen, or it will eat you alive. He'll probably only need an apology, but you will need to follow our customs for this, no matter how hard that might be."

"Now who is constantly stating the obvious?"

"You're slow. I must speak slowly and spell things out or you'll continue to blunder about in the dark."

Shanti rolled her eyes. *"I should've left you in the Graygual camp."*

"Yes, I have found that idiots are often happier in a puddle of their own stupidity. Say no more. From now on I will simply smile and nod when you say ridiculous things."

Shanti gave him a light shove with her mind, then envisioned giving him a tight hug. He smiled as he felt it. *"I missed you, Chosen. Very much."*

"Me, too."

"Talking in a language I don't know is rude," Sanders said as he pursed his lips. "Nice horse, by the way. What'd you do, steal it?"

"Yes," Shanti replied.

Sanders grunted then braced his hand on his thigh. His eyes drifted up into the trees, making sure the sentries were doing their jobs. "They're good animals. We need to get them into our breeding lines. That'll wipe that smug grin off the Duke's face. He won't be the head in horseflesh for much longer…"

The walls of the city reached into the sky as they drew near. A guard nodded as they passed through the large, wood gates. His gaze glanced at her, paused on Rohnan for a long time, and settled back on her. She felt his suspicion.

"It hasn't been long, but I'd forgotten how some of these people viewed outsiders," Shanti said in a low tone. "Especially female outsiders in men's clothing."

"Yeah. You don't fit in real well." Sanders chuckled. "But don't worry—the ones that do know you are also aware that you took off in the middle of the night after stealing all the Captain's gold. They might not trust you so much."

"Sanders, you are a real treat, you know that? Always with the sugar coating." Shanti chewed her lip. As the meeting approached with Cayan, all she wanted to do was turn around and run again. Something about the man turned her into a coward, and she had no idea what it was.

Cayan still hadn't moved from his location in the park. His assistant had checked in to briefly go over accommodations for everyone. They'd set up barracks for the new soldiers, but there were the four additional bodies, including a prisoner, to take care of. He felt Shanti and another threading their way through the trees quickly. Moments later, a small movement ruffled the leaves before Shanti stepped into the clearing.

Cayan's breath caught. She moved with the sleek, predatory quality he remembered perfectly. Her curves defined her as woman, but the stealth in her steps and her economy of movement cried hunter. It also spoke of an unconscious sensuality.

"Hi," she said in a low, sultry voice.

He nodded in response.

She took a step to one side. As if on cue, a man stepped through the foliage and appeared where she had been standing. His mind was that of a sensitive and caring soul and yet he moved like someone born with a sword in his hand, sleek and balanced. His gaze traveled Cayan's limbs and paused briefly on his palms laying relaxed in his lap, cataloging. Identifying the threat.

"This is Rohnan." Shanti ticked her head toward the man. "He is my Chance—like Lucius. Except, he has held this role since… forever. Since childhood. He is my brother in everything but blood."

"You thought him dead…" Cayan said slowly.

"Yes." She walked until she stood directly in front of Cayan, and then gracefully sank to the ground. Rohnan didn't move. "He took a wound to the stomach, but as soon as he was mostly healed, he came looking for me."

Cayan shook his head as confusion enveloped him. "Where did you find him?"

"I heard rumors of a ghost." Doubt crossed her face. "I heard many rumors. I knew it must be him, though. He was likened to me—they thought there was some connection. That similarity is rare so far east."

"So you followed his trail instead of continuing on your journey?" Cayan kept his voice level, careful not to make it sound like an accusation.

The man spoke up in a voice that almost sang even though Cayan could not understand him.

Shanti waved her brother away. "I can read him just fine, Rohnan."

She put her hands in her lap. "The other rumor I'd heard was about the rightful Chosen. An Inkna. The duty given to me by my people has been forfeit. We were mistaken."

"So you decided to track down a ghost, instead."

"That's right. Hoping it would be my brother. And it was—I freed him from a Graygual camp, even though the great lummox had put himself there in the first place. I also freed the man who is still waiting in the trees. He is the reason Rohnan was in that camp."

Cayan felt a moment of embarrassment as he *searched* for the person in the trees. Embarrassment turned to confusion when he didn't find anyone. His gaze hit Shanti's again.

"He has a special *Gift*. Burson, come out please," she said.

The trees rustled as an older man stepped into the clearing. He wore a wool sweater and a big smile. "It is wonderful to meet you, Captain. So far you live up to the records, and let me just say, I didn't think that would be the case. The *Seers* were mostly women, and women… well, they can embellish when describing heroes. Remarkable."

"He's…" Shanti shook her head. "I'm not quite sure what he is, exactly, and he won't say, but his *Gift* is one I haven't seen. One I didn't even know existed."

Suddenly, Shanti's mind disappeared. Vanished, just like the old man's. Cayan tensed. "He can mask minds?"

"Not only that, but he can suffocate someone's *Gift*, or shield people from it." Shanti's full lips quirked. "He was a great steal. He would've made it incredibly hard to kill Xandre."

"I see," Cayan said in a noncommittal voice. Her confidence was shattered, and she still came bearing gifts. The woman was one of a kind.

Burson looked at the sky with a smile. "Answers are many, but time is short."

Shanti scowled. "He constantly speaks in riddles, or

some kind of code. He seems to have studied some doctrines about a person called the Wanderer, who he thinks is me." A wave of hopelessness washed over her. She turned so she could see the other two men in the clearing. "You can go. I wish to speak with Cayan alone."

Rohnan spoke again in what must be their own language, but Shanti shook her head. "Rohnan, you need to start speaking in this language so you get used to it again. I'm just as safe with him as I am with you. Maybe more so. You can go."

"My task stay by you. All times. I wait in trees." Rohnan turned to go.

"Rohnan." Shanti's voice filled with a warning. "I need to speak with Cayan alone. I'll meet you outside the park."

Rohnan stared down at her for several moments. The edge in his eyes sharpened and his jaw tightened. Cayan smirked—he was the image of Shanti when she dug in her heels, which she was doing now. She held the stare, unblinking, with that same edge. Her gaze also held violence, and she was prepared to chase him out.

Without a word, Rohnan turned and silently walked out of the clearing. He obviously knew her well. Burson, still smiling, went after him, shaking the branches and rustling the leaves as he went. Shanti faced Cayan and bowed her head. She looked at her hands.

"You came back," Cayan said quietly.

He barely heard the answering, "Yes."

After a moment she lifted her gaze to meet his. Her eyes were deep and remorseful, opening up so that he felt like he could look through them down to her soul. "I have to begin by saying that I apologize. I was a coward. While I did feel the duty, I did not properly explain myself to you. You were right—I was running out of fear. I've done a great many things out of fear. I realize that now."

"But if it wasn't for the Inkna posing as Chosen…?"

Shanti barely shrugged. "I would've continued on, I suppose. I would've stumbled along blindly, without a real plan, and probably landed into Xandre's hands. I wasn't thinking."

Her eyes stayed fixed on his as she reached forward with her fist. Her hand turned over. Slowly, her fingers peeled away to reveal something metallic glinting in the moonlight.

"My people have a custom," she began. "When someone acts in cowardice, and puts others at risk, it reduces our honor. It lowers us in the eyes of our fighting brethren. When we also cripple trust, we put other lives in danger. That is not acceptable. In this situation, we must either ask to be severely punished, or we must offer something of great value to us. By presenting something of great value, it acts as a gateway to healing. You can hold onto the medallion, as long as you need to, to rectify your feelings. That may be never, and I will honor that. But when you heal, you can offer it back with a request to communicate openly about the issue, or to just let silence descend. It is all in your hands." She looked down at her palm. "I realize you won't punish me. It's not in your nature, even if I was a man. Plus… that would be the easy way. This is infinitely… more perilous to me."

With a shaking hand, Shanti pushed her palm closer to him. "This is my amulet. Besides Rohnan and my father's ring, it is the only relic from my home. It is the only personal item I possess that captures my heart. This represents all that I am, and I have worn it since I was two years old. Please accept me back."

Her gaze lifted to his. Even if he couldn't feel the guilt and regret emanating from her, he could see it in her face. He could see the fear of an uncertain future, and the hope that he would help her get through the next stage, in her eyes.

He took a deep breath. "What happens if I refuse to take it?"

"I am dead in your eyes. I do not exist."

"Wouldn't that make practice sessions in your village difficult?"

"This has only happened once, and Shanus, the coward, drowned himself at sea. He chose his own punishment."

Cayan's eyes widened. Without intending to, he put his hand on Shanti's knee. "What about a knife? Or your clothes? I could easily take those. It's cold—I'll let you almost freeze before I allow you to return home."

"Giving weapons are forbidden for a fighter. And these clothes aren't mine. I had to trade my clothes for that of a prostitute's. She was twice my size, however, mostly in the chest, so I then exchanged those for what I'm wearing. It's a long story."

Cayan leaned forward. Her direct and honest gaze held his unflinchingly. She wasn't joking. "I'm going to need more information. A whore?"

Her lips quirked again. "Some other time. I'm tired and my body hurts. I've been tied to a bloody horse twice in the last day."

"Why were you tied to a horse?"

"Because I'd ground myself down to zero energy and fell off." She gave a slight shake of her hand. "Please take the amulet, Cayan. Please forgive me."

Cayan leaned a little farther forward, his face now only a foot from hers. His eyes trained on those lush lips as he brushed his fingertips over the tender area of her wrist. He saw goosebumps prickle her exposed skin. He laid his palm flat to hers, feeling the sizzle of electricity pass through their touch. "Every time you look at this amulet around my neck, you will be reminded that I hold a piece of you?"

Uncertainty muddled her mind. Heat wormed into her eyes. "You plan to wear it?"

"Yes."

She licked her lips. He leaned just a little closer.

She said, "I will be reminded of my cowardice, and hope that your forgiveness is forthcoming."

Cayan's thumb brushed hers, stirring something deep in his body and coaxing that electricity higher. She gulped, but did not back away. He focused on those lips. On her heat. "I will wear it as a sign that you are forgiven, but keep it so that you won't run again."

A crinkle wormed between her eyebrows. He was bending her custom, and creating new rules, but he wanted her to be reminded that he held a part of her. More importantly, he wanted her to grow familiar with him holding that part.

He stroked his fingertips across her palm. The metal rolled over her skin. Their energy heated and sparked as he let their touch linger. Finally, his eyes locked with hers, he took the amulet and fastened it around his neck.

"Have you decided what comes next?" Cayan asked softly.

Her eyes were round. She hadn't taken a breath. Fear and uncertainty rolled from her mind, along with something else he couldn't quite place. A deeper feeling, but it wasn't taking shape. Even with access to their minds, he still had a hard time reading women.

"Shanti?" he coaxed gently, dropping his palms. His fingertips rested on the edge of her knees.

She took a breath and backed away from his touch. Her eyes flicked to his neck. She wanted to run again.

Cayan almost laughed.

In a voice that started out weak and wispy, but quickly gained strength, she said, "Xandre cannot have the Shadow People. If they join his cause, we are lost. There will be nowhere either of us can hide. Nowhere I can go. He would track me into the underworld and drag me back out for his benefit if the rumors of the Shadow People are true."

Cayan let the gravity of the situation steal the moment. "The Chosen is responsible for leading the Shadow People, correct?" She nodded. "Then how can that be prevented?"

"I will kill this new Chosen. He matches my power, but he is Inkna. I doubt he can fight."

"But he is surrounded by an army."

Her tongue rolled over her bottom lip. The uncertainty was back. "I realize your offer of aid may no longer be on the… um. Table? But I've come to ask it, anyway. I have qualities you need. I can train you. I can fight with you. I can work with your men. I know more about Xandre than most—I've studied him. I have more like Rohnan and me. They are the best and brightest. I also have some sort of network blossoming because of this Wanderer title. And I have Burson, who is mad half the time, but his *Gift* is valuable."

"And you require my army."

"You, and your army. You are my power's mate. We're stronger together. Much stronger... like you said." Her gaze flicked to the amulet. "There's something else—I'm being hunted. One of Xandre's Superior Officers is on my trail. He aims to take Burson and me alive. He'll kill everyone else with me, except for maybe Rohnan. I don't have much time."

Cayan stood, waiting for her to stand with him. Then he stepped closer to steal a little more of her heat before they headed back. Their conversion had turned to business, but he was a man—part of his anatomy stayed active regardless of the topic. "I'd heard about this Chosen. I have plans in motion to move in that direction and deal with him."

"I know. And I want to go with you."

"Is Sanders that easy to read?"

"Rohnan's *Gift* is... irritating, to say the least, but extremely helpful at times. Especially when fighting. He can read intent, having him reacting before the punch is even thrown. You might spar with him—it could humble you."

Adrenaline spiked through Cayan's body. He flexed,

having Shanti's eyes rounding again as her gaze left his and found his chest, then arms. She backed away. "I'll just head to my new… quarters."

"One more thing," Cayan said, stopping her as she tried to quickly slip away. She didn't turn toward him. "Report to the practice yard tomorrow. I want you training. In the afternoon, at your usual time, you will meet your Honor Guard there. Be warned—all but Leilius hate you. The day after tomorrow there will be a farewell ball. It is customary. You will be there. Visit the dressmaker and have something designed and made for you and your Chance. The morning after that, we leave. Is that soon enough for you? Will this new danger find you before then?"

"Let's both hope not." With that last, somber sentence, she disappeared into the trees as silently as death.

Cayan took a moment to reflect on her parting words. Whoever was chasing her, he had to be worse than the Inkna for her to use that tone. Cayan had thought the Inkna were incredibly tough adversaries. He couldn't imagine what might be worse.

CHAPTER 8

THE NEXT DAY DAWNED CHILLY but bright. Shanti awoke to a fire and a full change of clothes. Most she recognized from her previous time in the city—faded and stained, they were conditioned to fight in. Some, though, she knew were a sort of joke from Cayan, as the shirt and pants were bright pink.

Her gaze drifted out of the window at the far end of the large and richly furnished room. She felt so out of her element. Like water on hot cobblestone, her life's purpose had evaporated upon hearing about the new Chosen. Since then, there had been one strange piece of news after another: new titles, a different set of milestones, an underground group of people looking for a leader… It was as if she'd been ripped out of one future and placed in another.

The only stability was Cayan. The one place that hadn't changed, even though the world was changing around it, was his city. Somehow he had become the one constant in her life.

After breakfast she, Rohnan and Burson made their

way through the immaculate city to the training grounds. Rohnan muttered and chirped about the layout, the cleanliness, and whatever else, but all Shanti could focus on were the knots in her stomach. Her Honor Guard would arrive in a few moments and she was terrified they'd slipped back into uselessness. She worried that she'd deserted them, and left them with a new style no one else could teach in a place that valued fitting into a hierarchy, when she had led them in a loose structure where everyone was heard.

"I wasn't thinking, Rohnan. When I left, I wasn't thinking about anything but a pale duty handed down in old and faded documents. I had five boys who could be shaped into an incredible group of fighters, and I left them in the middle of the night. I had a powerful ally that could join with me and take out an Inkna clutch, *and I stole his money as a silent farewell."*

"You and he could take out a clutch?" Rohnan asked quietly. *"That is more than twelve—incredible."*

"Your leaving was necessary. This unbalance is necessary," Burson said as the expanse of the practice yard came into view beyond the shops lining one of the four main streets. *"When the phoenix emerges from the ashes, it can burn all the brighter."*

"Super. We'll roast a pig." Shanti let her fingers slide over the hilts of the knives in her leg harness.

"I find it amazing that a city of this size, with this

much to offer, doesn't have more travelers and traders." Rohnan's eyes were dancing over the bustling practice yard.

"They are too far north, I think," Shanti said. *"They get visits, but often they are the ones traveling to trade. I've never asked Cayan if that was by design."*

"This is a large, spacious practice yard full of stagnation," Rohnan said in an even tone. Doubt poured out of his emotions. *"What do we hope to accomplish by being here?"*

"This is how they practice. I suspect Cayan has an ulterior motive, as far as we are concerned, but I couldn't decipher it."

Shanti and her people had always practiced in the trees. There were no set areas, no organized starts and stops, and no standing still. Everything was on the move, like in battle. Waiting in line to throw a knife wasn't anything they had experience with, and for good reason.

"We will stand out, Rohnan. Prepare yourself."

"Is that why you're wearing that insanely bright... garment?"

"Partially."

They stepped onto the dirt of the practice yard. Shanti glanced at Burson, still beside her. *"What do you plan to do?"*

"Watch. You must understand, I've lived with an

outline of possible future events—many variations are possible on any one outline. I'm now fortunate enough to fill in the space between the milestones. It is both exciting and necessary to future decisions."

Shanti stopped as gazes drifted her way. To the far left lay the Pit, the most stationary of practice areas. Those waiting for their turn to throw a knife at a target had turned toward Shanti, some with open-mouthed stares. *"Are you a* Seer *Burson? Is that why you directed us toward Sanders yesterday?"*

Burson gestured for her to keep walking. *"Let's get you working. I suddenly find the number of large warriors looking our way... terrifying."*

Suspicion fell off Rohnan in sheets as he looked at Burson. Shanti felt the same. *"Soon I will rip away this cloak of mysteriousness you surround yourself with, Burson,"* she said.

"Soon, yes," Burson waved them on. The hard edge was creeping back into his darting eyes. *"But not yet. First you must regain your footing. Answers come as the questions arise."*

"I just asked the question," Shanti pushed.

"Please start working. I don't like the looks some of these men are giving you. They're obviously not used to women in their midst, and don't like you flaunting your femininity."

"He's right, Chosen. By stepping onto this practice

yard, tension has started to rise." Rohnan's hand drifted toward his own set of knives. He hadn't brought his staff, preferring to work with the sword today, something he wasn't as accomplished with.

Shanti waved away their thoughts as she started toward the Pit. The soles of her shoes made a soft sliding sound as she increased her stride across the yard. Her thoughts of fallen comrades and her uncertain fate fell away as she felt the drive and push of fighters with their swords. Her fingers tingled and her adrenaline surged, not just ready, but anxious to get back to the one thing in her life that was always certain: training. Fighting. Dominating.

A path cleared as she swept through the lines of men at the Pit. She moved with an edge in her eyes and a killer's grace in her bearing. A large man with a scar across his forehead watched her approach with a sneer and a chuckle.

"The pretty lady come to play with knives, is it?" the man taunted. "Watch out you don't break a nail. I only date presentable girls."

Shanti stepped forward and punched him in the sternum with her right hand. She elbowed him in the face with her left before ripping his knife from his hand. With economical movements, she knocked him in the head with the hilt, punched him in the gut, ripped his big body to the side, and stepped around him with a smooth movement. The knife made a loud *thunk* as it found the center of the target painted on the wooden post twenty paces away.

"You should never be flat on your feet," she said in an instructional voice. Rohnan walked toward the post, stopped halfway, and turned to her. He took out two knives in the styling of this town—Cayan must've left instructions for Rohnan to be outfitted with weaponry. "Even in practice, you should always expect to get attacked. Always."

Rohnan ran at her, knives flashing. She stepped toward him, ripped a knife from its sheath, dodged the first swipe and blocked the second. She tried to get a throw off to the distant target, but Rohnan had already shifted. A blade swung down toward her cheek. She flinched back, but the tip sliced across her chin.

"Move faster, Chosen!" Rohnan prompted in the local language.

"No shit, Rohnan." Shanti kicked at his foot and stabbed toward his middle.

"Shit..." he murmured as he blocked her thrust and stepped back.

"Bad... word... for—" she thrust at him again, then pivoted and threw. The blade stuck in the target, off-center, as he gouged forward. "Poop." She blocked with an empty hand and ripped out another knife. She did a backhanded slash to back him up.

"You distracted, Chosen," Rohnan panted as he took two fast steps with knives jabbing and swinging. "*Focus!*"

Shanti let the world dim further. She pushed out of her mind the eventual confrontation she'd have to have with the Honor Guard, her amulet on someone else for the first time in her life, and the incredible odds against them defeating this new Chosen. She shoved it all away and let the moment sink in.

The trees called from the not-so-distant wood. They sang through her *Gift* and seeped into her blood. The soft breeze cooled her hot face. She felt the hard dirt beneath her feet, lifting her up—offering its services to help her on this day. The knives in her hand felt like a friend's touch. The target waited twenty paces away.

Shanti focused on the sparkling green eyes of the enemy in front of her. She bent her knees a little more. The knife shifted a fraction in her grip. The battlefield and the goal realigned in her mind's eye. She winked.

"That's better." Rohnan smirked. "Let fun begin."

Shanti stepped forward in a gush of strength and precision. She slashed with her right hand before punching with her left. Rohnan leaned back and swirled around her. She spun, threw a knife, hit the edge of the target, and ducked under a swinging foot. She punched upwards and connected with his inner thigh.

Rohnan winced and staggered. For their mock battle, his leg would now be useless.

Shanti threw her own kick, knew it would miss, but then lunged, punching him in the gut with the hilt of the knife, and then ripping to the side. She spun again and threw the next knife. It hit off-center.

A heavy weight tackled her from behind. She twisted, but couldn't break the iron grip. She hit the ground full force. Her cheek bounced off the dirt. Pain radiated through her face.

Two fast punches hit her ribs and gut. It didn't matter, though. As she stood, panting, she acknowledged the truth, "We'd both be dead. I failed."

Rohnan stood in front of her. Sweat darkened his shirt and dirt marred his face.

And then without warning, she punched him. She'd always been a sore loser—it was one of her more aggravating quirks.

His head jolted back, but as she hadn't put much into it, he only took one step back. After a beat, his head tilted forward. A smile scratched at his lips. His brilliant green eyes started to sparkle. "Added experience hasn't made you grow up."

"Using your *Gift* when I'm not is cheating," she said in sullen defense. She couldn't help the answering smile, though. She knew what was coming.

And then it did.

Rohnan charged. Arms moving so fast she could

barely keep track, he threw a punch at her face. She flinched to one side, just before his body barreled into her. He took her to the ground a second time, knowing she wasn't as good a fighter on the ground. He didn't know about her scuffles with Sanders, and she'd had a lot of practice since she last tumbled with Rohnan. And she'd had a dirty cheat as a teacher.

She yanked Rohnan's hair as his punch landed in her rib. With the heel of her hand, she pushed his chin up and yanked his hair again, wrenching his head to the side. He grunted and raised his hands to ward off the assault. She twisted her upper body to get him off-center, having him scrambling over her to keep his position. She jammed a fist into his kidney, then his ribs, then under his armpit, aiming for sensitive areas. He pushed her down, getting his face too close to her. She head butted, smacking her forehead off his mouth. His lip split and he grunted again.

She strained and twisted before bucking, throwing his body off her. She was up a moment later, kicking him in the middle. He grabbed her foot, but she fell on him with a knee, landing right in the center of the back.

"Aw—yield! I yield!" he yelled in their home language.

Shanti climbed off and wiped the drool from her chin, then realized it was blood from her previous wound. She took her sleeve and dabbed while Rohnan arduously picked himself up off the ground. Dirt coated his front and his once-perfectly shaped lips were swelling and cracked with blood.

"When you learn how ground fight?" Rohnan asked with a smile. He winced and dabbed at his split lip.

"Watch Sanders fight sometime. He cheats." Shanti couldn't help a triumphant smile.

"You more brutal, I think. Fight style, I mean. Coarse."

"Nah." Shanti walked toward the target to retrieve her knives. "I changed my style to offset yours. Cayan does that. I had to get savvy in this place—they have some unique and good fighters."

As Shanti turned with her knives, she realized that the usual bustle of the practice yard was completely absent. Rohnan must've noticed it too, because he looked out over the still grounds as he slowly sheathed his knives.

All the men stood erect and motionless, staring in her and Rohnan's direction with rounded eyes and gaping mouths. Swords and knives hung loose at their sides, almost forgotten. Burson, alone, had a huge smile.

"Um." Shanti looked at the men standing in the line next to them. "Someone else's turn? We cut in front…"

A tall, thin man holding a knife slowly shook his head.

Shanti couldn't help a twisted smile as she shrugged.

"Well Rohnan, looks like it's your turn."

"WELL, IT'S OFFICIAL—SHE'S CRAZY and so is that twin of hers," Sanders said, his arms folded over his chest.

Cayan and Sanders stood at the edge of the practice field watching Shanti charge Rohnan with two knives. The goal was simply to get as many knives into the target as possible while also trying to thwart the attack. It was a level of multitasking in battle that his people weren't practicing. It mimicked fighting against overwhelming odds, something Shanti's people had always anticipated.

Sanders said, "Why would you even need to throw a knife when you've got an enemy trying to gut you. If you're going to throw a knife, throw it at the guy in front of you. Or girl, in that nut-job's case."

"You've seen her work—she kills the enemy in front of her, but her eye is always on the larger picture. If someone is trying to get by, or is about to kill one of your men, you'd want to stick a knife in their neck while you fought the man in front." Cayan shifted and crossed his own arms. "This is a level of skill we don't have. That we haven't trained for. These two have seen the enemy in combat and have prepared for the worst all their lives, yet they still lost most of their people. Even with the level of skill I see in front of me, they all died.

We are in way over our heads."

"They only had a few against a large army, though," Sanders countered. He shifted his weight, spat, and dropped one hand to the hilt of his sword. "And took on way more than their number. The sheer size of an army will win over individual skill. Besides, they were defending a forest village, or some other tiny place. They just let the enemy tromp in."

"They had traps laid—no one just tromped in." Cayan watched as Shanti finally reached Rohnan and flipped him over her shoulder. He landed flat on his back. The jolt must've chased the air from his lungs, but he didn't stop, or even pause. He swept with his foot, trying to catch Shanti's legs. She jumped the kick before a knife appeared in her fist with a flourish. She stabbed down, but Rohnan had already moved. He caught her forearm and wrenched, forcing her hand loose. The knife skittered away. Some of the nearby men in the gathering crowd cheered.

"They are so intense when they fight," Cayan marveled. "They look like enemies trying to kill each other, not siblings reunited after the worst happened."

Sanders grunted as two of the Commanders walked up with stern expressions. Sterling, tall, broad and great with a bow, clasped his hands behind his back as he looked on. "I don't think we're prepared enough."

Daniels, an aging man with a strategic mind the like

of which Cayan had never met the equal, focused intently on the pair fighting. "I couldn't help but overhear you and Commander Sanders speaking, sir. I would like to point out that even with our allies united peacefully and purposely, we will still be grossly outnumbered by our enemy. This dictator—the Being Supreme he calls himself—"

"What a ridiculous name," Sanders barked.

"He's trying to align himself with the divine. It is genius when you think of it. Common people fear a higher power. The name itself inspires fear as do the atrocities done in his name. He conquers cities before he ever asserts his presence. This Xandre has already conquered half the land. Many of those conquered are already at the poverty level, that is true. Even if he made them fight, they would just be fodder for the front line—easily killed and hardly missed. His general battalion is diseased of mind and body, according to Krekonna—brutal and disgusting. Barely human. They would pose little trouble for a civilized army with proper organization."

"Desperate men are unpredictable," Sterling said.

"Yes." Daniels pursed his lips. "Still, those… men, we shall say, are used to maintaining a presence in the conquered territories. They are doing unspeakable things—burning houses with families in it and the like."

"Is there a point to this, Daniels?" Sanders glanced

around Cayan to glare at Daniels. "You're ruining my mood. And it wasn't great to begin with."

Daniels cleared his throat. As a man from a highly cultivated, wealthy, influential family, he wasn't entirely comfortable dealing with someone like Sanders, whose father was a miner, and his grandfather a leatherworker. But because Cayan's army stripped away social titles and heritage, and promoted on merit alone, they found themselves constantly struggling to get along.

"They are a force we need to eradicate to clear the conquered lands, but they are many," Daniels went on. "However, the two warriors in front of us haven't trained all their lives to fight a group of diseased troops. I doubt they would've lost such high numbers if they had. No, they trained to defeat Xandre's elite group. The higher level of his army."

"I met one of them—two actually. Yeah, they were trained." Sanders glanced at Cayan, indicating the conversation they'd had shortly after Sanders had returned last night. "I cut the guy's arm off, and still he tried to fight."

"He bled out," Cayan said in a low voice. "The Duke's man couldn't keep him alive. He can't give us any information."

A throat cleared to their side. As one unit, they all turned, expecting a soldier who was about to be sent back into the practice yard with a long list of punishments for interrupting his superiors. Instead, it was the older man that had arrived with Shanti. He stood a few paces away with a smile playing across his lips and glittering eyes, as if he was enjoying a joke with himself.

"Yes?" Daniels asked with a haughty tone.

The man edged closer. "You were discussing an army you know little about. I thought I might help fill in the blanks." The man gave a lighthearted chuckle. Cayan reached out to his mind, but found it as blank as it had been previously.

"You know how his officers work?" Daniels asked in the same tone.

The man edged closer still. "I have studied them a great deal, as have Shanti and Rohnan. They are a cultured group of people, as is Xandre. All are highly intelligent and excel within an organized structure—not unlike those here. They are much fewer than the growing horde, but they still number more than you. Even lower-tier officers will present a problem for your men, and there are many of them compared to your own. When you join with other armies, Xandre will simply fill his ranks with the horde. That will thin you down in battle, and Xandre will finish cutting you down. These officers are spread out. They are not always reputable but they are not as hated or as feared. This means the army of the rebels has not yet reached as far east as I would've liked. But I am certain that the coming of the Wanderer will bring people flocking. And then there will be the battle of the Chosen. The changes will spread like wildfire when the Shadow is once again released upon the land. To get to this battle, to travel east, you will need a crew of your best and brightest. You will need your most cunning, your most skilled. You will be outnumbered always, and are now hunted by one of their best."

Another cheer went up from the practice yard, but Cayan barely heard it. All his attention was on this older, smiling man. "How do you know all this?"

"The Wanderer—I've heard whispers of this." Daniels squinted in thought for a brief moment. "Krekonna brought it up, I believe. I then asked some of my contacts in other cities—my family has extensive connections, of course." Sanders rolled his eyes. Daniels didn't notice. "This is something of an old wives tale, this Wanderer. It speaks of a woman wandering the land, gathering the oppressed and grieving. Something like that."

"Like the Old Woman and the Wand?" Sterling asked. "My mother used to tell me that story."

"It is more than a myth, I assure you." The old man's gaze changed slowly, from glittering absence of thought to poignant. "The Wanderer is the subject of intense study. There are those of us who are the keepers of the Wanderer doctrines, just as there are those who are keepers of the Chosen doctrines. And they are just two parts of four, but we are not there yet. All in due time."

He paused for a moment looking deep into Cayan's eyes. "We must teach you to crawl before you fly. You need to learn to control your extensive power. You are stronger than Shanti, I think, which was not foretold. I can feel untapped reserves in you. Rohnan will be able to unlock them. It is all coming together."

"Who is this hunter you speak of?" Cayan asked, stepping forward.

Burson smiled again. "Ah, yes that is more pressing. He is a Superior Officer in Xandre's army, and he seeks both Shanti and myself. I'm sure Rohnan would be a boon as well. Should he find out about you? The opportunity for a Superior Officer with a full dose of the *Gift?* You cannot produce *Gifted* heirs, no, but your value will almost be that of Shanti."

Cayan's mind raced, remembering Shanti's warning from the night before. "He's one of the elite, you said. One of their best?"

"Yes. We will need to move on soon. He is not one to shy away from a chance to gain entry into Xandre's inner circle. The perks are said to be endless."

"If we move on, what's to stop this officer from moving in?" Sanders asked.

Burson smiled again. "Numbers, to begin with. He

doesn't have enough to move in, as you say. He needs Shanti and myself, above all. We are the prize. He will do whatever is in his power to secure us—staying behind as we move on would hinder his goal. He was sent to guard me. If he fails, he will be killed or punished severely. If it is revealed he had Shanti in his grasp and let her get away… well, his death will be horrible. He will not risk anything by taking over a city that is not yet scheduled to be conquered. Xandre is an exacting man—everything is planned down to the last detail. No, our hunter will follow his prey, which is why Shanti said we must leave quickly. She was not lying. Danger will follow her to death unless she cuts out the root."

"Never a quiet life where she's concerned," Sanders muttered.

"You asked how I know all of this," Burson went on, "and I will tell you. I know this because I have studied, I have traveled, and I have been held captive. You can really learn a system when you are caught within it. You can understand a people when you live amongst them. I have spent my life that way."

The man ticked the sky with his finger. "We will need a small number. Shanti's five young men should go, her adopted brother, and me. She makes a unit of eight. I will be hers until the Chosen comes forth. Cayan—excuse me. How rude." The man giggled, a startling contrast to that cutting stare. "The Captain will also have eight, including himself. Any larger and we will be noticed and taken down if we try to get to the lands in the east. Any smaller and I fear we may not make it. No, eight each is the correct number, and Shanti's men must be traded for youth."

"How can we hope to confront the army of the other Chosen with so few?" Cayan asked as Lieutenant Lucius, a man Cayan's age with dark hair, walked into their discussion.

"That is why the smaller number." Burson's hard brown gaze surveyed Lucius before finding Cayan again. "We will sneak into the Shadow Lands. They are protecting their Inkna-Chosen, hoping to claim the Shadow. There will be various stations set up between here and our destination. The Superior Officer will make use of those—we will never be safe. Not ever. They will try to cut us down before we reach the sea. But if we sneak, we can get into the lands, and the battle of the Chosen will commence. Once on the island, the prospective Chosen and her entourage cannot be killed. Not in plain sight, anyway. The hopeful will go through the trials. Whoever emerges is the Chosen."

"Not killed in plain sight… How do we keep her safe?" Sanders glanced at Shanti as she walked toward the archery area with Rohnan.

"Ah. To that question, I don't have the answer. All I know is there can be no obvious battles. I hope you have a poison master, who is also excellent at making antidotes, because he or she will be needed. I would suggest looking to the women of this city…"

Sterling gave Cayan a hasty glance before looking out over the practice yard. Daniels tapped his chin in thought. Sanders said, "Why would you look at the women?"

"We'll talk about that later, Sanders," Cayan said in a low voice.

"Secrets within secrets. What a treat this journey has become." Burson wandered away. Sanders stared after him as the color drained from his face.

"Best keep suspicions to yourself until you and the Captain have a chance to talk in private, Commander," Sterling said in a quiet voice. He gave a quick glance behind him. "It's best not to go voicing women's business—it can end badly."

"Yes, it can. I'm better off for the knowledge, but wish I could unlearn some things," Lucius said. He gulped. His gaze trained on Shanti as she nocked her bow. He said, "She's back."

Cayan nodded as he watched the practicing pair. He ignored the sick realization Sanders must've been having, if the sudden spiked fear that radiated off him was any judge. "And here come her Honor Guard."

"And I hear she has her Chance back," Lucius said quietly. Cayan could feel his uncertainty.

"I'm sure you can share the post, Lucius, but you'd need to choose. You can't be an army man and her man at the same time." Cayan stopped himself from putting his hands in his pockets. Losing his friend to someone else, regardless of whom, would kill him. But Cayan would not stand in the man's way. Lucius needed to decide his fate, and Cayan could see the allure of staying with Shanti. She was the pivot around which this whole war revolved—she would always be in the action, and Lucius craved excitement.

There were so many things in the air right now, so many elements drifting. Danger was coming at them from all sides and the possibility of survival was dwindling into no hope. Cayan suddenly knew how Shanti felt.

"I TOLD YOU!" LEILIUS SHOUTED as he shoved Xavier. "See? Now who's hallucinating? I told you I saw S'am last night. I *told you!*"

Marc watched as the color drained from Xavier's face and his mouth dropped open. Marc followed Xavier's stare then stopped dead.

"Holy shit, I don't believe it," Rachie said.

Leilius was right—there she was. Marc blinked and shook his head, but when he looked again, she was still there. Shanti stood dressed in a horrible pink pantsuit with dried blood on her chin and blond hair run through with black streaks. She looked thinner, but that could've been the weird clothes she was wearing. There was no doubting those striking features. Even from there, he knew those violet eyes. She stood with a man taller than her but with similar features and white-blond hair. He moved with the same grace. Dangerous. Marc wouldn't even be able to lift a sword against him, he'd just run away. As fast as possible.

"She found a friend," Gracas, the youngest of them, muttered. "And he's a head-turner."

"What, are you into guys now?" Rachie asked.

Gracas punched him. "No, you dick. I'm sizing up the competition. I bet he gets all the ladies."

"How would that affect you, idiot?" Rachie retorted. "You can't get girls now: what will change if he's hanging around?"

"Actually…" A smile soaked up Rachie's features. He started nodding slowly. "Actually, no, this could work. The girls will get turned down by him—because he won't have time for all of them—and then they'll have no choice but to go for me."

"Dumb idea." Leilius stood with his hands on his hips. "They'll still go for Xavier, because he's way better looking than any of us."

"Nah, he thinks too highly of himself. He'll be pissed he's second-best. Me? I'll take anything I can get, pity-sex included. I don't care."

"Me, either." Gracas grinned.

"What if that's her boyfriend, though?" Rachie asked.

"I think her boyfriend died," Marc said through numb lips. Why had she come back? She said she had her duty, and all that pressure, so why had she returned? And why was she wearing that horrible pink thing?

"Shut up, you guys." Xavier straightened up and put a heavy hand on his sword hilt. "That guy is way older than you, and even if you could get girls, which you can't, you won't be going for the same ones he will. And it doesn't matter why she's back. She didn't come back for us. So who cares? Let's get to work."

"Why else would she come if not for us and the Captain?" Leilius said.

"She didn't let us know she was here." Xavier led them toward the Pit with a tight mouth.

Marc knew that look on Xavier's face—he was sulking. Why? Marc had no idea. Nor did he care.

He followed with stiff legs as they walked through the slow-moving men trying to watch Shanti while attempting to appear busy. The Captain and commanders were all at the other end of the practice yard, talking and staring at the pair. People at the sword practice area had cleared to the side, even though there was room for a several people to practice at once.

Marc watched in fascination as the blond guy picked up a practice sword and surveyed it. Shanti picked up another and hefted it a couple times. Without warning, she lunged. Marc couldn't help releasing a squeal. She moved so fast. The woman was terrifying.

Her opponent didn't baulk. He reacted immediately by blocking the lunge and thrusting a counter-attack.

"I'd forgotten how fast she was," Rachie said in awe. "And that guy reacts *too* fast."

"She's still quicker than him, though," Leilius said as he looked on. Only Xavier bothered to wait in line to throw a knife.

"You can't be *too* fast." Gracas glared at Rachie.

"Yeah—look! He's reacting even before she gets moving, anticipating what she's going to do."

Marc watched as Shanti initiated a lunge, but before the move was begun, the guy was already moving to block. He countered, and Shanti reacted with her usual speed. Her next strike went the same way—she'd barely even begun the movement and the guy was already moving to intercept.

"See? I didn't even know what she was going to do, and he already had the answer. How do we learn *that?*" Rachie continued his unblinking stare.

Marc couldn't help staring, or the thoughts crowding in his head. Part of him thought he'd never see her again. Now that she'd come back, he couldn't help but feel that window inside him open again.

He'd been moping and stuttering and wasting away, and she'd look at him with that contained disappointment before rolling up her metaphorical sleeves and getting him on track. Even if she hadn't ever planned on coming back, he should've been continuing to make himself better. She'd started him on the right path, but why was it up to her to keep pushing? He was old enough to look after himself.

Marc voiced the thought. "I'm way behind."

"Tell me about it," Gracas said. "She's going to be pissed. I've been messing around."

"I haven't, but I hate just standing in line with the 'yes, sir' stuff. It's boring," Rachie whined.

Xavier looked back at them, spared a glance for the sword work between Shanti and her friend, and then turned back. "We don't need her."

"Oh blow it out your ass, Xavier. You've fallen behind the most. You need her, you're just mad she hasn't fallen madly in love with you." Rachie braced his hand on his hip in irritation.

"Aren't you guys still the least bit pissed she left without a word? You've, what, just forgiven her because she came back eventually?" Xavier asked.

Gracas and Rachie both shrugged. Marc followed suit as he said, "She did come back. And she's got a lot of stuff on her plate. And it's not like we really did our part. She took the time to get us started, and then we just crapped out. She should be pissed at us, too."

Gracas rubbed his hands together. "When do we start practicing, do you think?"

CHAPTER 9

QADIR WALKED SILENTLY THROUGH THE trees. He glanced up at the sentry to his right, not even ten paces from his location. The man was scanning the area with a practiced eye. Alert, though there couldn't be much activity in this rural setting. Usually a mind would slow down from long hours of boredom, but this man seemed sharp in the way his eyes scanned and occasionally darted. To test this theory, Qadir tossed a rock into a nearby bush. A tiny rustle sang through the otherwise quiet afternoon.

The sentry glanced in that direction immediately, focusing on the waving leaves. After a moment the flora stilled and quiet resumed. The sentry returned to his scanning.

This was the second sentry Qadir had tested, and his reactions were the same. A small, mostly inactive town it might be, but the guards were kept vigilant.

Plans shifted within Qadir's mind. He withdrew, careful not to disturb anything that might make a sound. Once he was back within a thick grove of trees and shrubs, away from the watchful onlookers, he allowed himself to sit in quiet contemplation.

The violet-eyed woman had surprised him. That was exceedingly rare. She'd taken a well-traveled lane instead of a smaller, less-traversed route. It was gutsy. When Qadir realized the mistake, making haste to catch her was a futile effort. Especially because she'd run right back to this place. The Westwood Lands.

What brought her here, he wondered. What was it about this city, and these men, that she returned here for a safe harbor?

Qadir thought of the large, solid gates. Defense was in mind when those were made by skilled craftsmen. Even from Qadir's distance, he'd seen scars that could only have been caused from battle. The walls, built with good stonework and seemingly impregnable, were an effective deterrent to an attack. For a city without a great deal of traffic, the defenses were well thought out.

Thoughts filtered through Qadir's mind. Memories flashed by. Facts and rumors rolled.

The Inkna had inspired an attack here, Qadir remembered. They had watched the city for their goods and commodities. To gain access, they'd used a decrepit people close by.

Qadir scratched his chin. He didn't recall the name, which meant he'd probably never heard it. It didn't matter, though. They were immaterial.

With the violet-eyed woman's aid, this city had laid waste to an Inkna settlement. Her power had rendered them defenseless, and the warriors with her had pulled the Inkna out by the root. It was an impressive feat for two reasons. One was the woman's power. It must be everything the Being Supreme thought it was. Several powerful and expertly trained *Sarshers* would be needed to take her down.

Second was the prowess this small city of warriors must possess. There couldn't be many within an area this small, but they must be well-trained. Taking on the Inkna was a job for fearless men. With wealth and assets included, it pointed toward a solid, organized leader with a head for business as well as defense.

A tally flashed through Qadir's thoughts. Raven flights and travel times were added to the force already on its way. Each day the size of his battalion would grow with specialized *Sarshers* and trained men with excellent pedigree.

His mind called up the images of the various gates, always open but constantly watched. They had but one mind-worker. His *Sarshers* could merge and desecrate the sentries as his squad on horseback raced toward those gates. By the time the city was alerted to the attack, Qadir's men would be through, cutting down those who posed a threat. His *Sarshers* would bring up the rear as one solid force, focusing on the violet-eyed girl. With her incapacitated, they could drop the city to their knees and reestablish order.

There was only one issue. That old man.

An uncomfortable flare of fear burnt up Qadir's back.

The Being Supreme had appointed Qadir to guard that man. If Qadir failed in his duty—

The thought cut off as the clawing fear started to eat away at his gut.

Death would be an easy way out if the Being Supreme learned of Qadir's failure. This situation needed to be rectified.

Qadir took a deep breath and closed his eyes, refocusing on the numbers of men and the various travel times. Two days was all he'd need. With his plans already in motion, two days would see this city conquered and the priceless captives in his hands. Until then, he'd stay out of the woman's range, letting her relax in the thick illusion of safety.

She was already captured; he had but to spring the trap.

CHAPTER 10

*"*THE CAPTAIN WAS WATCHING US *pretty closely,"* Rohnan stated as Shanti and he made their way through the large park to the clearing she had once used to train her Honor Guard. *"He is an interesting man. Half-calculating, half-impulsive, I think. He will be trouble in a fight."*

"He is *trouble in a fight."* Shanti rubbed her stomach. Butterflies raged as she got closer. Guilt dripped through her middle like acid. *"Do you think they'll forgive me?"*

"You said he changes his style to match that of his opponent. And he has the Gift. *Will my natural defense not be as effective, do you think?"*

Shanti's brow furrowed as she realized Rohnan was still talking about Cayan. *"Rohnan, regardless of his shift in style, you can feel intent—how can he hide that?"*

Rohnan's eyes barely squinted—it was his version of a shrug. She smiled. *"These people won't hold it against you if you get beat by their beloved Captain. It's getting beat by a girl that they find worthy of scorn."*

"These people are small-minded in many ways, but I'm not worried about appearances. I've studied this Captain. I've seen how he moves, how his mind shifts. Did you realize that he studies all of your movements, and is always aware of your presence? He learns from you even when you don't teach. When you trained in your Gift *today, before we left the practice yard, he stepped away from his commanders to focus more closely on you. Not us,* you. *He knows you are the key to unlocking his potential, and his mind is sharp. With his power, and his various gifts, he could be great—he could rule half the world. All he needs is what you possess—he just needs you."*

Shanti stopped and turned to her brother. Fear and concern poured from him. His eyebrows dipped low over solemn eyes. She reached out her hand and waited until he took it. The contact made his deeper emotions open up to her.

Fear and inadequacy raged within him, clinging to her being alive with a wild desperation. He'd thought her dead, and that had raged war on everything that kept him rooted. Shanti had been his backbone growing up, she knew that, helping him cope after *feeling* his parents killed right in front of him at age three. She woke him up and held him when the screams of their deaths overcame his slumber. She'd bestowed on the fair boy with a strange *Gift* who never spoke and often cried, the rare and coveted title of Chance. A duty that would change the makeup of the world. A title heavily sought and prized. For the first time, she was learning that he thought she'd made him *something* to their people.

When he thought he lost her, all the strength had gone out of him. The nightmares had raged on, day and night, a fear of the future mixing with that of the past. He had no one strong enough to drag him out of it. He'd lived from one torturous day to the next, finding no comfort in the warm embrace of strangers, or the hot blood of his enemies.

Shanti felt it all, welling up and spilling over, as she shared his touch.

She smiled as tears came to her eyes. She wrapped her arms around her brother. *"And now you are worried Cayan will rip me away again, is that it?"*

"He has the ability, Chosen. If he so chose, he could learn all he could, and then strike you down. You may be creating a new nightmare to destroy this land."

Shanti laughed despite Rohnan's shaking fears. *"Creating a new nightmare, maybe. But not to destroy this land—to wreck my head."*

"I'm serious…"

"I know you are. I know." She rubbed his back, transported back in time to those early years when they were both newly orphaned, just trying to survive the

pain together. Keeping her Grandfather was a small consolation for losing everything else from that first battle.

“He could *be great, Rohnan, you are right. And I hope he becomes so, because to take down Xandre, we’ll need it. Cayan has so many rare gifts all blended into one. He has what I lack when it comes to organization, strategy, and overall economics. I worked with a small group—he is able to maintain a much larger one. I need him. For our side to win, he has to be a part of it. He has to fill in the holes I cannot. Do you understand?”*

“But what happens when he learns what you have to offer, and realizes he doesn’t need you anymore?”

“I doubt that day will come. I can churn out some truly remarkable fighters with little more than a basic spark. That is one of my gifts. And that is something he lacks. He needs me as much as I need him. We need each other to fight the war machine Xandre has created, and he’s smart enough to know that.”

“And when he tries to dominate you?” Rohnan asked in a solemn voice.

Shanti felt a flash of fire fueling a mad grin. *“Oh, he tries. He tries all the time. It’s one of the few things about him that is completely predictable…”*

Rohnan backed away and wiped his face. Shanti let him take a moment to look into her eyes, rebuilding his strength. He nodded once and looked at the ground.

"You are no longer an outcast. You have found a mate for your Gift.*"*

"Pah." Shanti waved her hand through the air. *"Did you see the practice yard? If I'm anything, it's an outcast. But now you have Burson, who also has a strange* Gift. *You are never alone for long, Rohnan. There are strange people everywhere."*

He smiled, looking out over the trees. Lightening up, thankfully.

Rohnan took a deep, shuddering breath. He said, *"I never understood why the Elders chose me to protect you. I'm not built for it. Kallon, your Battle First, would've been a better choice—he's confident, strong and sure. He's a warrior. I don't deserve to be your Chance, Chosen. I'm not fit for it."*

A dark chuckle welled up inside her. *"What a pair we make. I never thought I was the Chosen—I didn't ask why the Elders chose me; I didn't think they did. And just when I shed the title, I'm strapped with another, which I can't hope to understand. I can't even fight that one, because I don't know what it is."* She sighed. *"I don't know what comes next, Rohnan. I have no idea what our future holds. But we'll face it together, okay? Our people need us."*

"And so do a band of young boys, I hear."

Shanti started walking again, the butterflies springing to life and fluttering around her ribcage. *"I think I've widened the most eyes making this particular group of boys into something commendable. Or… at least… I did. Before I left.”*

“Your turn for self-pity, then?”

“Yours took long enough—can’t I have some time?”

Shanti stepped through the branches and into the clearing where five boys budding into men waited for her. Leilius, tall and lanky, beamed when he saw her. “Hi, S’am!”

She smiled at his greeting and looked to the person next to him. Gracas stood with a half-smile and raised eyebrows like he was waiting for something. She nodded, and received one back. Then Gracas elbowed Leilius.

“Ow!” Leilius rubbed the offending spot. “What’d you do that for?”

“Violence.” Gracas’ smile got bigger. He hadn’t changed at all.

Jubilation bubbled up as her gaze found Rachie. He stood with his hands in his pockets and a sullen expression. She looked at his hands, then back at his face, without saying a word. The youth yanked his hands out of his pants and scowled. Gracas laughed.

Next she looked at Marc. He stood with his head bowed, shooting furtive glances up through his eyelashes. “You came back,” Marc said in a quiet voice.

“Yes. We’ll get to that in a minute.”

Finally, removed from the others, with his hands firmly lodged in his pockets and his shoulders hunched, stood Xavier. Easily the biggest of them, though not the oldest, jagged pain radiated from his mind. He'd put on a couple pounds of muscle since she had last seen him, and in the next couple years he'd put on a lot more. His frame closely resembled a youthful Cayan's; though he might not grow to be as robust or quite as tall, he had such potential.

"Start with the... young man with the large shoulders," Rohnan advised. *"He feels betrayed. He takes your leaving as abandonment. His budding confidence was knocked out from under him. His ego is damaged, which means his self-worth is fractured."*

Shanti started forward and stood directly in front of Xavier. She looked up into his dark eyes full of angered insecurity and laid a palm on his heart, a gesture in her homeland pleading forgiveness before words were ever spoken. He didn't know the sentiment, but the confusion that was quickly overshadowed with a deep comfort meant he craved personal contact to make things right.

Holding his stare, she said, "I left you, and I know that. At the time I thought it was the thing I must do."

"You didn't even say goodbye," he accused with a slightly quivering voice. To attempt to cover up his emotion and pain, he scowled down at her.

"I know. I was afraid. I left in cowardice. I have a lot to answer for."

Xavier's jaw tightened. Shanti heard Rachie whisper, "Did she just say she was afraid? Oh my god—can you imagine if Sanders admitted something like that? He'd probably kill us all for hearing it."

"Do you think she's going to kill us?" Gracas whispered back in a harried voice.

Shanti felt Rohnan's humor drift toward her. *Was I ever this young?* Shanti would've asked him. But Xavier didn't think any of this was funny. His eyes held hers like they might a lifeline; like he was afraid she wasn't really back, and he was still drifting like he had been when she was gone.

The parallels between him and Rohnan were uncanny even though they were from totally different worlds, with totally different paths. Both of them mimicked how Shanti felt after she'd left Cayan. She'd been lost. Drifting.

Shanti shook her head to try and focus. She stepped away and walked to the other end of the clearing where she sat down and rested her forearms on her knees. She swept her glance across the boys and said, "In my homeland, when we make an error such as this, we either request punishment, or give something personal to the offended party." She explained what that personal item represented and finished by saying, "I have nothing to give, however. I have no possessions, save my weapons, and a warrior is forbidden to give items of battle. So I must beg for a punishment—"

"You do have something to give," Xavier interrupted. He stared at her with burning eyes. "You can give us your word." He stepped forward. The muscles on his frame flexed. "Give us your word that you won't do that again."

"She has more to worry about than being your nursemaid, Xavier," Marc said in a sullen voice.

Xavier's eyebrows lowered in frustration and determination. "I'm not saying hold back for us, I'm just saying let us know before you charge off. Give us the option to go with you."

Shanti leaned forward as she assessed the fervent young man in front of her. She noticed Marc's face tilt up, his eyes glued to her. The other boys stood silent, waiting for her response.

Rohnan gave her a small nod.

She sighed in resignation. "I will give you my word that I won't leave without some sort of farewell. I will not give you the option to go with me, but I will keep you informed."

Xavier stared at her. His dark eyes held her accountable. After a silent beat, he looked at Rohnan. "Who's he?"

The weight drifted off Shanti's shoulders and

cleared from her middle. With a smile she couldn't help, she stood. "He's my brother, Rohnan. I thought him dead. Apparently, he's hard to kill."

"Just like you, S'am." Leilius walked forward with excitement. "I'm really good at hiding. I've been practicing. I even got the Captain."

"Got strangled by the Captain, you mean." Gracas came forward, too. "I'm terrible at everything but throws, S'am."

"I only got strangled because I scared him." Leilius scowled and put his hands on his hips. "I probably could've gotten a knife in his ribs. He was preoccupied."

"How can he read you so fast? Rohnan, I mean," Marc asked in a sheepish voice. "We watched him fight you today—he seems like he reads you before you're fully moving."

Shanti let the gratitude for quick forgiveness clear from her mind. Without wasting any more time than she already had by leaving, she began explaining about Rohnan's *Gift*. She physically moved the boys around the clearing before putting them to work fighting, throwing, and most of all, learning.

LATER, AS ALL THE BOYS were paired off and working on what they'd learned, Shanti divided her focus and let her *Gift* push out past the walls, making sure each of the sentries were vigilant. Reveling in the added power Cayan lent her, she pushed further still, testing her range and trying to analyze the detail. Animals moved about their business or flitting through trees but other than that, all seemed quiet, almost peaceful. She let her power drift, taking her mind from the training for a moment so she could focus solely with her *Gift*, calmed by the rustle of the trees and sounds of training. She almost felt like the breeze, easy and tranquil.

She took a deep breath, then gave one final push with her power before pulling it all back in. That's when she felt shadows of minds at the edges of her awareness. Patient but watchful, male humans sat in groups around the city. Past the sentries and hidden, one sharp and cunning mind laid in wait. Expectant.

The Hunter.

A blast of fear stole her breath. Her adrenaline spiked and her fingers started to tingle. "He's here! How did he find us so fast?"

Rohnan's head snapped up. His eyes opened wide and her mirrored fear blasted from his awareness. "So soon?"

"He's expectant—waiting for something." Shanti put her hand on her sword's hilt. "He's going to come in after us. Why else would he be hanging back?"

"We can't let him." Rohnan stalked toward the edge of the clearing. "I get Burson. You get Captain."

"I am here." Shanti started at Burson's calm voice, from just beyond the rim of the clearing. His mind wasn't blasting the conflicting emotion she'd grown to expect. He was completely shut off, and had approached without a sound.

Shanti turned to Xavier, unpracticed but still undeniably the leader of this crew. "We've been followed by one of the best. He's outside the city. I have to leave again soon. We are journeying east. Now you know."

Shanti turned to Rohnan with instructions on her lips, but was cut off by Xavier. "We're going too—I thought you knew. The Captain told us shortly after you left the training yard earlier."

Shanti rounded on Xavier with an incredulous expression. "No, you—"

Burson cut Shanti off. "They are going as your guard. As I am. As is Rohnan. I believe the Captain has already notified those leaving with us. Although, he expected to have more time."

"They are still learning—this will be a dangerous journey," Shanti seethed.

"We're leaving *now*? I haven't even packed!" Gracas spit out.

"Chosen, we don't have time argue. We must get out," Rohnan pushed in an urgent voice.

Shanti filled her lungs and forced calm. Ignoring the fear of a lethal enemy just outside the gates, and the danger it posed to these people, she focused on Rohnan. "Pack our things. Get everything ready. I'll get the Captain and send word where to meet us."

"The boys?" Rohnan asked.

Shanti didn't even spare them a glance. "Send them home. I need to speak with Cayan about it."

She ran, bursting through the trees while *searching* for Cayan with her *Gift*. The Hunter was at the very edge of her range—he'd chosen his spot well. He couldn't be ready to move in yet, but how long did they have? And what did he have planned?

SHE FOUND CAYAN IN THE heart of the city. His emotions flitted between expectant, eager and partially aroused. As she sprinted to the location, she was confused when she realized he was at the tailor's shop in which she'd visited earlier that day to order her dress.

She burst into the shop. The bell above the door clanged, announcing her presence. Cayan stood in black slacks covered in white dashes and lines. He turned, shirtless. Thick cords of muscle on his sizable frame rolled and flexed with his movement. Large shoulders tapered down into a thin waist and trim hips. Every ounce of his upper body was perfectly defined and unerringly cut. Her mouth momentarily went dry with the sheer power she could see in his body.

Her logic and fighting mind restarted, cataloging that power and obvious prowess as a needed asset.

"Yes?" he asked in confusion. The tailor scoffed at the interruption.

"He's here—the Hunter. The Superior Officer pursing me. He's already outside the city walls just out of Burson's reach. We need to leave. *Now!*"

Cayan's mind exploded out, taking hers with it. The effect, unexpected, dizzied her for a moment. Lightheaded, she staggered forward and reached, bracing a hand on his warm pec. The skin contact solidified their link. Their *Gifts* boosted, extending past her earlier reach until the quantities of men as well as their emotional state became clear.

Cayan honed in their combined focus on the sharp and cunning mind. "Is that him?" He grabbed her shoulders to steady her.

"It is. Do you feel his intelligence—the sharpness of his mind? He's a highly strategized thinker, and has years of experience and the best training Xandre could impart."

"Have you met him before?"

"No. Just run from him. I'm basing it on his intelligence, his position, and my knowledge of Xandre and his army."

"We have many more than he has. We can easily take him down."

Shanti broke contact and stepped away. "He has more than a dozen *Sharshers*, all spread out. With them are men that are no doubt excellent with blades. You don't have an army of Sanders, and even if you did, Burson can only protect one area at a time. They are too far away, and too spread out, for us to kill that many. We'd have to fight in groups, and this officer will have prepared for that. You think Daniels is excellent at his craft? You've not met anyone like a Superior Officer. Daniels has a lot to learn still, and will need to learn it from the master that is waiting outside your gates. Soon the Hunter will start killing sentries. You aren't far from losing men, Cayan. And for what? Just to run, anyway. We have to leave."

"If he's planned to withstand my men, he's certainly planned to keep us here."

The bell jingled again as a blast of chilled air assaulted Shanti's back. Sanders and Lucius burst into the shop, making the tailor frown in irritation. Shanti looked at Lucius, the man she'd named Chance the last time she had been there. When he met her gaze, she felt as much as saw his regret. There was a distance there that hadn't existed before, and when he glanced at Cayan, it became clear. He'd had to choose, and he had chosen his Captain and his city.

A pang hit Shanti's heart, but she didn't dwell on it. He'd chosen family and his home, and if she was honest with herself, he was probably better off. Death rode her shoulders—he didn't need any part of that.

She nodded once, indicating she read him, right before Sanders stepped further into the shop. "One of the sentries saw something. He said he could've sworn it was a man in a black uniform, but he only caught a glimpse. He didn't want to check it out—everyone around here knows what a black uniform means. He called for a shift change and got to me as fast as possible. Can you use that mind thing and check it out?"

Shanti glanced at Cayan before she said, "It *was* a man in a black uniform, and we have trouble."

CHAPTER 11

MARC WAITED BEHIND SHANTI AT the front gate with white knuckles clutching the reins of his horse. With every swallow he choked on his own terror. He'd done this before, and battle terrified him. He wasn't good with a blade, and could barely ride a horse. The Captain and Shanti had made a grievous error bringing him on this journey.

Horses shifted around him, sensing the anxiety of their riders. This was it. They were going to storm out of the city and try to run down the enemy while the twilight confused the eyes. They would face down one of the smartest, most cunning enemies with only one mind-warrior person, and she couldn't ride a horse well either.

Marc tried to swallow the knot of acid rising in his throat.

He took a deep breath then ran over the plan that had taken more than two hours to hatch. Shanti and the Captain would break up into teams. Shanti would exit the front, toward a person called the Hunter, his two

Sarshers, and a few other Graygual. The Captain would go out the back toward a few Graygual and four *Sarshers*. Burson would shield the Captain and his crew from the mental warfare, while Shanti *thought* she could handle the two *Sarshers* out the front.

The Captain had asked, "What if you can't?"

It had been a good question, to which she replied with a terrible answer: "There are always risks."

The sides of the city had the least protection, with only one *Sarsher* each and a couple Graygual. That was because the enemy at the front and rear could easily run to head off anyone fleeing out the sides.

The most surprising thing was the last-minute addition. She was a girl. Not a warrior girl like Shanti, either. A girl of no more than Marc's age from the orphan house. Marc couldn't fathom what her role might be, and no one was talking about it. He could tell Shanti had been confused, too. She'd asked repeatedly why a young woman with no training was going with them. Why weren't they taking an experienced fighter instead? Apparently this girl, Ruisa, had a special talent they would need in the Shadow Lands. That had started Sanders muttering, but no one would say what that special talent was, despite Shanti threatening to hurt someone if they didn't share.

Marc glanced up at the darkening sky and shifted in the well-worked leather of the saddle. "I don't like this. I think I would've rather been pushed off to the mines."

"That's because you've never been in the mines," Xavier said in a low hum. His hard eyes were on the middle of Shanti's back, his knuckles just as white as Marc's.

"You have the map?" Shanti asked Rohnan.

Rohnan didn't so much as glance at her. He stared straight ahead through the open gates. "Yes. The meeting point is noted. The Captain sure he get through?"

"Yes, though since the Hunter is probably certain we'll go that way, I'm sure he has someone covering the roads leading out of here."

"He'll follow the wild game trails," Tobias noted, a warrior who was good with a sword and better with a bow. His eyes were hard and expression grim.

As far as Marc knew, Tobias didn't shy away from danger, but he also didn't enjoy running straight at it, unlike Sanders, who waited with crazy eyes filled with expectation. The Commander was unhinged, and Marc hated being in battle with him. Sanders made a guy think he should have no fear. And often, it did erase the fear, which led to doing stupid things.

"Okay, it's about time." Shanti absently patted her horse before nocking an arrow. "How is your aim, Rohnan?"

"I not the one who fall off horses, Chosen." Rohnan

nocked an arrow. "How is head?"

"I wish I knew how strong the *Sarshers* are." Shanti's fingers whitened on her bow.

"Only one way find out."

"Yes, Rohnan. Very helpful, as always." Shanti winked at Marc, nodded at Xavier, and then to Rachie. They had been chosen to go out this way. The rest of the Honor Guard had gone with the captain.

Marc knew from experience that when she smiled, or winked, or hugged, it meant she was preparing for the worst. That meant this was going to be one of the worst.

His stomach pinched and he breathed deeply to stop himself from throwing up. It was barely working.

"Are you going to tell us who to shoot at, S'am?" Rachie asked in a whisper.

"Usually, I'd call you an idiot for that question, Rachie," Shanti said in a flat voice. "But in this case, you aim for anyone in an all-black uniform."

"Do they know we are coming out?" Xavier asked.

"They will be ready." Shanti glanced back. "One of the sentries sent through an alarm an hour ago by shooting an arrow. He wasn't as clever as the sentry before him. The Hunter's mind-path changed shortly after that. It appears the Hunter does not need much to figure out his enemy's movements."

Silence filled the space when Shanti stopped talking.

Men shifted on the walls, bows in hand, waiting. If this Hunter killed Marc and Shanti and the rest, and decided to attack the city, the defenses were ready. The Captain had prepared for failure.

"We be okay." Rohnan's sing-song voice was almost as pleasant as his soft gaze when he turned back to glance at Marc. It didn't help.

"Okay, here we go." Shanti kicked her horse. It neighed and pranced sideways. "Bloody stubborn animal. What does it want, a *please?*"

She kicked its sides again. The animal jolted forward suddenly. Shanti barely grabbed hold of the saddle, crushing her bow to her chest, as she struggled to hold on. Laughing, Rohnan urged his horse after her.

"They're both crazy," Marc said as he leaned forward to get his horse moving.

"Crazy is good, boy. Crazy gets things done." Sanders' horse started forward.

"It'll be okay, Marc," Xavier echoed Rohnan in a low tone as he kicked his horse forward. His voice was shaking. "S'am is the best, and Rohnan seems almost as good. We have Commander Sanders, too. They'll get us through."

Marc nodded as terrified tears welled up in his eyes. He kicked his horse, following the others. He wouldn't let Shanti—S'am—down. He would do his part, to protect his city.

"I wish she gave us that boost where we don't feel anything," Marc mumbled.

"She had to save her strength. It's okay. We don't need it." Xavier said.

Confidence low but determination high, Marc followed the group as they started with a trot. When they cleared the entrance to the city, the gates shuddered into action, closing behind them. Locking them out along with the enemy.

Marc's adrenaline rose as they started to pick up the pace. The horses neighed and huffed, in response to the tension of the riders. The sentries nodded or saluted as the eight passed. Marc noticed them shifting, adjusting their bows. The sentries would be the first line of defense if the enemy came toward the city.

Their speed increased. The trees flashed by and the ground shook within his vision. S'am's long braid swung back and forth on her back. Rohnan's white-blond hair flared in the wind. The horses started to pant. And then S'am grunted and leaned forward.

"They're strong!" she yelled at Rohnan. Marc could barely hear her voice over the pounding of the hooves as the wind tried to steal her words. "Each at about three-fourths power level of mine!"

"Can you hold them until we close?" Rohnan yelled back.

"Get your arrows nocked!" Sanders yelled. Somehow his voice cut through the air and vibrated down Marc's back.

Marc's teeth chattered from the horse's jarring strides. He found himself nocking a hasty arrow even though he couldn't hit a tree from fifty paces away. Still, he had to try. They all did.

"Spread out," Sanders yelled. "Don't kill the person in front of you."

Marc urged his horse to the right, toward Sanders. Xavier and Rachie did the same, wanting to stay in earshot.

"Faster!" S'am's words whipped out of her mouth and swirled behind her. Marc caught them, though, and leaned forward. His horse put on a burst of speed, as did the others.

But S'am's took off. One minute, she was bouncing all around her saddle. The next, she was flying in front of them smoothly on a horse that defied nature's constraints with speed. Rohnan urged an almost equally fast horse after her.

"C'mon!" Sanders roared. He kicked his warhorse.

The thunder of the animals, and the wind slapping Marc in the face, had his heart hammering and palms sweaty. Then he saw them. A line. Ten of them, all but two with black shirts and red circles. The one in the middle sat astride a spectacular shiny black horse. Those to the sides of him had no circles on their chest.

"Aim for the *Sarshers*!" Sanders ordered.

Marc barely heard. Or maybe he didn't hear and it was a memory.

His mind went blank except for the sound of his thumping heart. His horse found a clear lane and ran. Ran with all it had. Straight at the line of men on their tall steeds. All with flashing swords. Two with bows.

Shanti loosed an arrow. Usually an excellent shot, this time the shot went wide. It hit the man next to one of the *Sarshers*. The arrow stuck in his arm and his own shot went wide, barely missing Xavier who had found himself on the end of the line.

Rohnan loosed. Then ducked. His arrow stuck into the chest of one of the *Sarshers* as an arrow whizzed over his head. Shanti slumped in her saddle ahead of them. She was still running directly at the enemy.

"Get those *Sarshers*! They're too strong for her!" Sanders screamed. He loosed, nocked, loosed, nocked, loosed. Over and over. Fast and expert. No fear. The enemy was on the move. Their horses running, making them harder to hit.

Bouncing around, Marc had trouble nocking his arrow. When he did, he raised his bow and drew the string to fire at the man directly in front of him. S'am was headed toward the same man at an angle.

Breath coming in hoarse pants, Marc pulled his arm back and tried to sight his arrow. The horse jostled him, making him struggle. His vision jiggled. He could barely focus on the shaking figure in front of him. He loosed the arrow. It sailed high over the enemy.

Marc swore under his breath and grabbed another. The figure ahead was raising his own bow, aiming for S'am. She wasn't aiming back, though! She looked like she tried to straighten up, but she seemed strained. Those *Sarshers* had clearly taken a lot out of her.

Panic shot through Marc.

He sighted again, closer now. The tip of his arrow waved through the air. His bow as steady as a boat in huge swells. His body bounced frantically on the horse. Marc could see the Hunter's blank face, perfectly composed. No passion, like Sanders. No determination, like Tobias or Rachie. No fear at all. His arm pulled back as the last *Sarsher* fell from his saddle.

Shanti tried to raise her bow, but Marc had seen her this depleted before. She was close to passing out. She'd be easy prey, then.

Sweat dripped into Marc's eye, stinging. Without the time to wipe it away, he closed that eye and used the other to sight. The Hunter's arm pulled back. Adrenaline spiked within Marc. He let go of the bowstring. His arrow made a *thummmm* sound and was gone.

The Hunter flinched back as S'am drew closer. His arm jerked, releasing the arrow into the ground, before the bow tumbled down the horse's flank.

I did it!

Marc had shot him in the shoulder!

S'am thundered down on top of the enemy, not in control of her horse. Rather than fighting the animal, though, she dropped her bow and ripped her sword from its sheath. The blade glinted in the failing light, wobbling at the end of a weak arm. She had nothing left.

"Run away, S'am!" Marc screamed, trying to nock another arrow.

With something Marc could only describe as an un-horselike war-cry, her horse rammed into the Hunter's own mount. The Hunter's horse bucked wildly. The Hunter, agile on his animal, still had to grip the reins and held on.

S'am's horse didn't relent. It screamed again, this time turning its rump to the other animal before kicking the Hunter's horse with a powerful strike.

The Hunter's horse screamed in response, a sound filled with pain and agony, jarring the Hunter as it lurched.

Only then did S'am's horse finally run on, with S'am clutching frantically to its back.

Marc's horse, much slower, kept its same course, still running at the Hunter.

"Oh no! No, no, no!" Marc yelled, trying to turn his horse.

Too late. Marc's horse ran right by. The Hunter, still

looking majestic on his injured, baying animal, turned his head to watch Marc pass. His arm hung limp at his side, Marc's arrow still lodged in his shoulder. A cold, hard stare, devoid of any pain or emotion, hit Marc like a brick to the face. Dead eyes sliced through Marc's body all the way down until it tingled his toes. He could feel that stare promising retribution; promising a life of agony to himself and his family. That stare promised far worse than mere death; it promised that the Hunter would remember Marc's face and add him to the list of prey.

Shaking, hands numb, Marc lost all sense of direction. He didn't know where his horse went. He didn't notice where everyone else was or even look around to see if there had been any casualties. He just stared straight ahead with the memory of that look echoing through his body and burning his bones.

He'd never been so terrified in his whole life, and he knew, without a doubt, that it would never go away. Neither would that Hunter.

CHAPTER 12

SHANTI WAS SO TIRED SHE could barely feel her body. Limbs plagued with a tremor she couldn't control, numb feet, eyelids coated with iron and trying to lock shut—she was a mess. Even her horse was spent. The animal's sides heaved, its breath puffing white through the chilled air.

All eight fighters had escaped with their lives. Tobias had sustained a gash on his leg from a sword that wouldn't be too big of a deal, and Jaime, a man Shanti barely knew, had taken an arrow to his left arm. The arrow had barely sliced into the flesh just below his shoulder before it fell away, the barb not sticking, but the wound would hinder him. Marc could patch him up, but he'd need rest to make a full recovery, something he wouldn't get. He'd just have to make do.

Cayan's crew had already arrived by the time the horses walked into the designated meeting point. As they neared the other horses, Shanti slumped even further into her saddle, almost lying on the neck of her horse.

"What's wrong with her?" Cayan stalked up with decisive movements to accompany his harsh tone. "Is she hurt?"

"The *Sarshers* strong. Very strong. Strongest we have seen. They nearly overcome her." Rohnan slid to the ground as Cayan came to the side of her horse.

Shanti felt his hands slide around her middle gently, careful not to jostle her.

"I'm fine, Cayan." She feebly pushed at his unyielding arms. His hands hooked around her waist and upper shoulder before sliding her over the side of her horse. As her balance tipped, she clutched onto him with numbed arms. Her legs dangled as he hoisted her like a child and cradled her next to his body.

"It's a good thing you treat me like your equal and let me walk on my own," she muttered, focusing all her power on not dropping her head to his shoulder.

"You'd just fall down. You're a woman—letting you crawl toward the fire would make me look bad," Cayan said softly.

"Oh great. Look after *your* reputation."

"What happened?"

Shanti pushed through the tired fog of her brain, ignoring the spicy feeling of their mated power bubbling up, to the quick skirmish with the Hunter. "He couldn't have meant to sacrifice those *Sarshers*. They were incredibly strong for Inkna. Xandre won't be happy we took them out."

"Rohnan couldn't help?" Cayan walked up to a roaring fire surrounded by stones to keep the blaze contained. Somewhere close the smell of cooking wafted up and flirted with Shanti's senses.

"His *Gift* doesn't work like that. He can give me some power and energy, but his *Gift* is all receptive. When Burson masked your power, it mostly cut me off from you, and then there was the distance. I had a hard time blocking their attack."

Her head felt like it was full of water, heavy and slow-moving. Cayan's warmth, and the strength of his arms surrounding her, made her eyelids droop in fatigue. Her arms tightened around his neck as the thought of sleep, cradled in warmth in safety, stole her focus.

Her scoff had her eyes fluttering open again. Safety, what a pleasant fantasy. "Put me down, Cayan. I'm not a toddler."

"Act like toddler," Rohnan said, standing close—probably monitoring Cayan's hold. Regardless of what Shanti had said, Rohnan still didn't trust Cayan's motives.

Shanti sighed as she was set on soft furs near the fire. Cayan's people always did everything to extremes, including comfort. In the future, it would just eat time, but for right now, she was thankful. "Marc saved the day. It was his shot that prevented the Hunter from finding his mark."

"And everyone else? Tobias is limping slightly and Jaime is grim…" Cayan said, straightening.

"I'm good, sir. Just a cut. Marc said he can put some salve on it," Tobias called from behind them.

"Marc will see to me as well." Jaime's voice held strain. Shanti knew that he was trying to ignore the pain.

She sat with a hunched back as the warmth from the fire seeped into her skin. Burson sat opposite her poring over a map. Gracas and Leilius stared at her with solemn eyes and thin lips. Leilius had seen action before, but she knew it scared him when he thought about it for any length of time. This was the first time for Gracas, and though he'd probably start to love the excitement, the first plunge had left him in quiet contemplation.

Or maybe it was just being in the vicinity of the Captain. It was hard to say with the spirited youth.

The rest of Cayan's group must've been at the small fire on the other side of a line of trees. She could see the glow and the shadows of men, but she was too far away to make them out. Rohnan was seated beside her. He put his hands near the fire and rubbed them together.

"The Hunter?" Cayan asked, finally sitting down.

"Alive. Wounded, but not terminal." Shanti looked

at Cayan. Dressed in a barely creased blue shirt and pants, he sat tall and firm, like he hadn't just fought his way out of his city. "His men ran at us in perfect formation, herding me into the center while the others were shepherded out. Marc happened to be right behind me, or I would've been left alone. He is… cunning. An excellent tactician," she shook her head. "He worries me."

"Do you think he'll follow?" Cayan asked with tight eyes. He worried about his city—about leaving it unprotected.

"Yes," Shanti said with certainty. "We killed those two *Sarshers*, and taunted the Hunter. He'll come after us. He won't worry about your city, not yet. There's nothing there for him."

A vein throbbed in Cayan's jaw, but he said nothing as he turned his gaze to the fire.

"Did you kill all your *Sarshers*?" she asked.

"Of course. The two stationed on the sides, as well. They chased us, so Tepson and I hung back to dispatch them with our bows. All the *Sarshers* are accounted for."

"And you weren't followed?"

A small smile twisted Cayan's lips. The fire danced in his eyes. "You're the only one who left anyone alive."

Shanti couldn't help her huff as she turned back to the fire. "I'd like to see you kill one of the elite while combating two huge powers and trying to hang onto an insane horse who would rather stop and kick another horse than run on out of danger."

"S'am's horse was vicious!" Rachie laughed as he sauntered up to the fire. "Gracas, I did it! I showed up Tobias, *and* I did my part!" He sat next to the other members of the Honor Guard with a goofy grin.

Xavier walked into the firelight next with a smug swagger of his own. His eyes took in who else was sitting around the blaze. As soon as he noticed the Captain, his walk straightened and his shoulders hunched. He quietly sank down next to the others with a bowed head. Rachie, having noticed the same thing, albeit belatedly, snapped his mouth shut. All the boys' eyes found the flickering flames.

Shanti rolled her eyes—she'd never understood the deference the boys showed, but she'd learned to ignore it for the most part. She turned to Cayan, "I need energy. You can provide it. This will be your first lesson because you are way behind."

"I will monitor," Rohnan murmured, scooting closer and putting a hand on Shanti's neck.

Shanti jumped and shied away. "Rohnan! Get that block of ice off me. Warm it up, first!"

"Do we get lessons, too, S'am?" Gracas asked. Leilius elbowed him before pointedly looking back at the fire. Gracas scowled and looked at his attacker, not understanding the abuse.

"Yes, but not tonight," Shanti answered. "We have a long journey ahead of us. In the lulls, I'll help train you boys, as will the others."

"To which others are you referring?" Tobias dropped a saddle away from the fire. The light flickered shadows along the indents of his face. Sanders dropped another saddle next to him.

"Why didn't you have the Honor Guard look after the horses?" Cayan asked Sanders with a hard stare.

"Figured I'd let them get used to battle, first. They've got their adrenaline up right now, but when their heads start replaying events, they won't be so keyed up." Sanders walked over to a tree behind Daniels and Burson and leaned back. He bit into an apple.

Cayan's gaze followed him. "That's the best time to keep busy."

"Yes, sir. I also wanted to look over the animals myself, to see if any were hurt. Two have shallow scrapes. A little blood, but nothing too bad. One was Shanti's horse. That thing has great breeding. Fast as lightning, muscular, seems fearless—I'd bet it was intended for a war horse but fell short with its attitude. I've never seen a finer horse—never in my life, sir. Mean as the blazes, though—thing tried to bite me! Rohnan's horse is nearly there. Good stock. And that Hunter's horse was sure a pretty thing with the added bonus of following its master's command. We can learn a thing or two, there.

The Duke would be buying *our* stock."

"Always hearing gold coins jingling, huh Sanders?" Tobias smirked as he took up position at the tree next to Sanders'. He let his good leg take most of his weight. Marc was probably working on Jaime.

Sanders grunted. "When I see something worth seeing, I remember it."

"If we have the opportunity, we'll try to… acquire more," Cayan said.

Shanti and Rohnan both started to laugh. Shanti said, "Steal more. Just say it. If you get the chance, you'll steal more."

Tobias started to chuckle. "Let the blondes do it. They seem to have had practice."

"I do. Much," Rohnan said. He placed his fire-warmed hand on Shanti's skin.

Shanti met Cayan's eyes. "Okay, we need to start. Are you ready?"

The dancing humor drained from Cayan's gaze. He shifted so he faced her and flipped his hand so their palms were touching. Shanti sucked in a breath as his fingers entwined between hers. Electricity spread throughout her body. Warmth pooled in her core.

"You allow so intimate a hold with him?" Rohnan asked in a murmur.

"He fears losing control. This makes him feel more grounded. And since I've already relived the horrors of

feeling this hold again, I'm immune to it now. Surely you can feel the comfort he radiates when he does it?"

"That's rude, you know," Sanders growled. "Why don't you talk in a language we all know?"

"Why don't you learn more languages?" Tobias shot back.

"Are you trying to be a bard? Because if so, you need to find a sense of humor first." Sanders took another bite of his apple.

"Just spreading the good cheer of a narrow victory by running away." Tobias winced as he shifted his weight.

Sanders snorted. "We did at that. I didn't like the look of that Hunter. Didn't seem human."

"His fear is growing." Rohnan ignored the chatter around him, focusing on Cayan through his link through Shanti. *"As your power merges with his and blossoms, he can feel the power at his disposal through you. The two of you have a large well of power, but his is deeper. His deepest reserves... bottomless, it seems. But locked up. Covered, somehow. We need to break through that barrier to allow a surge—a deep undertow—of power. He is stronger than you, Chosen. Much stronger. I've never seen the equal."*

"You'd never seen my *equal, Rohnan."*

"And I hope I don't see his. I wonder if he can feel what lays deep within him—if he has always felt it, and is

afraid of the free-fall into it, worried the power will overcome him. Or maybe he is afraid of what else resides down there. He lost his parents young, did he not?"

Shanti closed her eyes and focused on Cayan's touch. She felt the hum between their skin, and the electricity that originated at her hand then spread out. She pushed harder into his mind, trying to get deeper. Rohnan could see things without trying that most people couldn't find, even with a deep connection. Still, she had to try.

Her mind whirled and spiraled, sinking deeper into his. He enveloped her presence, welcoming her in, holding her within himself. The spiciness saturated her body, humming. Erotic stirrings tickled private places, mirroring his deeper desires. Fire erupted in her core and her skin broke out in a sweat, making her breath come out in fast pants. She leaned in as he stroked a thumb across her skin, relishing that pulsing heat she'd never felt before.

"That is an effect of your succinct mating, and will probably be very pleasing one day, but it is not why we are here," Rohnan warned. *"Focus."*

Shanti fought the tightening in her body. She fought her yearning and his lust. Above all, she fought the begging need for completion by his touch. Instead, she weaved within those emotions until she found what Rohnan had recognized while she had been siphoning off some of his energy and replenishing her *Gift*. Some sort of blockage nestled within deeply scarred emotions. Jagged and cutting, she sensed pain. Loneliness. Uncertainty. And beneath that the world almost seemed to drop away. She felt a void so deep it sucked her toward it.

Rohnan was right. Power. A vast store of world-shattering power. She wasn't the most powerful in the land by far. He was. He just didn't know how to access it.

"This would overcome him. If he doesn't know how to use his current power, he shouldn't break into an even bigger store of it," she surmised. Rohnan grunted his assent.

Out of curiosity, and maybe because he had been scraping away her defenses and pain to get at the roots of her since she'd known him, she honed in on that scarred place, on that loneliness, just to get a glimpse of what he was hiding.

As if she'd triggered a trap, his defenses reacted. He crushed her within his mind. Jagged edges stabbed at her consciousness. Claws pierced.

Heart hammering, she pulled back and yanked herself free. She ripped her hand out of his and felt Rohnan pulling her body away. Her eyes blinked open, shocked and shaken. Cayan stared at her, confusion filtered through a haunted, desperate sorrow. His eyebrows drew low over his pleading eyes.

"So, that's a do-not-enter area, then?" she asked lightly, straightening. She gave him a smile, trying to ease the situation. Rohnan took his hands away and turned toward the fire, giving them a little privacy, such as it was.

Cayan reached toward her again. "I still don't have any control, but… yes. That's…" He glanced at those around the fire, most staring at them. When he looked back at her, strength and power overshadowed the soft vulnerability she'd seen moments before. "Did you get what you needed?"

Yes, she had, but the commanding air he was using to replace a deeply rooted humanity—the tough, almost coarse treatment of his vulnerability—sparked her stubbornness. No way was he going to spend months dragging out the harsh realities of her past, and then try to shrug off his own problems. His people might find men crying a weakness, but she wasn't of his people, and she would make this big, tough bastard blubber like a baby.

Rohnan started laughing, reading her. *"This is what I meant, Chosen. You crave to dominate, or be dominated. There is no middle ground. There is no soft approach in your mating dance. There is war and release, only."*

"I didn't ask. Mind your own business." Shanti focused on Cayan. "No, I didn't." She took his hand again

and resumed their connection. "Kick me out again and I'll be forced to teach you a lesson."

A glimmer sparked in Cayan's eyes, the usual blue turned an eerie purple in the firelight. The man always rose to the challenge.

Rohnan chuckled again, a sound that grated under the circumstances.

When they entwined their *Gifts* this time, Shanti didn't touch that jagged place, but she went deep until she felt that hint of bottomlessness peeking through his tight defenses. "Now, do you feel my mind within yours?"

"Yes," he said in his hard voice.

"You should do this away from his men. That was shortsighted of you," Rohnan said in an offhanded way.

She ignored him, mostly because he was right. To Cayan, she said, "Can you feel me sucking a little? Drawing on your power?"

"Can I try this next?" Tobias said. "I wouldn't mind a little suction."

"She's the wrong sort to get mixed up with," Sanders commented. "Too much of a headache."

"I can feel it," Cayan said. He was tightened up, though. He didn't like having to learn something in his men's presence.

The air of gloating she felt coming from Rohnan was annoying. He loved it when he was right.

"I had enough strength to connect with your mind and draw what I needed," Shanti explained to Cayan as she backed out slowly. "If you—not I, *you*—had very little strength, I would initiate a connection like this, and then I would feed you power. Feed you energy. With an enemy, if you are strong enough, and deft enough, to create this type of connection despite their attacks and defenses, you can suck their energy away. A few of the Inkna attempt that trick—I learned it from that disgusting little mouse you captured a long time ago."

She withdrew totally and took her hand away.

Cayan took a moment to stare at her, his uncertainty of his *Gift* making his emotions turbulent, but he recovered quickly. "We'll go over our journey tomorrow morning," he said. "You should get some sleep. We'll need you at full capacity."

"It's as if you think this is my first time traveling," Shanti said, thankful for the excuse to slip away and into her sleeping furs.

"First time traveling with a group." Cayan rose.

"Well, not the *first* time, right, Captain?" Tobias spoke up. "But hopefully it's the first time she *stays* with a group…"

Sanders smirked. "Remains to be seen. We'll need a sentry for the camp, and another to watch her."

Rohnan matched their laughter as Shanti stood.

Shaking her head, she left the warmth of the fire in search of her saddlebag and bedding. The journey had begun, and today might prove to be the easiest day they'd have. The Hunter would be dogging their steps despite his injury, and organizing men to cut them off whenever possible. She'd thought getting through the Graygual to get across the sea would be the hardest part. Now she wondered if they'd even get that far.

CHAPTER 13

SHANTI MOANED AS SHE CLIMBED into her saddle. Her back ached, her hips and groin were stiff, and her quads couldn't be tighter. They'd been riding through wood for the last two days, often taking tiny trails and constantly ducking branches. Her body wasn't used to sitting in a saddle for extended periods of time, and it showed.

Rohnan had offered to tie her on. She had offered to break his nose.

It was just her luck that her horse hated everyone but her. And because it tried to bite everyone that touched it, she had to stow its saddle, brush it, and give it food and water. As a fellow leader of this journey, those chores should've been delegated to one of the boys. She should've been relaxing by the fire as someone else looked after her ride. But no. Her horse was a bastard. A really fast, well-bred bastard, flunked out of pedigree for its personality.

She did not appreciate every one of the fighters pointing out the similarity between her and her horse.

"Okay, Shanti…" Daniels stepped close to her horse with a studious expression.

Her horse sounded its strange, equine growl.

Daniels' gaze jerked up, focusing on the horse's head with round eyes as he quickly scooted away. He was one of the few not to have been bitten, and he seemed to want to keep it that way.

Clearing his throat, he stretched to hand Shanti up a map from as far from the horse as he could. "We have about another half-day through the trails, then we have an open stretch of land before our next sheltered area."

Shanti glanced at the well-drawn map featuring a great many small trails marked in red. A couple of larger trails were colored blue. They all led into a treeless area with a black line running through it. She put her finger on that line. "This is a main road?"

Daniels nodded as Cayan joined them. The horse made his complaint known once again. This time, Cayan stared at the animal for a moment. He didn't move away.

The horse didn't press the matter. It probably knew Cayan would resort to violence, much like Shanti did.

"Oh yes, piss off my horse. Thanks." Shanti studied the map.

The horse blew out a breath and shifted right, forcing the others to move with it.

Shanti rolled her eyes and followed the black line

with her finger to a large thoroughfare. "He'll have people waiting for us on this road," she tapped the black line, "and an army on the larger trading route. This won't work. I thought we went over this last night?"

"We aren't following the road. We're crossing it." The sparkle of humor from the horse situation left Cayan's eyes as he stared up at her.

Frowning, Shanti visualized crossing the road into what looked like another thick wood. "When was this decided?"

"Burson," Rohnan said as he moved his mount up beside hers. "He spoke with Daniels this morning."

Shanti glanced back toward the fire pit where Burson sat on his horse. Gracas and Rachie rehearsed new moves they'd learned the night before. Shanti hadn't lied about keeping their training going, and they'd responded to her methods as they had before—immediately and with vigor.

"When he makes recommendations, they sound so logical. It sounds like this is the only way we can go and live." Daniels glanced back at Burson. He shook his head. "It's suicide, this way he's identified, but I've gone over how this Hunter works. Traveling any large road is death. No question. We have a small force, and nearly half are no more than children. We have two mental workers, and one we cannot use until the most dire of circumstances so we don't give away his talents too soon. We have a nulling effect mental-worker, which is useful, but he does not fight. All the Hunter needs is space and he will have us."

"Then what is this?" Shanti pointed at the edge of the wood in which they traveled. She let her finger travel the large open space between covered areas. "He will have these maps. Maybe not so detailed, but he only needs the easily traversed routes. He'll see that there are three places we can enter the cleared land. Only three. And they are not so far away from each other. You can bet he's setting up a force to intercept us. We need to go a way he doesn't expect."

"There is no other way. Not if we want to keep heading east," Cayan said in an even tone. "Any other route would put days on our journey, maybe weeks, which would just give him more time to heal, and to arrange a force to the East."

Shanti let her eyes travel the other wooded area on the map. "If the trails in this other area are like the trails in this, it's going to put days or weeks on our journey, anyway."

"That's the Dreaded Lands, Chosen," Rohnan said quietly.

Cold dribbled through Shanti's middle with the name. She pictured the map of the land in her mind, placed Cayan's city, put in the wood they were in, fit the map over it, and then dropped her head. "Stupid.

Without a larger map I didn't even—" She handed the map back to Daniels. "Absolutely not. No way. It's suicide."

"It is the only way," Cayan said in a low growl.

She stared into those crystal blue eyes as she said, "Have you not heard the stories and myths surrounding the Dreaded Lands, Cayan?"

"Do you believe in myths and ghost stories?"

"Yes, when there is nothing else, or when traders will add weeks onto their journey to keep from going through. Even the Graygual won't enter those lands, Cayan. That should tell you something."

"Shanti—" Cayan stepped closer and lowered his voice. "In normal circumstances, I wouldn't have left my city with Graygual at my door. I'd planned to send you first, and follow when I knew it was safe to leave. I will admit Burson has a candied tongue, as Daniels said. But he was right. Everything he said was right. I've heard he made changes to your journey that seemed foolish, and because of that, Sanders is alive. Burson… has more than just a nulling effect on our power. There is something else to him. Just by the fact that he's never been wrong. I feel in my gut that we should trust him. There is no other way that makes sense."

"It mostly swamp," Rohnan spoke up. "We need a map to guide us through. Without it, we die, anyway."

Daniels reached into his satchel and took out another map. "Compliments of the man himself." He nodded at Burson, who watched Xavier trying to emulate Leilius' tactics of blending in. His big, stiff body looked even larger amid the thin twigs and branches he'd chosen to hide amongst.

Shanti felt Rohnan's unease. "Something's not right about this. Do you remember anything in the scriptures about a man like Burson?"

Rohnan's troubled eyes fell to the ground. "No—but none of this was mentioned. This current journey—it's like it all skipped. We should be in Shadow Lands now, from what I study. Where we are seems another journey. The Captain and his men are needed addition. His army, and his allies—essential. Burson's *Gift* has to be on our side. I *feel* that. But we are lost right now, Chosen. We are wandering. And he has become our guide. It all as he says."

"Fuck." Shanti didn't know what else to say. She was traveling completely blind without a clue of what came next. She wasn't in control of her journey, her fate—nothing.

So she said it again. "Fuck!"

"I don't like this, either," Cayan said. His mind tickled hers like a feather's touch. Warmth and comfort infused her thoughts and spread through her body in waves from his *Gift*.

She'd continued to train him for the last few days

too. Now he had down the mental stimulation that could emulate safety and comfort.

It was a nice gesture, but it didn't fool her. Their journey was about to take a perilous turn.

Shanti pushed his mind away and kicked her horse. The animal swished its tail at the two humans by its side, neighed, and started walking. "Let's go," she yelled. "If we're running to our death, I'd like to get there before supper."

THEIR PACE WAS QUICK THROUGH the widening trails. It was almost as if the wood wanted to spill them out into danger so it could watch what happened. Everyone had heard where they were headed, and knew what Shanti and Rohnan called it. The Dreaded Lands. The place where travelers ventured in, but did not make it out.

Every part of the vast land had a place where myths and stories talked of raiders and thieves and murderers. What made this particular place different was that no one returned to spread rumors. No one. There were no tall tales of what lay inside.

"If anyone can come out of this place, Toolan, it's you," Leilius said as the sun passed its zenith and began its slow fall.

"I've heard of *Sarshers* entering and not coming out. Warriors. Experienced men. All went in, not believing the myths, but none came out." Shanti let her unfocused gaze sweep to the side as anxiety ate at her guts. Then something occurred to her.

"What did you call me?" She turned in her saddle so she could see Leilius. He rode like a sack of potatoes not properly tied on. She really hoped she didn't look like that.

"Too-lan. Tute-lan?" He struggled with the sound of whatever word he was trying to spit out.

"*Chulan*, dummy," Marc called up. "Shoo-*lan*."

"Shoooo-*lane*," Leilius tried.

Rohnan turned in his saddle in front of her. *"I've been teaching Marc our language. He is extremely intelligent—just needs a soft hand for encouragement."*

"I've used… the opposite hand for encouragement."

Rohnan laughed and turned back around. *"That is because you don't have a soft hand. Anyway, he picked up that I call you Chosen."*

"You call me Chosen in his language, too, so everyone knows what I am supposed to be, even though we now know it's false. Why is Leilius using our speech for the title?"

"They have adopted Chosen as a name. That name comes from your home language, and so they are trying to celebrate your origin. They have faith in you."

Shanti scoffed. *"You put them up to this because you hate me, is that it?"*

"Love, Chosen. I love you. I just don't always show it when there is a joke to be had."

"We can get through this place because we're a team, Shoolan. And we have the Captain. These other people, they didn't have the Captain." Leilius sounded so sure. The kid was the most trusting, positive person Shanti had ever known.

"Cadet, if you keep talking like that," Sanders said in a voice that could cut through a monsoon and still reach the intended ear. "People are going to think God scooped out your brains and replaced them with rainbows and horse shit."

Shanti couldn't help a bark of laughter. Rohnan echoed it. Smiling, she said to Leilius, "We'll do the best we can, and hope Burson is the holder of miracles."

THE SUN WAS NEARLY TOUCHING the horizon when they dismounted and gathered on foot before the large expanse of clearing. The road was easy enough to see. More than a hundred paces to each side had been scraped clean of trees. Whenever a new sprout shot up, it had been cut and burned away again. No one on that road wanted the Dreaded Lands to encroach any closer than they already were.

Blocking the road stood at least thirty Graygual. Ten were on horseback. But those on the ground did not stand straight and tall, they did not have crisp uniforms, and were unshaven.

"These are disposable," Shanti murmured to Cayan.

"What do you mean?" Cayan whispered.

Shanti raised her voice enough for it to carry far enough for the others to hear. "The officers had to be used to keep the men in order, but those officers are middle-aged and still in the lower ranks. They either perform poorly, or were grunts recently, not to have advanced further. The grunts are sloppy. They don't hold the normal standard of Xandre's prized warriors, which means they're probably from a conquered nation, there only to help get answers to questions. Today's question is 'how does the violet-eyed woman and her hired men fight?' How do they move? Do they work together, or is there dissension within the ranks?

"We aren't meant to die, today. We're meant to show what we're capable of. What direction we'll go. How we deal with a threat. The Hunter did not expect to be beaten last time—he is now learning about his prey so as not to make the same mistake again."

"If that's true, he'd have to watch us in action himself," Sanders said. He ducked so he could get under the hanging branches and look farther into the field.

Burson pointed, also ducking down to get a better view. "On the small hill out to the right."

Between two groups of fighters who were blocking

two of the three possible outlets, sat a man on a horse. Shanti couldn't see the details of his face, but the way he sat, and the way his arm was bent across his stomach in a sling, proclaimed exactly who he was. Two men in black sat on horses to the sides of him. The Hunter's guard.

"He's smart." Shanti chewed her lip as her *Gift* lapped at his senses. She was careful to keep it light—she didn't want his minions alerted to her mind's presence. "But he isn't all-knowing. He's outside of Burson's range, and I'd bet he's outside of those *Sarshers'* range, too, but not mine. He underestimates me. Good."

"I don't like crossing this open space in clear view," Sanders said.

"We don't have choice," Rohnan replied.

"The Hunter does not know of the Captain's fighting prowess," Burson noted in a dry voice. It was his 'survival' voice. "It is best if we keep that to ourselves until we have no choice but to reveal it."

"Exactly," Shanti agreed. "He can't know anything of the Captain yet. Those that might have seen him in action are dead. Burson, keep his mind looking normal. We'll pass within range of those *Sarshers*, and they'll be checking for power, if they can." Shanti laid her hand on Cayan's arm as her mind catalogued what lay in front of them. "Cayan, you should ride with the others, but try to keep from fighting if you can."

"The enemy outnumbers us by nearly two to one, more with our number of inexperienced, and you're suggesting I stay out of this fight?" Cayan's voice was light, but a warning blasted from his mind.

Her hand resting on his arm wasn't enough, apparently. She squeezed, hoping it would have the desired effect. "These are throwaways. These people can't fight. They'll be disorganized and as likely to stab each other as us."

"We have five boys that fit that same description," Sanders growled.

"These boys are not the same five you led through the burned forest, Sanders," Shanti snapped. "They'll rise to the occasion. Hell, Marc is the reason I'm still alive. It was his arrow that rendered the Hunter useless."

"We wasting daylight," Rohnan chided gently.

"Let's get in position," Cayan commanded, stepping away from her attempt at a placating touch.

They turned back to the horses. Cayan fell in beside Shanti. "You're not making this journey easy, Shanti. You're operating with knowledge I do not possess."

"I've had the unfortunate benefit of spending my life learning about Xandre. We're on the run—I don't have time to clue you in every moment. Even if I did, Burson is constantly changing the rules."

"Not good enough." He gave her a firm stare to drive the point home before he faced his people. His eyes hit Ruisa first, then glanced over the boys before stopping on Burson. "We'll form a vee. Shanti will be at the head, with Rohnan and me next. Commander Sanders—"

"Yes, sir." Sanders stepped up.

"Organize everyone else for the most effectiveness around Ruisa, Burson and Marc. We need them protected. I don't want them affected by this if we can help it."

"Yes, sir."

Cayan nodded. "Let's get mounted. Shanti assures me these troops don't know how to fight. Even so, we will hit them hard and fast. We will burst out of the trees and kill immediately. Our object is to cross the clearing without losing anyone. We do not need to kill all of the enemy, we simply need to get by."

"Yes, sir!" the men and most of the boys chorused.

"Yes, ah—" Leilius' voice trailed away as he realized he was too late.

"Let's go." The circle broke as Cayan moved toward his horse. He grabbed his bow. Without looking at Shanti, he said, "I will use the bow unless my sword is needed."

Shanti sighed. It was a compromise, and it wasn't up for negotiation, but at least it was something.

She needed to work on that placating hand thing.

She kicked her horse to get it moving.

Wrong move.

The beast launched forward. It sideswiped Cayan's animal as it started to trot. The trot gradually increased in speed until the branches were *thwapping* her in the face. "Slow down, you…" Her eyes widened as the opening to the clearing loomed ahead of her. The horse sped up. "Slow down, you bloody… *bastard!*"

It sprang out through the trees and into the clearing. She ripped her sword free as the animal charged for the first enemy in their way. The man glanced up, but Shanti's horse was on him, barreling him to the ground. Its hooves crashed down on the man's sternum. A sickening crack cut off the scream.

"Straight! Run straight!" Shanti screamed, holding on as the horse veered toward the next Graygual. She slashed down as she rode by, cleaving his head.

"Where—?" They veered again, toward two men holding their tarnished swords in unpracticed hands. The horse sped up. One man dropped his sword and squatted, covering his head. The other man bent his knees, holding his sword ready.

Shanti's horse ran him down, knocking into him at full speed.

"What the hell are you doing, you blasted animal?!" Shanti roared.

An arrow zipped by her head. She glanced up to see an officer drawing his bow from his standing horse. Before she could react, an arrow struck his neck and blossomed red like a rose in the failing light.

Cayan caught up with her, nocking an arrow into place. “Aim for the trees,” he ordered.

“I have no control over this animal,” she yelled back.

Her horse gave its strange war-cry as it veered toward a cluster of Graygual. All brandished their rusty steel. The foremost started swinging his sword wildly. Shanti’s horse screamed and slowed.

“Run! Run, damn you!” she yelled. She kicked at its sides, But the beast was in a world all its own.

Without thinking, hating the damn animal, she leapt off and hit the ground with a quick stagger that turned into a run. She attacked the side of the cluster while the horse flailed its hooves at them head-on. She battered a sword strike out of the way before lunging and sinking her blade into flesh. A hoof cracked a Graygual head beside her.

The horse pushed into the group, separating two out to one side, where Rohnan was swooping in on his compliant horse, his staff whirling above his head. Shanti lost sight of him as she faced the remaining Graygual, slashing down across his face. She stuck her blade through his stomach before she ran on.

Cayan was covering her right, riding gracefully, quickly employing his bow. He fired, nocked, drew, fired, nocked, faster than thought and deadly accurate.

And giving himself away!

"Stop Cayan, we don't need you!" she yelled as she sprinted toward the next group of terrified Graygual.

The nearest man screamed and dropped his sword, turning to run. She let him.

Etherlan didn't, riding with his long brown hair flaring out behind him. He swung down his sword and cut the enemy down.

"Keep moving—go to the other side!" Shanti roared as thundering erupted behind her. She looked back with a pounding heart and wide eyes, afraid her horse was about to run her over. Instead, it neighed as it drew up beside her, matching her pace perfectly.

"This bloody animal," she muttered. Having no choice, she hooked a leg into the stirrup, grabbed the bridle and half-jumped up into the saddle.

She leaned forward and was soon catching up with Cayan as they crossed the road, everyone else either branched off to the sides in their loose formation, or stayed in close to those who couldn't fight.

The way was clear in front of them. The remains of the enemy was behind or sprinting away as fast as they could. Shanti had a second to marvel at Cayan. He rode the horse like the animal was an extension of himself.

His movement and sway was so flawless it looked easy. Natural. At a full gallop, he turned his upper body. Muscle rippled across his broad back. His arms and shoulders flexed into large boulders. He sighted his bow and released in one fluid, perfect movement.

It couldn't be any more clear how skilled he was. His prowess on the battlefield was unrivaled, his confidence clear in his calm, almost tranquil movements when confronted with the enemy. He was greatness in the flesh, and any fighting man worth his sword would see that.

The Hunter was not just a fighting man—he was a master. The only thing they had successfully hidden during this ride was Cayan's *Gift*. Everything else was on display for the calculating mind sitting atop that berm—the Hunter's plan had worked.

Shanti couldn't stop herself from laughing at the absurdity of trying to hide the obvious. The Hunter was looking directly at her. She couldn't see his eyes, but she knew those soulless, cold, dead things were staring at her nonetheless, watching her progress. He thought he would find her weakness somehow and use it against her.

Little did he know her weaknesses were masked and protected by Cayan and all his men. She wasn't prey, not with Cayan and Sanders behind her.

Still laughing, she swept up Cayan's *Gift* in her own

and *blasted* out. High and hard and wide, she *punched* his mind and that of his guard, not able to kill at this distance, but able to send a painful message. She held her arms wide, sword in one hand, palm open and inviting on the other.

Come and get me, Hunter. It'll be the last thing you ever do.

CHAPTER 14

QADIR PASSIVELY WATCHED THE WOMAN spread her arms in challenge as she rode the last few meters into the cover of the trees. Her movements were silky and smooth, even on the jarring animal she rode.

She laughed at him.

An unexpected flash of rage had Qadir tilting his head in surprise.

He wasn't used to being laughed at. He couldn't remember ever having been so, especially by the subject of his attentions. The woman knew he analyzed her, and yet she laughed.

Qadir took a moment to let the unhelpful emotion drain from his body. Then he replayed the battle in his mind.

She had ridden her horse like a novice. She had been bounced and jostled, flopping forward and back depending on the speed. Once she got into the thick of the action, though, and her mind engaged in her task, her movements became natural. Speed helped. Her brain operated most effectively when she acted on instinct. More than that, she had an innate ability to read the battle and move accordingly. She had leapt from her horse when necessary, dispatched men of average skill with quick efficiency, and then jumped back onto her transportation without a hitch.

Yes, a highly effective warrior. Extensive training, experience in battle, and a natural ability set her above those around her. What she lacked in strength, she made up for in speed and battle-hardened intuition. No doubt she was also resourceful.

To best her, he would need a slew of advanced warriors facing her at once, or deal with her himself. She was too good for anything less.

That was not accounting for her mental prowess. This woman had many facets, and he already knew that he would need more than a few strong *Sarshers.*

What an interesting mix he would need to bring down one woman.

The Being Supreme had been right, not that anyone would doubt him. She was the one prophesied, and she would gather the masses to her side. If she was permitted to reach the Shadow Lands, the Being Supreme's domination would be in jeopardy.

Qadir tapped his fingers on the edge of his saddle.

The woman personally affronted him. She rode a horse specifically bred for him, for its courage in battle, speed and steadfastness. The animal was bred to act as a weapon. And it had. It had tried to kick and bite its way through the battle, acting as another warrior. The woman hadn't known how to work with it—what exactly each of their roles were—but that horse had turned out exactly as it was meant to. Sleek and vicious, the animal was a natural defense against the enemy. Unlike other horses, who simply followed commands, that horse was geared to combat adversity, keeping warriors from its rider by any means possible.

It might have been just a touch overzealous in that battle, but it was young. It would mellow with age.

Irritation welled up in Qadir, a familiar emotion when dealing with incompetence. He had been told the beast wouldn't take a rider. And yet, a novice had been accepted just fine.

Qadir's trainers had much to answer for. This would not go unpunished.

The old man had been in a protected place within the battle formation. His worth was known, and not because of his self-appointed role of finding the Wanderer and guiding this person to their destiny. Wanderer, Chosen—it all amounted to the same thing. Titles were for fools and simpletons. The violet-eyed woman knew of his mental power, and as such, ensured he was guarded. Picking him off as a discarded member of their crew would be out of the question. Pity.

Qadir wondered if he had flushed her out of the

Westwood Lands, or if it had been the Being Supreme putting up the false Chosen. She would want to defend her title, but hadn't planned to leave in such haste.

Haste was good. Half-thought-out plans meant mistakes. He could capitalize on those.

A smile graced his lips. He would, without question, be hoisted up into the Inner Circle and given anything his heart might desire. He already had his eye on a certain fair-haired prize captured from somewhere in the southern nations. She would produce for him some strong heirs and many nights of pleasure.

He was getting ahead of himself.

Qadir focused on the few items that had him unsettled. They all traced back to the man with raven hair tied at his nape. He was not what he seemed, but Qadir could not explain exactly what it was that alerted him to danger.

He moved as well as the woman—he had much skill in battle. His technique with his bow was perfect. His aim was true. The sword he carried, though not used today, had certainly been used against an enemy. It was within perfect reach and the man wore it like he might a sash, completely comfortable with its weight and presence. Qadir suspected the raven-haired man was just as good with that sword as he was with the bow, if not better.

But he was still just a man.

Something else pinched Qadir's gut uncomfortably. Was it the way he moved with the woman?

He had reacted to each of her subtle cues—he worked around her when she made a decision to engage, and cut out those on her flanks. She, in turn, played off his decisions and took up the slack when he was the one to engage. They used each other in a way that seemed almost choreographed, but Qadir knew it was completely improvised. The man was not from her land, and had a completely different style, but even so, they worked together effortlessly—more so than her countryman, who was clearly just as well trained and excellent as all those from her land.

But the raven-haired man…

What was it about that warrior that wasn't what it seemed?

Qadir turned his horse as the night stole the sun's light. To the *Sarshers*, still pale from the woman's awesome power, he said, "Kill the survivors. They are no longer needed."

CHAPTER 15

THE PATH INTO THE FOREST was wide and bare of vegetation. Small grasses fought through the trodden dirt, trying to sprout new life, but Cayan had no doubt they'd be ripped out as people passed this way. This wasn't a path made once and forgotten. People and horses used it regularly, and the tracks a cart made were etched into the land in many places.

"Commander Sanders," Cayan called.

A foot stomped and a horse grunted in frustration before Sanders was able to get his brown stallion next to Cayan.

"That woman's horse is crazy!" Sanders barked. He shook his head. "The thing is a menace. If it hadn't tried to take out the enemy on its own, or had damn good blood lines running through it, I'd say let's eat it."

Cayan coughed out a laugh. "I think you might get backlash on that decision."

"Not from those who've been bitten by the bugger. Or Shanti for that matter. She can't control that thing."

"She has no experience with horses. She'd be useless

on any of them."

"I can hear that," her soft, sultry voice said from behind them.

Sanders grunted and let his gaze travel out to his right, taking in their surroundings. Cayan said, "Have you noticed the ground?"

Sanders' gaze shot to the path they were on before drifting back to the trees. Shadows descended and pooled at the bases of the trunks, masking anything that might be hiding within. "Yup. There are people living in these woods. Parts might be a swamp, but there have to be habitable areas as well, or they wouldn't have carts coming and going."

Cayan strained to see in between the reaching branches to pierce the darkness beyond. Shanti's power flirted with his as she blossomed out to get a sense of their surroundings. His mind drifted with hers, winding into her currents. Almost immediately, that spicy feeling deep in his stomach started to simmer. His power surged and wound tighter within hers, pushing their reach farther.

The minds of animals lit up within the forest. Other minds, distant and watchful, blinked into existence as Shanti and Cayan's combined power drifted over them. Those Cayan felt seemed anxious. Perhaps they already knew strangers lurked within their midst, even though none of the sentries were close enough to see Cayan's party.

"People might live here, but those not invited do not leave," Cayan said softly.

"If anyone has been permitted to leave, they aren't boasting about it," Sanders replied. After a moment, he added, "Feels wrong, though. This place feels… off, somehow."

Cayan nodded as Shanti started reaching, able to *search* farther that way. There were more people off to the distant north-east than anywhere else, but a few dotted all over. Their spacing seemed random, but Cayan suspected it had something to do with the various paths and the number of travelers on any given path. The minds they were feeling seemed sharp as well as watchful. This was an organized effort, which spoke of army. Cayan doubted the locals would invite everyone to join their party, in which case the people on watch could most probably fight.

"Rumors have a way of keeping people away, though," Sanders speculated as he glanced behind him. He resettled in his saddle. "A good tall tale will keep out most of the thieves and curious passersby."

"There aren't rumors so much as missing people," Cayan said as his and Shanti's mind reached out behind them. Fear blasted out in sparks, wild and savage, from various minds. Pain often took over, before the mind-path blinked out altogether. "The Graygual are killing their own army."

Sanders looked at Cayan. "What's that, sir?"

Cayan felt another mind die, blinking out after a swelling of pain.

Shanti said, "Those men were used in some kind of experiment. That experiment has been carried out. The Hunter no longer has need of his pawns now that he has seen the results. He's cutting them loose." Shanti directed her mental gaze back to the area where she'd found the most people.

Sanders grunted and nonchalantly braced his hand on his thigh as he looked forward. "Once upon a time I would've found her complete lack of interest in killing one's own troops cause for alarm. I might've worried she'd slit my throat in my sleep. Now that I know she probably will, I find I'm not as concerned."

"I wouldn't slit your throat in your sleep, Sanders. I would do it when you were awake. Think of the sport it would be." Shanti's voice was colored with humor.

Sanders snorted.

The encroaching night sifted down into the lane, reducing visibility and blending the path into the trees. Cayan mentally counted a cluster of twelve people at the farthest reaches of his and Shanti's combined power, where the path came to a fork. Both routes were of a similar size, leading out into the trees at a gradual curve left and right. To the left, the emerging blanket of stars twinkled between the treetops. Moonlight shone down, sprinkling the path with soft light. The light haze of fog gave the scene a surreal quality Cayan found strikingly beautiful. A great artist would spend all night trying to capture that play of light as it danced within the haze.

In comparison, the other path looked like a gloomy death trap. Branches stretched over the route, creating a deep and dense ceiling that didn't allow light to penetrate. Jagged thorns reached across the torn-up ground, stomped and twisted until the darkness swallowed the scene.

"I'd say go right," Sanders said into the sudden hush.

"I would love to hear why," came Burson's voice as his horse moved up through the ranks. The sound of the hooves deadened within the press of the trees.

Sanders gave an irritated glance back before looking at Cayan. Cayan barely nodded for him to go on.

Sanders looked at both paths before pointing at the canopy of the lighter route. "Those trees have been pruned. Look at how they end in jagged stumps. Some are old pruning and starting to regrow, and some are newer. The branches that might've reached over the path have been broken and torn away."

He pointed to the closest example. The ripped-away branch was cast to the side of the trunk. It looked like a new break.

Sanders glanced at the other side. "This path is wild. It grows as it should. No light, no welcome beacon, no promise of safety. Nothing is engineered over here. This would tell a traveler that the path most loved is the left one. He would go that way."

"But you are suggesting the other way," Burson said in a sing-song voice.

Sanders jerked his thumb at the ground as he looked behind him. "That's because I'm not a fool. Look at the chewed up ground to the left. Carts have traveled that path. Horses, people—that path has been used as often as the path we are on. If it wasn't, it would have weeds all over it. Those who come here often go left. The other path is mostly even. It's got some scars that look like it's been brushed or something, but weeds are sprouting up, see? Someone probably comes through when the ground gets wet and messes it up enough that the weeds don't grow back for a while. And in the interim, they probably pull them as they prune. No, this is a trick to draw the traveler left. I'm almost curious to follow, too, because I want to know what trap awaits."

"It might be a vicious trap, though," Cayan tempered.

"I didn't say I *would* follow it, sir. Just that I was curious."

"Nice save, Sanders." Shanti chuckled.

"Then, we'd better go right," Burson said.

Shanti sighed. "Burson, you don't fool anyone. You wanted to come through here. You've been looking in the direction I've sensed people. You know more than you're letting on—you know which direction we're supposed to go."

"Fooled me," someone said in the back.

Before Burson had a chance to say anything, Shanti continued, "And if you are leading us into a trap, I will kill you. Do you understand me? I don't care about trust and belief and the war. If you are trying to harm these people, I will rip your throat out regardless of what it will mean to my cause."

Burson giggled, of all things. "Such ferocity. That Hunter has a lot to ponder this night, I am sure. Yes, right is the correct way."

"Always with the nonsense," Sanders muttered as Shanti directed her gaze at Cayan.

She said, "We go right, but who goes first? Him, or one of us?"

Cayan didn't even have to think. "Him. If there are traps or pitfalls, he'll avoid them. If he has an ulterior motive, it'll be revealed in his actions. There aren't any people this way for at least half a mile—this part of the path isn't watched. We don't have to fear an attack."

"Sir?" Tobias called from the back. "My horse isn't great in the darkness and I can't see much up ahead—"

"Apart from horse butts," someone muttered.

Sounded like Rachie.

"—should we get a light?" Tobias finished.

"We should camp here for the night," Shanti said in a low voice. Or maybe it just seemed low within the oppressive trees. "I have a feeling we'll meet whoever inhabits this wood tomorrow. I'd rather do it in the daylight."

SHANTI CRAWLED OUT OF HER sleeping fur into the hard chill of the morning. The thick canopy of trees parted in the center of the clearing, enough to reveal the lightening sky. Shanti brushed her hair from her face as she glanced at the glowing embers nestled within the ash of last night's fire.

Finding a large enough clearing hadn't been hard at all. They had been on the path barely a hundred spans before Burson pointed off to the right and announced a nice little clearing that would fit everyone. He entered first, without fear, and pointed out the best areas for horses, fires, and sleeping furs. It didn't take the Elders to know that he had been along this route before, and he'd slept in that very clearing.

She'd felt Cayan's mistrust, and his burning need for answers, but Cayan had said nothing. He simply nodded, glanced at her with hard eyes, and organized his men. He must've known it wasn't the time to push for answers—not with so much unknown before them. They couldn't risk Burson freezing up and turning back into the mindless mute Shanti had first met. They couldn't risk losing advice on the best ways to make this journey.

Maybe he was waiting for her cue in the matter. It was hard to say.

Shanti was one of the first awake. She quietly made her way through the sleeping, and snoring, men to the young man huddled in a ball within his furs. Shanti knelt by him as Rohnan stirred on his other side, poking his head up and looking at her with the immediately alert eyes of someone who'd been traveling dangerous lands in the last year. Rohnan silently righted himself to a sitting position as Shanti laid a hand on a shoulder.

Marc stirred before sleepy eyes peered out of his bedding. They blinked as he recognized her, then flashed wide open. He scrambled up into a sitting position, looking around wildly.

"What is it?" he asked in a frantic hush. "Are we under attack? Why is everyone sleeping? What's going on?"

Shanti laid a firm hand on his shoulder. "I wanted to talk to you for a moment about the Hunter. Your head hasn't been in the right place since you saw him."

Marc glanced around before his eyes squinted in suspicion. He glanced behind him. His mood turned sullen as he recognized Rohnan. "Your twin seems like a mind-reader. He's always hanging around me, lately."

"He doesn't read minds, but his *Gift* is very potent. He knows what you saw, and can read how you are reacting. As can I. You're afraid. And that's okay." She coated Marc's mind with comfort, and tried to stitch that feeling into her speech.

"Did you see that guy, though, S'am?" Marc asked in a low, fearful voice. He glanced at the sleeping Xavier not far away. In a lower voice still, he leaned forward and said, "Did you get a look at that Hunter?"

"Yes," Shanti replied. "The Graygual officers are very special people. Even before their rigorous training, they are the sort of men who have no morals. They can do unspeakable things to others without a hint of shame or remorse. They do not feel like others feel, Marc. They are excellent manipulators, too. They lie and feel out those around them to curb their behavior and get what they want. One moment they might be helping organize a town and keeping the peace—keeping the worst of the Graygual army in check. The next, they might send in their men to rape, pillage and murder to inspire fear. I've heard of officers threatening children to get the cooperation of their parents. If they don't get that cooperation, the child is killed in front of them. This is not programmed into them, this is something they already are. Xandre takes this type of man and turns him into a weapon."

Marc gulped. "A personality disorder."

"Yes. It is not a personality that functions well in a civilized society."

"It works very well in civilized society," Rohnan cut in softly. "But not in a good way."

"They are trained," Shanti went on. "Rigorously trained in mind and body. They are hurt, they are battered, and they are molded into the sort of man who does his job no matter the odds. He does not fail, because failure would be worse than death. He is not afraid of pain, because he has learned to conquer it. And he does not fear for his comrades, because he does not care about them."

Marc looked at the ground. "I never believed someone could be soulless. You know, because… that's just kind of silly. But…" His deep brown eyes sought Shanti in desperation. "If ever someone was soulless, it would be him. He was just… empty."

Shanti patted Marc's shoulder. *Should I hug him?*

Rohnan nodded.

Shanti hugged him, and started when Marc threw his arms around her. He was turning into a man, but part of him was still very much a boy. Shanti patted his back. "I've seen some bad things," he said. "When we went into that place the Inkna occupied, and I saw how the people were treated—I was scared. That could happen to us. But now… this guy…"

Shanti backed off to look the youth in the eye. "It helps to get angry. To let the rage over his wrongs fuel you and override the fear. That's what Rohnan does. I…"

Shanti settled back into her heels. Fire burned in her memories—flames swallowing her home and her village. Bodies writhed. Blood dripped from faces like tears. Her people lay in heaps on the ground, run through with swords and then discarded.

Instead of helping, she'd run. Left them all behind to rot in the open because no one was left to nestle them into the ground and make their journey up to the Elders easier.

A tear dripped down Shanti's face as she hung her head. "He doesn't scare me in that way. I look into his eyes and see a mirror. I see a woman who over and over again deserts those she loves, over and over again. I feel the emptiness inside me that I see in his eyes. So no, he doesn't scare me. How could he?"

She rose, avoiding Rohnan's eyes, trying to push away his concern and sorrow. Instead, she looked down on Marc as the emotions threatened to overcome her. "But I ache. I ache for what I've done. I know that I will never be like him. I will never reach a place where I can no longer feel the destruction I've caused to those I love most. That I continue to cause. When you look at him, hold onto your humanity with both hands, and know that as long as you can still feel, you are better than him. You may not believe it most of the time, but as long as you can *feel*, you can find your way back to grace."

Shanti felt Cayan's warm mental embrace as it tried to entwine within hers. He was trying to wrap her up and cradle her within himself to protect her.

For once, she let him. She allowed what felt like his strong, unyielding arms encircle her body, cushioning her against the unspeakable horror in her mind. She couldn't escape her past, but this time, she welcomed his comfort to endure it.

Shanti walked away from the area. Without realizing where she was going, she ended up in front of her horse. Without thinking, she slapped it across the face, picking a fight. It responded as she knew it would—by releasing that weird growl and trying to bite her. It stamped its hoof. She slapped its face again. It kicked its front foot forward and nearly clipped her thigh.

Fast bugger.

Another hoof kicked out, almost getting her arm. She shied away and hunched as the sobs bubbled up.

She'd run. Like a coward. She'd turned and run away from all of her people.

She sank against her horse and threw her arms around its neck. She didn't care if it kicked her, or bit her. She just wanted a moment of escape from her past.

Just one second of sinking into the unfeeling world the Hunter occupied would seem so luxurious.

Instead, she gained a few stolen moments of hugging a stubborn bastard of a horse, and felt a surge of gratitude for it letting her.

AS THE DAY PROGRESSED, THEY came to several forks in the path. To test him, they had Sanders continue to choose which path to take and each time Burson followed his advice, indicating he was right.

"Any idiot can see which way the supply trains are going," Sanders said. "But that could lead us right to a camp full of armed and dangerous people. So who's the idiot? The one that follows the path, or the one that doesn't?"

It had been a good question. One that had everyone looking at Burson.

Burson looked at the sky with a smile. "Only few choose the right paths. I was one. There have been only a handful of others. But I had the doctrines on my side. And the *sight* as it comes with my mind-power. You have only brain. Yet that is enough, it seems. Remarkable. The other paths lead to traps and they do the work of a large army. I wonder if this group of warriors and insightful young women would have found the signs to avoid the traps? Maybe."

Shanti had looked back at Rohnan at the mention of *sight*. Burson was a *Seer* in some way, not solely relying on his doctrines as he'd led them to believe. It gave more credibility to his decision-making.

Shanti's horse edged around a bush laced with a glimmering spider web. The dank, moist forest smelled like it has been scrubbed clean with moss. Dust particles sparkled in the snatches of light filtering through the canopy. The dense foliage seemed to *press* in on them, as though nature was trapping them into a tight embrace.

Tingles worked up Shanti's back and arms as the eeriness of the surroundings toyed with her mind. Unseen eyes peered out at them, watching from natural hideouts. She could feel the minds all around them, wary and hostile. It had been like this for a quarter hour. They were being stalked by those unseen, but no move had been made.

"Can you see anything?" she asked Cayan.

He shook his head.

"Can't you just chase them out with your mind-thing?" Tobias asked in a hush.

"Burson said no, remember?" someone replied in a loud whisper from the back. "They have let him through at least once already."

"I don't like this hiding bullshit," Sanders growled.

Shanti didn't either. She had a grip on all their

minds, but Burson had told her to maintain peace. Peace was the only way through the wood without bloodshed.

Tell that to the people waiting with weapons in the trees.

The rasp of branches sounded off to the right. Cayan's head snapped that way, trying to see who made the sound. Shanti's focus went to the other side, in case the noise was a distraction. Behind them, leather creaked as tightly wound men shifted in their saddles. A slow slide of a sword from a sheath mingled with the clomp of hooves on dirt.

"Got movement," Tepson called up. "They're definitely watching us."

The itching between Shanti's shoulder blades intensified. She strained her eyes, looking into the trees for the telltale glint of eyes. For bodies. For *anything* that might give these people away. They were like ghosts, silent but ever-present, stalking them through the woods. Dangerous ghosts, at that.

Shanti's horse neighed. It pranced to the right, either sensing her apprehension, or feeling the people waiting just off the road.

"Do any of them have that mind-weapon?" Sanders asked quietly.

"No. But none are scared like Marc is—they're experienced." Shanti let her fingers play across the blade of her sword. "They think they have the upper hand."

"Saw one—I saw one!" Gracas hissed.

"What are they waiting for? They have us surrounded." Cayan asked in rough voice. He took out a throwing knife.

"Wariness. I'm getting heavy doses of wariness. Some recognition is also evident, though soft," Rohnan said. "Tension is higher, though. It's building. Something is coming. They're waiting for something."

"They can hear us, right? They're close enough to be able to hear what we say?" Marc asked from down the line. "If so, let's not give too much away. They're not giving us anything."

They're giving plenty away, Shanti thought. *And that scares them because they're used to lying in wait, undiscovered. We've blown their greatest asset—concealment.*

"Here we go—" Rohnan said. He stood in his saddle and pulled his staff free. Cayan whipped out his sword from its sheath, signaling those behind them to do the same. Metal slid against leather.

A group of fifteen or so entered Shanti's tight mental focus, sprinting. "Here they come and they're coming fast!"

She stood in her saddle, brandishing steel. She glanced at the ground—stay on or get off?

"They have no horses—stay on your horse," Cayan growled.

A thrust of stinging mental power slapped her mind. Everyone behind her groaned. Marc and Leilius both shrieked. As the runners drew near, the power intensified, pounding her with waves of mental needles that felt like they were piercing her whole body.

CHAPTER 16

"THIS IS NOTHING—GRIT YOUR teeth against this!" Sanders roared. He swung a leg over his saddle, ready to jump off and attack.

"React!" Burson shouted. "Do not kill."

With a lifetime of experience, Shanti fought the attack until she could identify each of the participants. As Sanders was jumping from his horse, she found the source and gripped each of their minds, ready to softly end the attack.

Cayan had also reacted, but unfortunately his maneuvers weren't so subtle.

Without warning, a deep rumble *blasted* into the trees. Like a shockwave of invisible fire, power blistered toward the attackers, mental-workers and fighters alike. Those waiting within the trees recoiled from the thick, heady power. One toppled out onto the path, clutching his middle and screaming. Another wave rolled from Cayan, the subatomic thunder unlike anything Shanti could duplicate. It hit the runners like a wall, stopping their progress. Shrieks and screamed filled the trees, and still he pumped out attacks. His eyes glowed, flickering with the power that left him in steady torrents.

Shields slammed home to protect the attackers, but they were nowhere near strong enough to withstand Cayan's might, especially with her mated power to bolster him further. He pounded into them, dropping them to their knees. Shanti felt the agony as minds pulled into themselves, like bodies curling into the fetal position.

"Enough, Cayan," Shanti yelled, pulling back. She wrestled his mental power, turning it from its path as best she could and pulling it into herself. His mental presence wrapped around hers. The spicy quality of their mated powers fizzled and tingled her limbs. She sucked in a breath as a flood of warm comfort and support radiated through her core. He must have been thinking of her episode earlier that day, and their intimate mental contact had brought out his concern.

This was not the bloody time!

"Cayan, pull *back!*" She ripped out of his mental embrace before jumping from her horse as her *Gift* blossomed out once again. "Secure the first row of attackers—do not kill!" she said to the others.

She pinpointed the *Gifted* as they tried to rebuild their defenses, though some were undoubtedly still curled up on the ground. Cayan's *Gift* joined hers, back under control now that the immediate threat was gone.

She let it swell her power, and then *pierced*. A thin stream of intense strength hammered into the center of their defenses. Their mental shields shattered. She clutched their minds in a steel grip. When one or more tried to shake her loose, or put up further defenses, she *twisted*. New shrieks rent the air.

"Follow the game trails, Chosen," Rohnan shouted as he veered to the right.

Shanti jumped over a form huddled on the ground moaning. His sword lay in the dirt. She ran around another who sat with her arms around her knees, rocking with eyes closed.

She saw the trails Rohnan referred to, crisscrossing like a spider web. They weren't for game, they were for ambushes. Clever.

"Rohnan, go farther right. There are two there. Cayan—"

"I got it," came Cayan's reply. He was running left with his sword at the ready.

Shanti burst through a hedge, and nearly stumbled onto an arm lying across the trail from a fallen body. She hopped over, took a few more steps, and turned with sword in one hand and knife in the other. There were four people, from ages twelve through forty, all kneeling or lying on the ground. A man, the oldest, looked up with pleading eyes. *"Please spare my wife and son,"* he said in the common trader's dialect. *"He's only fifteen and she—"*

"Not me," the boy spat with a raised chin in grim defiance. *"Spare my mother."* He pointed to the woman lying on the ground, heavily pregnant.

A shock of horror engulfed Shanti. Without thinking, she screamed for Marc and ducked to the woman.

"Is she weak in power?" Shanti asked in a rush, rolling the woman off of her stomach.

The son made a quick movement. A fisted hand holding a rock lashed toward Shanti's head. She ducked and punched, clipping him on the chin before *blasting* him with her *Gift*. He grunted and clenched his jaw before she thrust into his mind for a deeper connection. With one fierce *tug*, she sucked his *Gift's* essence into her. She could latch on and use his mind's control center to wreak havoc with his body, or she could keep sucking until he passed out, cutting off before he died.

She opted for the second. She only wanted him out of the way.

"No!" the man shouted. He lurched for his son before hesitating and leaning back toward his wife. Tears rolled down his cheeks. *"Please. Please don't hurt her. She's eight months pregnant."*

"I'm not going to hurt her, and your son is just sleeping. You people really should trust a little more. Surely you realize I could've killed you outright. MARC!"

"S'am?" Marc crashed through the trees like a

wounded deer.

"Here," she called.

Finally he stumbled through dense bushes with a sword and a white face. He looked around with wild eyes, saw the man raise his arms in defense, and stabbed forward. Before Shanti could jump up to intercept, he veered the thrust away to the right. "Is he surrendering?"

Marc turned around, still wild-eyed, and saw the woman on the ground. "What happened?" He knelt to the woman in a rush of movement. His eyes cleared of fear immediately, but his hands still shook with adrenaline. He felt along her belly and pinched her eyes open. She moaned and moved her head.

"It's her *Gift*. Her mental thing. She's exhausted, like you get sometimes." Marc went back to feeling her belly. His eyebrows dropped low over his eyes. He jumped before ripping his hands away. "Weird. I've never felt a baby kick before. It has some punch. But, the baby is alive. And her pulse is fine. She just needs to rest, I think."

Shanti bent with a lung-filling sigh. If she'd killed a pregnant woman, not even the underworld would welcome her in.

"What were you thinking having her out here? Are you insane, or just stupid? Get her home."

"They said you were powerful. That we all had to

come or else they couldn't hold you," the father said in a quivering voice. He crawled over to his wife and grabbed her hand, shooting furtive glances at their son.

Shanti shook her head. *"They should've known that the few extra people wouldn't have helped."*

Rohnan returned, his weapons already put away. He glanced at the people on the ground before dropping down to the woman. "What happened?"

"She's weak in the *Gift* but she's okay. Help Marc get her to her home. I'm going to go see what's going on with the fighters—see if we can expect any more violence."

"This how they been able to keep strangers out," Rohnan said as he felt the woman's pulse. "With their *Gift*. All together they are powerful. Is enough for many, but not powerful enough to keep Graygual out for much longer."

"No. Not with the Graygual armies moving this way in greater number." Shanti kept her sword out. She didn't know what she'd find back with the others, and her people were still outnumbered.

"The Captain's *Gift* is... unique..." Rohnan said. His tone was even and his shield was up tight. There was subtext to his statement, his body language and blasé attitude made that clear, but he intended to keep it to himself.

She absolutely hated it when he did this.

"I can see that you are trying not to make a point, Rohnan, and, succeeding in being irritating." Shanti looked at Marc. "Are you okay to stay with him, Marc?"

Marc didn't bother looking up. "Is he a doctor? He's being pretty thorough. Seems like he knows what he's doing."

"He's a healer, of sorts. His *Gift* lends to that discipline. Also that of working with kids. He—"

"I cover that, Chosen," Rohnan interrupted. "You have other things do."

"*To* do, ingrate." Shanti hefted her sword and stalked back toward the earlier fray. As she left the others, she heard, "Did you call her 'Chosen'?"

Not only did someone speak the Mountain Region language, he knew of the title. Great.

She felt Cayan making his way along the path and looked right as he emerged through the lush trees. His gaze traveled her body before converging on her trail, directly behind her. "Easy take down," he said.

"Yes. The wonders of working with a *Gift*."

"The Inkna will no doubt think the same when they need to use this wood as a thoroughfare. Going around eats days."

They slowed when they found Tepson, one of their men who was known for his luck, standing amongst a group of ten. He had his sword out and his captives tied with their wrists behind their backs. The rope connected one to the other, and they each knelt, women and men of all ages, with pressed lips and tight eyes. Wariness, fear and sorrow radiated from the group.

Tepson glanced up when he saw movement. His gaze went right around Shanti to the Captain. "Sir, we have them all situated. Waiting for instruction."

Cayan scanned those on the ground before settling on a man in his mid-twenties with short-cropped hair and a square jaw who bore a scar on his neck, as if someone tried to slit his throat and failed. He had wide shoulders layered in muscle, and thick arms.

"Who's in charge?" Cayan asked.

Before Shanti could translate, the man's jaw tightened. Defiance sparked in his eyes. "I'll cooperate if you release the women and children."

Cayan stared at him. He was undoubtedly sizing the other man up, deciding how best to work with him. He must have seen potential and wanted to win his trust.

And he would. Cayan was great at that sort of thing, but it could take time. Shanti didn't have any more patience.

"Look at my eyes!" she barked. "Do you think we're the sort to harm women and children?"

With a hard gaze haunted with battles lost, he met her eyes. She read desperation there immediately. Hopelessness. He wasn't just hiding, he was lost. Exiled of his own volition. Waiting to die.

He must have seen the Graygual in action. And it had crippled his resolve.

Without thinking, she stepped forward and slapped him across the face. "Your fight isn't done yet! You're young. And you're able. You don't have to hide here with these families. You can take your life back!"

His eyebrows dipped low as his cheek started to turn red. His gray gaze traveled her face before resettling on her eyes. Surprise lit up his features.

"That's right," she said "I'm on the run. I've seen what the Graygual can do, too. But I can't hide. I've wanted to. Kiss the Elders, I've wanted to. I've wanted to let Lord Death claim me—to let my past bury me with those I left behind. But I can't let what happened to me happen to anyone else if I can help it."

She waited, giving him a moment of silence.

"They took my wife. She was newly with child, and still they took her." He blinked as his eyes started to glisten. "They slit my throat, but without conviction. One of the survivors revived me. They killed my wife after they—" He cut off in a strangled sob.

Shanti envisioned wrapping a warm blanket around his shoulders. She knelt in front of him and laid her hand on his cheek. In a soft voice, she said, "They killed all of my people. I know what you are going through. I won't lie and say that ache will go away—I don't think it ever will. But hiding isn't the answer. My brother and I were given the duty of getting help, and then tearing down the Graygual. Join me. For your wife. For all the wives. For all the survivors. Help me."

A tear rolled down his cheek as he stared into her eyes. His nod was so slight she wouldn't have noticed it if she hadn't been touching his face. She bent forward to kiss his forehead, then gave him a hard slap on his shoulder.

Men couldn't mope for too long, or they turned into horrible whiners. A little violence went a long way with a fighter.

"What nation are you from?" Shanti asked as she stood.

"Dirkshore." He cleared his throat. In a steadier voice, he continued with, "On the south-western coast."

"Then you were one of the first. I am from the north-western coast. We were the last on the coast to be conquered."

"I've heard of you. The little girl who knocked Xandre down."

"Not for long, I didn't." Shanti took a deep breath and looked at the others huddled together. Their fear had completely dissipated. So had the hopelessness. These people were all hiding; that's why they guarded this area with such a heavy hand. They were afraid of their enemy coming in and dragging them back out. And with the *Gifted*, that's exactly what would've happened. They would've been entered into the breeding program, and their lives would be spent in a gilded cage.

"I hate the Graygual," she spat. She looked back at the gray-eyed warrior who was watching her expectantly. "Yes, I am that little girl. And that 'victory' cost the lives of everyone in my village. The only victory as far as Xandre is concerned would be one resulting in his dead carcass. That's it. As long as he is alive, he will keep going. He'll keep killing. He might wait years, but eventually, he will revisit all who wronged him and rip their lives apart."

"Then we must kill him," said a slight woman with a bow lying next to her. Her eyes were hard, and just as haunted.

"Are you all survivors of the Graygual?" Shanti asked in dismay.

"In one way or another, yes," the woman replied. "But you should talk to Yeasmine. She's the one who started this place. She is the one who guards us."

"She failed today," the gray-eyed man countered.

"Be thankful she failed with me. It could've been worse." Shanti started forward.

Cayan said to Tepson, "Untie them. But good thinking with the rope."

"Didn't want to cut it up, sir. We'll probably need it again," Tepson responded.

"He's a fast thinker," Cayan said as he followed closely behind Shanti.

"Because he didn't cut the rope?"

"Yes. That took foresight. You probably would've cut it."

Shanti glanced back in time to see those dimples accent his smile. She scowled at him. "Shows what you know—I haven't needed rope. Nor do I have a desire to tie anyone up."

"Being tied up can be fun. I could show you sometime…"

Shanti's eyebrows created a shelf over her eyes as she processed both his tone, and the humor rolling around in his empty brain. He was calling her naïve. And blast if he wasn't right.

Why hadn't she and Romie tried rope? Huh.

Cayan's laugh grated.

She slammed up her shields as they walked into the clearing. Quickly, she noticed that her horse was standing all by itself. No other horses, and no humans, stood within ten paces of it, but it seemed perfectly content. A line of twenty men and women sat right in front of the tree line with their hands tied behind their backs. Sanders stood at the head with an older woman. She stood regal with her chin raised, her back straight, and shoulders squared. If she knew she had dirt smeared across her face, messed gray hair, or a large rip in the knees of her pants, she didn't give a sign. Or perhaps she just didn't care.

"Xavier and Rachie cut the rope to tie people up before I got here, sir," Sanders said as he jerked his head to the line of captives. His eyes simmered with temper. Xavier and Rachie stood with shoulders hunched, staring at the ground.

Shanti approached the woman. "Are you Yeasmine?"

The woman, shorter than Shanti, turned her gaze to Shanti then broke her demeanor by gasping. "The violet-eyed girl! Burson was right—he's found you."

"The Wanderer has commenced her journey. People will flock to her in droves, readying for the coming of the Chosen." Burson looked at the sky.

"I hate when he looks at the sky," Rachie murmured. "He looks crazy."

Sanders swung his glare toward the young man. Rachie's mouth closed with a click. He shifted down the line of captives.

"Yes, I am Yeasmine. Do you wish us harm?"

"No. But neither do we wish to die today. We will defend ourselves, as you saw, and we're far more powerful than you." Shanti glanced back at her horse, who had stomped the ground in impatience.

"That is a Graygual horse," Yeasmine said in an offhanded way.

"He's a bastard, that's for sure. I stole him."

"We don't trust outsiders," Yeasmine continued. "Often they are after gold, food, or our mental-workers. We cannot risk our secrets being revealed outside of this wood."

"They'll come through soon looking for a shortcut across the land," Cayan said. He stood, perfectly relaxed with his hands at his sides, his sword in his sheath. His eyes, though, held an edge. He surveyed his men, and then the captives. "My men would've found you without our mental power. Your mind-warfare would've taken them out, yes, but they are not the Inkna. You're only safe here from thieves, traders and travelers. Not the Graygual. They just haven't had a chance to deal with you yet. Or me. They are too focused on Shanti and Burson." Cayan glanced at Burson to get his point across. "But they know me by name. They know my city by name. And they will want access to this wood. Ghost stories will do nothing to deter them."

"We've seen Graygual through here," Yeasmine countered. "They didn't find their way back out."

"They wandered through, sure. They were either trying to get somewhere quicker and thought themselves invincible, or they were being used as an experiment," Cayan countered. "You know the end for this place is near. I can feel it. I can read it in both your eyes and your mind."

"You have to trust someone, sometime," Shanti said quietly.

Yeasmine lifted her chin slightly. She glanced down the line of captives, and settled her gaze on a man about her age with a faded blue right eye. Half his face had burn scars as well as his neck. He nodded without saying a word.

Yeasmine looked back, her reservations plain on her face. "Trusting has led to death in the past, but we don't have much choice. We will kill if threatened. You are warned."

"You're talking to the woman sought by the Being Supreme," Cayan said with a growl. "Her fate will be more disastrous than any of yours if she is caught. You will find no one less likely to switch sides than this woman."

Yeasmine continued to stand, regal and proud. Her worst fears were surely coming true. Their self-appointed exile was at an end. Danger could no longer be contained. The nightmares that haunted them at night would soon come in the flesh.

Shanti turned to Cayan. "Can you handle it from here? I have to do something with that horse."

"He's wild," someone from the line stated in a deep voice. "Like you."

"Knows you well already," Sanders said as he started untying people.

"I think I liked traveling alone, better. Less commentators," Shanti muttered.

She approached her horse with a scowl. She pointed at its face. "Don't give me sass, you bloody bastard."

It chomped at her finger. She slapped its face then jumped out of the way when it kicked out at her. "I'm going to find a whip and teach you manners!"

She stepped to one side, pushed its face away, and grabbed its bridle with a firm hand. "Now, be good, or I'll put you with Cayan's horse. That one really has a temper when goaded."

"She's just as mad as the old man," someone hollered.

Shaking her head, Shanti opened her mind and sought out Rohnan. The Elders were laughing at her, she could tell. It probably sounded a lot like the twittering captives behind her.

CHAPTER 17

SANDERS STOOD AT THE BOTTOM of a flight of stairs cut into the forest floor. Healthy ferns lined the path and lush green branches curved around the top, creating a sort of tunnel. At night, it would be eerie. In the middle of the day, with the sun sprinkling through the leaves, it was gorgeous. Junice would sit and marvel at it for a while.

"What are we waiting for, sir?" Tobias asked behind him.

"Just taking a moment. This wood reminds me of home."

"Yeah. They did more with it, though. Did you see those houses built into the trees? How long do you think they've been here?"

Sanders started up the staircase. "Years, at least. That older dame—Yeasmine—headed out of her town when the Graygual were first on the scene. She saw the way the winds were blowing. Didn't want to be a baby mule for those disgusting varmints."

They reached the top of the stairs and slowed to

look at their surroundings. A heavily trodden dirt path ran east to west surrounded by more healthy vegetation.

"Right, right?" Tobias asked.

Sanders glanced left, saw the same thing as when he'd glanced right, and finally turned right. "That's what they said. Let's hope they're not wrong—they haven't marked anything."

They'd been in the area for a couple of hours, and in that time Shanti had managed to create a following. She wandered through the people, stopping here and there, laying her hand on a shoulder or cheek, saying a few words, and a new admirer was born. It was madness.

But then, Sanders recognized that look in their eyes. He'd seen it in the wake of the Inkna takeover. Those eyes belonged to people who looked out at the world through broken and damaged lives. Who looked around them, seeing only pieces, and had no idea how to put it all back together.

In stepped Shanti.

She didn't have a clue what she was doing, where she was going, or what she would do when she got there, but her steadfast determination to keep moving had people nodding their heads and picking themselves up.

Whatever worked.

"Here we go." Sanders ducked under a branch and into a small clearing covered in purple wildflowers. The trees at the edges thinned out a little, giving depth to the area before being closed in again by the prolific plant life. Four boys stood to the left along the edges of the clearing, chatting amongst themselves. Ruisa, their expert in poison, stood in the middle, where they were all supposed to be.

If Ruisa hadn't been an orphan, there was no way she'd be there. Her parents would never have allowed a daughter to fight let alone go traveling on a dangerous mission. But her mother had died giving birth to Ruisa's twin, who hadn't lived, and her father had been taken by a sickness shortly after Ruisa had been born. She wasn't the oldest in the orphan house, or the only girl, but she was the only one who sought out the Captain and begged to learn to fight like the foreign woman. As the women of the city had taught her their secret arts of defense—something that shouldn't be kept from men, because that shit just wasn't right—she was perfect for this journey.

Well, as prepared as these under-trained boys were. She would probably be more useful, too, if they ever made it to the Shadow Lands.

"I still don't understand why we are bringing along a bunch of cadets and a girl with absolutely no training," Tobias said in a confused mutter.

"The boys are here because the old man said they should come. Arguing with him is like arguing with a madman—he'll drag you down to his level and then beat you with experience. The girl, because… well, apparently women need a way to stick up for themselves, and we're just supposed to take it, because if we don't, we'll shit water for a month until we agree to keep our mouth shut. For a bunch of gossips, they can really keep a secret when they want to."

"What?"

Sanders just shook his head and marched forward. Tobias would probably just have to find out the hard way. Thank God Sanders had a good, sensible woman as a wife. It helped that he would never, ever raise a hand to her. Sanders knew of men raising their fists to a woman, but none of those men were in the army. If anyone slipped up under Sanders' watch, they learned quickly what it was like to get picked on by someone stronger and faster. And they learned that lesson for life, Sanders saw to it.

He and Junice had their disagreements, but Junice was a level-headed creature. Her mother on the other hand…

"Right, let's go. Line up!" Sanders barked.

The boys looked up with wide eyes. "W-why are you teaching us? What happened to S'am? Or… anyone else?" Marc asked.

Sanders glared at the boys as his temper heated up his insides. If they didn't get moving, he'd *make* them.

Obviously sensing this, Xavier said, “C’mon.” He led the others toward Ruisa.

“Where’s Leilius?” Sanders asked.

“Right here—”

“Holy—” Tobias jumped as the voice sounded right next to him. Reacting, he turned, grabbed Leilius by the throat, and sent two quick punches into Leilius’ middle. He grabbed the kid by the collar and was about to throw him to the ground when he realized who it was.

With a twisted grin, Tobias relaxed. He slowly let go of Leilius’ shirt front. “Sorry, kid.” He patted Leilius’ back. “Didn’t see ya there.”

Leilius wheezed.

“Leilius has just demonstrated what happens when you jump out at an enemy,” Sanders declared. “If you plan to kill said enemy, you need to stick your knife in his throat before he knows you are there. If you do not, you need to get out of the way when he tries to stick a knife in your ribs for surprising him.”

“I was just standing here,” Leilius said with a red face. He held his arm across his stomach and hobbled toward the others. “I wasn’t trying to get the jump on you.”

Tobias shrugged, saying to Sanders, “The kid is quiet. I didn’t hear him.”

Sanders stepped toward the group of trainees. “Ruisa—” Her hard eyes looked at Sanders unflinchingly. "Pair off with Rachie. Hand-to-hand. See what you can learn."

"But, sir," Rachie whined. "She's a girl. I might hurt her."

Sanders stared at the young idiot. Rachie slinked off to the side. Ruisa followed with a straight back and a determined expression.

Sanders and Rohnan had been taking turns giving Ruisa solo lessons these last few days. She learned quickly. She was wiry, and incredibly fast for a girl. More than that, she was hungry to be the best. Sooner rather than later, the "for a girl" title would drop off, as it had with Shanti. When that happened, the girl would dominate them, Sanders had no doubt.

He looked at Gracas next. "You, with Xavier. Hand-to-hand."

Gracas flashed Xavier a grin. "Bigger they are, harder they fall."

Sanders grunted, looking at Marc and Leilius, next. "What can you two do?"

"I can run really fast," Marc ventured. "Sir."

"He's terrible with a sword though, sir." Leilius shook his head slowly. "Terrible."

"Well, you'd better learn, because if we get ambushed, which we no doubt will, you're going to have to defend yourself, cadet!" Sanders motioned toward Tobias who tossed two practice swords at the boys' feet.

"Get moving. You're both terrible with swords, so this should be an even match. When we're done with hand-to-hand, we'll work with knives and the bow."

Sanders stepped away and watched with a grin as Ruisa pulled Rachie's hair before punching him in the chest. She was a tomcat, raised in an orphan house with no rules. It showed.

Tobias stepped up next to Sanders and said, "She's not nearly as strong. We need to do some strength exercises with her."

"We're working on it. She's not effective enough with those punches, either. But she's only been at it for a few days."

"Oh?" Tobias rocked back on his heels as he surveyed her. "She didn't start back in the city, huh?"

"No. The Captain didn't want to train her until he knew Shanti would be around to do it. It was smart—she would've been picked on. The army isn't a place for a girl that's learning. Not yet."

"My, my, sir. I think the foreign woman has changed your mind about where women belong…"

Sanders grunted as Xavier went flying through the air. Surprise etched the kid's face. "I'll take whatever troops I can get. After working with that young girl, and seeing Shanti… Well, if she is up for the challenge, that's okay by me. I'd rather see an attack coming then a sneaky one you don't know about until you're half-dead begging for mercy..."

Tobias quirked an eyebrow.

"Go help Leilius and Marc. They look like fools," Sanders growled.

If these Graygual wanted to play with poison, they had better get ready for a master, because Ruisa probably knew some things Sanders did not want to know she knew.

SHANTI WAITED FOR CAYAN AS he finished getting his men settled within one of the empty tree houses. It was someone's home high in the trees, but currently the couple that lived there were traveling, getting to know the unrest in the land. Yeasmine had said that this settlement was safe from strangers, but she acted differently. She knew what was coming.

Rohnan waited with her his hands clasped behind his back. Together they would try and deal with the problem of Cayan's power. Shanti had tried to understand it when she and Cayan had their nightly trainings, but whenever she got close, his defenses kicked in and chased her out of his head. Not only was his control under pressure an issue, but access to that deep well of power within him would be necessary in the weeks to come. They needed to break through these problems, and today Shanti intended to apply a little pressure to do so.

"How long are to remain?" Rohnan asked in the Mountain Region's language as they waited.

"You've picked up the Mountain Region language fast. Still have a way to go, though," Shanti noted.

"Is coming back. Just needed refresher."

"Mhm." Shanti looked around the trees at the many houses. They were built around the largest of trunks and out onto sturdy branches. Each was a small dwelling, housing a family or a couple, but there were many of them. At least fifty or so people lived in these woods, but most of them were gathered here. The rest were spread out around the wood, keeping track of travelers and prizing a more secluded life.

"I'm not sure how long we'll stay, exactly," Shanti answered. "But not long."

"Many want come with us," Rohnan warned. "Many more want be sure you are who you say you are before they join ranks as well. They see a future in you. They see way to get their life back. Without you, they sit here and wait for the inevitable."

"I love when you lecture me about things I already know but don't want to talk about, Rohnan. It is so refreshing." Shanti watched the gentle sway of the trees tops. "I need to talk to Burson. He said he'd give us some information tonight."

"Did he say he been this way before?"

"Not that he had to, but yes. He's spreading the word about the Wanderer. Those from the western-coastal areas know of the Chosen, not the Wanderer. The titles are convoluted. But we can't take people with us. With the Hunter waiting to cut us off, we need to sneak through somehow and find a way of crossing the sea. With the Graygual on our trail, not many captains are going to want to do that."

"The man with the gray-eyes will come regardless. And he's handsome. Probably warm and eager to please."

"Tomous." Shanti called up the image of the man she'd seen earlier. Her core started to tingle with possibilities. It had been a while since she'd enjoyed any intimacy. She missed it.

She wiped the image from her mind. "Is that how you get your women, Rohnan? You prey on the widows and lonely-hearts?"

"If I need to, sure." A crooked smile crossed Rohnan's face. "There is one such vying for me attention. Well, a couple, but one I might visit tonight. She has promised a comfortable sleeping arrangement."

Shanti closed her eyes as the breeze brushed her face. Her core was heating up with the prospect of being close to someone, with the thought of skin touching skin. Her chest felt tight, but in a good way. She really had been without for too long.

"If you don't use what the Elders blessed you with, it might rot," Rohnan said in their language in a sing-song tone. *"And there he is. It is obvious how willing he is to keep you in good working order."*

Shanti shoved him as her smile burned bright. She couldn't help a girlish giggle. Opening her eyes, she saw that Tomous was standing across the leaf-strewn forest floor, talking to a woman with a bow. He glanced up, saw her looking his way, and let his gaze linger. A slow smile spread across his face. The heat in Shanti's core turned into a slow burn.

"There, see? He is undressing you with eyes. And he young—lots of stamina." Rohnan rocked back on his heels with an all-knowing air.

"Would you shut your mouth?" she giggled and pushed him again. She turned away from Tomous as a flash of Romie's face invaded her memories. She felt her elation dwindle.

"It hurts less," she said quietly, looking out through the trees. "I don't miss Romie as much. I'm healing, and half of me is disgusted by that fact. Like I'm shaming him. Like I'm shaming his memory."

She felt Rohnan's shoulder brush hers. "You are afraid to love again."

Shanti felt tears well up. She tried to call up those strong feelings she'd thought would be everlasting, and couldn't quite find their potency. "I feel like I'm losing him, and if I do, I worry I'll lose everyone else, too. That I'll forget all but the worst. I'm afraid that without remembering the love, all I'll remember is death."

"You won't. But with war comes memories of destruction. With peace, and love, come memories of the good moments. They there, but when you cut off possibility of loving another, you also cut off memories. You are locking yourself up with worst your past has to offer, instead of allowing new experiences to help heal."

Shanti let her gaze drift back to Tomous. To his strong arms and sturdy shoulders. His body would be warm and willing. Eager, as Rohnan said. As would hers. But that wasn't what Rohnan was talking about. That was a physical distraction. The intimacy would evaporate come the morning. The feeling would dissipate as the sun and reality peeked through the windows.

"But a pleasant distraction," she said as she pushed aside her pang of loss and focused on the moment. Her smile returned, if a little forced. "I don't want to meet Master Wonderful with rotted equipment, after all."

"There you go. Welcome back to body of my sister."

Shanti laughed as Cayan stepped up with a straight face. A small crease formed between his eyebrows as he glanced at her. A moment later his gaze lifted to Tomous. "Ready?" he asked with a rough voice.

"Will we fit?" Shanti asked, starting forward.

"All of us, yes. Your furs are already there."

Rohnan chuckled darkly. *"Does the Captain not like to share? I hope that doesn't extend to men..."*

Shanti elbowed her brother as they made their way to the clearing. The answer was no, Cayan didn't. Luckily, it wasn't his decision to make. This time her choice wasn't his to rule as Captain. He could do nothing to stand in her way.

CHAPTER 18

THE WOOD AS A WHOLE was dense, but there were plenty of small clearings with soft flowers and grasses underfoot to spread out. Many of them were largely undisturbed. Shanti took a deep breath, letting the natural environment soak into her *Gift*, rejuvenating. She felt Rohnan beside her, doing the same. Cayan walked to the far side of the clearing.

"Okay," she said, opening her eyes. Cayan faced off with her, his large body loose and ready to move. "Looks like you're ready to fight."

"We're fighting with mental power, correct?" Cayan clarified.

"He's anxious. He's holding his Gift *with every ounce of his control. He's suffocating it,"* Rohnan murmured.

"He's not going to tell me what he feels?" Cayan asked as he glanced at Rohnan.

"No. I've learned that telling you what you're doing makes you do it even harder," Shanti explained.

"Too bad you haven't given in and had sex with him—I bet you'd tell him exactly what he was doing.

Over and over again."

"Death's playground, Rohnan—you might visit two women tonight. Your mind is unraveling." Shanti shook her head to try and dislodge the image of Cayan's body over hers, as her imagination applied details she didn't want to envision.

Rohnan started laughing and said, "I'm not the only one. You too busy feeling sorry for yourself."

"Oh, shut up."

"Are you two done with playtime?" Cayan asked, impatience radiating from him.

"See?" Shanti muttered to Rohnan. "You've gotten us in trouble."

"You should be used to it by now," Rohnan responded with a smile.

She felt like a kid again with Rohnan. Unfortunately, Cayan was not amused by that fact.

In a firm tone she didn't necessarily feel, she said, "Cayan, you are already accessing your *Gift*, which is good. It's more natural to you than it was, but you're only working with a small portion of it. There are two milestones we have to cross. You need to work with all you have readily available. I do not mean all you are *capable* of working with, I mean what you are *comfortable* working with. Once you can do that, and I'm hoping we can do that quickly, you need to learn to access that deep well within you and use all you are *capable* of working with. Do you see the difference?"

"Understanding what you are saying, and accomplishing what you are saying, are two different things," Cayan said in a matter-of-fact tone.

"He's starting to feel helpless. He doesn't understand something—probably this deep well you speak of." Rohnan drifted toward the side of the clearing and sank down into a cross-legged, seated position. *"It is tied to something highly personal. Something old, I'd wager. Something to do with insecurities."*

"I'd like to know what he's saying." Cayan said in an even voice, but Shanti could hear the tightness in the words.

"No, you wouldn't," Shanti replied. "He's done this to me—he's done it to all the advanced fighters. He's pointing out weaknesses we hide from the world. I'm sparing you."

"But he's telling you."

"Fight him, Chosen. Charge him. He doesn't like admitting to weaknesses, let alone having others hear of them. Distract his mind and body, both. Hard and fast."

"Shanti—"

Shanti cut Cayan off with a quick *stab* to his unprotected and unsuspecting mind. She ran at him, and *twisted*. She envisioned slapping his face then punching his stomach as she reached him and kicked out toward his head.

His shields went up as the kick landed, flinging his head back and making him step back a pace. Shanti backed up and stood in a ready pose, waiting.

"I wasn't ready for that," Cayan admitted with a furrowed brow.

"Is that why you let me kick you in the head? And here I thought you were being chivalrous." Shanti gently *poked* his shield. "Come out, come out, wherever you are."

"Were you using full power?" he asked as he hesitantly dropped his shield. His shoulders were tight and his arms flexed. She'd unsettled him.

"No. Maybe half." Pausing with a thought, she relaxed and glanced at Rohnan. "Those that had mated power in our village, did they—"

Her words cut off as a fist neared her eye. She jerked back, the punch barely missing her cheek. Without thinking, she *blast* out in a focused beam of mental ability. It hit Cayan's mind like a shot from a bow. It then trickled down, covering his body in invisible acid.

He patted at his chest before realizing what was happening and, with effort, put his hands to his sides. Thick cords of muscle flexed down his body. His large shoulders rolled and his defined chest showed through his light training shirt. The strictly feminine part of her brain took in every detail. The receding warmth in her core roared back into life.

Flushed, Shanti cut off her *Gift* and ran her hand over her face. "Sorry." She backed away with a shaking head. "You startled me."

A crooked smile tickled his lips. His dimples made soft imprints in his cheeks. "Full power?"

"Full power would have killed you," Rohnan said, staring at Cayan with squinted eyes. "You show pride in her ability."

Cayan shrugged. "Of course. She's on my side."

Shanti looked at Cayan seriously. "Can I ask a question without you trying to take my head off?"

"If you make it quick." He winked at her.

Unsettled, and having no idea why, she turned to Rohnan. Watching Cayan out of the corner of her eye, not sure why he was chuckling, she finished her question. "Did those with mated power connect to the higher power even when fighting each other? Or does that work against the training?"

Rohnan was still staring at Cayan. "It work against training. You might as well tell the other what you intend."

"Oh, so it's like fighting you, then."

"Worse, because I do not know what mental assault you intend, I just know you intend something light or terrible, depending on level of frustration. If you were to connect with Captain, he would know more precisely what you intend. He would not get the practice of battling in real time with surprise encounters."

Cayan held Rohnan's stare, the smile dwindling from his face. He didn't like being the subject of scrutiny. "He's speaking well compared to a few days ago."

"We both learned this language in our studies—he just needed to get the feel for it again. He learns extremely fast. He hasn't really gotten a handle on the slang yet, though."

"Unlike you, who embraced it before even knowing correct sentence structure?" Cayan's playful smile was back.

The man was serious one moment, and lighthearted the next. She had no idea what prompted the mood swings. "Yes. Slang is more fun."

"As are dirty words?" Cayan circled her. His eyes turned hungry.

"Naturally." She remembered their sparring after the battle with the Inkna. Before he'd kissed her.

Her face burned red and a light sweat broke out on her brow. She remembered his playful teasing of her anatomy with his *Gift* and how good it had felt. It was not helping her already excited female anatomy.

"Fight him, Chosen," Rohnan said with laughter in his voice. "He's not only one who is trying to hide his weaknesses."

"He's irritating, isn't he?" Shanti growled before she lunged. She hammered a fist into his stomach and blocked a punch to her side as she danced out of his grasp. He had more strength and a longer reach—she had to stay vigilant not to get caught inside.

She swept the ground with her foot. He jumped over and threw a fist down at her side. She rolled away, hopped up, and *stabbed* his mind. He accepted the pain as he stepped forward. His elbow smashed across her jaw.

She put more power into the next mental *thrust*. She took two quick steps into his arms, gave three solid punches as her mind hammered his, before throwing her fist upwards toward the underside of his chin.

His head snapped back and her fist sailed into the air as his arms came around her. Ripping her fist back down, she landed one solid punch before he brought her into a tight bear hug, holding her body against his. Her arms were caught against his hard chest while his encircled her like steel bands.

She tried to head-butt him. He straightened up and leaned back so she could only reach the top of his chest. She stomped on his foot, which did nothing, and then stomped on his inseam, which did little more.

A warm feeling started to run through her body and pooled in her core. Shanti gritted her teeth as that spicy feeling flared to life within her middle. Her power started to simmer. More heat filled her body. Her core throbbed. It felt like a warm, wet mouth was enveloping her tight nipple.

"Oh…" she moaned. It hadn't been intentional.

Mortified, core pounding, desperation welled up. She leaned to the side until he had to step with her to hold her weight, and then shifted back with a thrust of her knee. At the same time, she focused most of her power into the form of needles. He wanted to fight with sex, she'd fight with pain.

Her knee struck his inner thigh, right next to his manhood. Millions of sharp, painful pricks pummeled his body. She reapplied the acid and coated that with fire.

His arms tightened around her in reflex. His body bent, as though trying to bring her in and shield her. His cheek glanced off hers, scratchy with stubble. Every muscle on his frame flexed, flush against her body. His grip tightened as his body wrapped around her protectively.

"His impulse is to lash out as he did earlier today when we were under attack, but he doesn't want to hurt you," Rohnan said in analysis. *"He is trying to protect you from himself, and he is taking the pain to do so. The pain is torturing him, but he will not relent. He will die before he strikes out against you—all my fears were unfounded. You were right. We must subject him to this a little longer. Try to access that hidden place, now. He's open to you. Do not uncover it; just assess it so you can*

find your way back to this willingness."

Shanti sank into his body—not because it would help, but it was impossible not to. She closed her eyes as muscles flexed around her. Winding into his *Gift*, she connected with her power's mate. Their power soared higher, amplifying her assault. She drew back on it at the hitch in his breath and the low groan.

"Too much, Chosen," Rohnan warned.

He welcomed her into his mind, wide open to her presence, as Rohnan had said. She sank in deep, and then felt a moment of fear as he wound her within his mind so deeply, so tight, she felt like she was a part of him. The world dropped away as she felt the pain she was causing him; needles dug into her body, causing flashes of excruciating agony. Clenching her teeth against it, she let him suck her so deep she felt like she was drowning. Emotions stolen from him flitted around her—fear that they were headed to their death, passion and desire for the body held close, compassion for her and Rohnan's plight, and a deep, resounding love for his city and people.

Taking a deep breath, she focused on that block, so obvious now that he was allowing her full access to himself. She felt the raw pain around it and the intense, soul-crushing suffering of losing his mother. His father's death scarred him, plunging him into isolation. She felt the effects of his constant struggle with loneliness, having no equal in position or physical ability. He'd taken his position so young—before he was even a man—and still felt the burn when people pointed out his mistakes. His inexperience. His inadequacies.

He never thought he'd be good enough.

Understanding and compassion welled up inside her. The physical pain she felt dropped away. It no longer mattered because she understood his suffering. She'd struggled with it constantly, herself. And when she reached one milestone, it seemed there was always another so far away. Another title she was burdened with. Another problem she had no idea how to solve.

She cut off her attack. Mentally, she wrapped herself around him protectively and tried to settle her power on that ache, so old. She tried to cover his fears and his loneliness with herself—to soothe it away.

The blockage vanished. The world went dark. A surge of power so pure, so intense, rose up around them like a flood.

"Oh no," she heard herself mutter. It sounded like a distant echo.

"Control it, Chosen. Control it!" Rohnan's panicked voice drifted through her conscious.

Cayan shifted as his power boiled in him and spilled over into her through their connection. Like flame to paper, his power flared within her, singeing her awareness and turning that spicy simmer into a pleasure-filled burn. Still the power rose. Engulfing them. He shifted again, releasing her hands. Instead of fighting, though, she held on. She clutched onto his back, squeezed her eyes tighter, and feeling the deep undertow of power that sucked at her consciousness. It moved in slow but strong currents. Like a huge beast, it crouched between them, its depths cavernous.

She tried to work it like her own, shaping and directing, bending it to her will, but its mass was too great. Too cumbersome. And still it built. Using its mate, the power merged and brewed, rising up. Overrunning Cayan. Pulling at Shanti.

This power wasn't made for dexterity. His wasn't the same as her *Gift*, maybe no two *Gifts* were the same. It certainly didn't work the same.

Fear tingled up her spine as the power kept growing. It poured out of him, into her in an ever-faster flowing torrent. They weren't ready to work with this—and it would have to be *they*. It was too big for Cayan's limited skill alone. Too extensive. This power could only be used to destroy. To demolish. There was no picking out an individual, he could only choose a direction and expel the shock-wave. She was the lightning, he was the thunder. Together they were a force of nature itself, so beautiful, yet full of unpardonable destruction.

The burning sensation within her amplified as she

held onto his power with everything she had. Tears dripped down her face from stinging eyes. She clutched onto his shirt. Fire licked her skin.

The power was eating them up. Without release, it would kill them both.

Desperate, her mind racing, she pictured their surroundings. If she tried to throw it upward, it would mushroom out and hit everyone around them. Rohnan would surely die, and so might some of the others. Instead, clutching onto her last resources of control, she tried to smother the rolling, churning power of Cayan with her *Gift* and seek out an area without human life. Minds flared into a crystal clear mental image. The power boiled. Her skin felt like it was melting off. Her mouth went dry as her vision went black.

She picked a direction and EXPLODED.

A hurricane of power tore from her and Cayan and rumbled the ground. It blasted through the trees, singed the air, and killed any animal life in its path. The torrent sucked out of her middle and extinguished like a candle in a windstorm.

Their panting breath sounded through the silence. They stood in an *absence.*

Shanti still clutched onto Cayan, shaking. Staring with wide eyes at the green around them, her hard inhalations rang in her ears.

She felt movement from the warm body pressed

tightly against her. Hardly able to think, she watched his chest get further away and felt fingertips on her jaw. Pressure had her lifting her face and blinking up at the soft blue eyes of Cayan. His high cheekbones and straight nose lent a beauty to his features that was made more masculine by his strong jaw and the small cleft in his chin.

She had one second to marvel at how much more handsome he was than Tomous when his shapely lips came down and connected with hers. Her eyes drifted closed as he opened her mouth with his. His tongue flicked and played before he tilted his head and deepened the kiss.

What started light and engaging turned deep and passionate. Her heart hammered and butterflies swarmed her belly. Fear lurked two steps behind, though. The feelings he called up—deep and consuming—reminded her of all she'd lost. Of how much more she had to lose.

And the guilt…

Shanti put her hand to Cayan's chest and pushed. He resisted for one moment, before relenting. He broke their kiss with a lingering parting of lips before stepping back. His pupils were dilated and eyes so deep they reached right down into that place where she'd found all his pain. The place he didn't admit entry to anyone, save her.

"Sorry," she said, tearing her gaze away from his. "I didn't mean to do that."

"Which?" he asked as a smile tickled his lips. "Rake me with pain, learn all my secrets, unlock a power I have no hope of controlling, or running your hands all over my body?"

"All but the first, if you're keeping tabs." She scowled at him. "But you started it with the mental sex stuff. You practically waved me in."

"No, I was hoping to get waved in." His eyes glimmered with desire.

She turned toward Rohnan, who was staring at her with a white face and mouth hanging open.

"What?" she asked.

Rohnan looked back and forth between Cayan and her. "He is… The amount of power…" Rohnan shook his head. "That was not foretold. He was not foretold. Have we taken a fork in journey, Chosen? The wrong fork…?"

"I'm sick of all this foretelling, and these titles, and having no idea what is expected of me." Shanti turned to Cayan in frustration. "Let's spar. Use your *Gift* if you still have it. Otherwise, prepare for pain."

Cayan's laugh was a rich baritone. "I'm the one with all the power, pretty little lady. You're okay, for a girl."

Shanti's eyebrows fell as she charged. Her mind *stabbed* and *wrenched* his. She kicked his upper thigh and stepped in for a punch but he blocked and stepped to the side. He delivered his own punch, hitting her side. She caught his wrist with one hand, grabbed his forearm, and pulled. He was so strong and heavy though, and barely stepped forward. She spun into him anyway, taking advantage of his imbalance. She hammered an elbow into his sternum, slapped down at his balls, and then gave him a sound uppercut when he flinched.

He staggered that time.

She maintained the mental assault as she started chasing him around the clearing. Then he triggered his own *Gift*, though this was no more than the portion he normally used.

It was more than enough.

Thick waves of power pounded into Shanti, shaking her bones, delivered with a rueful smile. Her instincts said to slam her shields home and curl into the fetal position to escape. Her instincts were wrong.

Instead, she gritted through the body-shaking pain and started a powerful mental assault of her own. She battered him one moment, and needled him the next, changing how she hit and attacked. Making him apply defense and weakening his outgoing power. He might hold the upper hand with brawn, but she had the sharp, painful finesse.

She could also multitask.

At the same time as she used her mental ability, she kicked and punched, keeping up a constant barrage of physical assault. His power wavered as he fought her off. Then his physical defense weakened as he tried to work with his *Gift*. She caught his shoulder with a flick of her foot, then put all her weight behind a kick to his thigh. His feet swept out from under him. He rolled. When he stopped she was ready with a punch to his face.

He expected it.

He caught her hand in a grip she could never duplicate, and yanked. Her momentum and his encouragement brought her down on top of him.

"I heard you aren't great at fighting on the ground," Cayan said through rapid breaths.

He rolled her under him and pinned her with his body. Her head butt hit home this time, splitting his lip. He shifted up and held her hands by her wrists. She bucked with her hips, but couldn't make use of his slight jolt forward. He pinned her thighs by bending his legs and putting his ankles above her knees. His groin pressed into her lower waist and his big chest lay over her small upper body.

She twisted, trying to create some space between them to maneuver in, but to no avail. She ripped her hands one way, and then the other. They moved less than an inch. Her legs were useless. That only left her head.

She relaxed. "I give up."

He bent enough so he could see her face. Those dimples really made him more attractive, but often she absolutely hated when they appeared. Now was one of those times.

He bent to her ear and said, "I win."

She turned her face quickly, and bit into the side of his neck. If it was good enough for her horse, it was good enough for her. She clamped down until she tasted blood. He started to squirm, pushing his face down into her.

"Okay, okay, truce," he said urgently.

"Get off," she said through skin.

His legs came away from hers. His hands released her. He started to roll to the side, squishing her. She released his neck and prepared for more battle, but he just finished his roll and slapped his hand to his neck. "Ouch."

Shanti grabbed her boobs. "I agree. I don't have much, but you flattened what I do have."

"You can work with me on my *Gift*, but I'm going to work with you on your wrestling. You're terrible at it."

"If I'm on the ground, I've done something very wrong," Shanti replied.

Cayan's humor fell from his face. The sparkle left

his eyes, replaced by fear and concern. "They want to breed you, Shanti. Getting you on the ground will initiate that. You will not kill yourself if you get taken—you will wait for me to come and get you. In the meantime, you will need to be able to get yourself out from under someone bigger."

"Is that right…?" Shanti said in a deathly quiet voice. "That's mighty presumptuous."

Cayan sat up. Blood dripped down his neck. "Yes. This is non-negotiable. I will protect you if the worst comes to pass, even from yourself, just as I have done since you were carried into my city. I will not lose you, Shanti—you should know that by now. Since they will not kill you, that allows me time. Xandre might be a battle lord, but he is only a man. If he harms you, he will be a dead man."

"Poetic." Shanti wiped her face from sweat and stood. "But you have no idea what you're talking about. He's not just a man, Cayan, he has elevated himself into a nightmare. One I can't seem to wake up from. I will not let myself be raped and tortured so you can try to play the hero."

"I will get my way," Cayan said easily as he stood. "In all things, I *will* get my way."

"Another fat lip, is what you'll get." Shanti turned toward Rohnan, and then stopped when she realized the edges of the clearing were filled with people. They stared at both of them with wide eyes and open mouths.

"They probably felt Cayan's power, first," Rohnan said, watching them with humor-filled eyes. "And they *surely* felt you two fighting with your power. You are not as careful as usual, Chosen. He flusters you."

"He's stronger than me, faster, has a longer reach, and has power greater than mine that is hard to defend against. Yes, I get flustered. Would you like me to show you how it feels?"

Rohnan stood, laughing. "Not really. Your love-bite look like it hurts."

"Burson wants to speak to us tonight before bed. He has some answers—or so he says. So maybe if you're not too busy *getting your way*, you can make that engagement," Shanti said.

"Careful, you sound petulant, Chosen," Rohnan said with a smirk.

"I noticed you didn't mention that I also have greater skill in fighting than you," Cayan said. His clear, blue eyes were sparkling again. "Or did your resorting to biting adequately portray that fact…"

Shanti's fists balled. She wanted to throw something at his head so badly it made her dizzy. She turned and noticed Sanders leaning against a tree. "Sanders—does biting mean I lose?" she asked.

"Not at all, Shoo-lan," Sanders answered immediately. "It means you are resourceful in your victory."

As Shanti threaded her way through the gawking people, she heard Sanders say, "Sorry, sir, but I would've done the same thing."

There was no way the real Chosen had to take this much flak. No way. Burson had better have some bloody good answers for her. There was no way this journey was worth Cayan's crap otherwise.

CHAPTER 19

As dusk settled into the woods Cayan found himself sitting around a small fire across from Shanti and Burson. Rohnan sat away from the flame, seemingly content to listen but not participate. After their sparring match, Shanti had spent the afternoon among the people of the village in the trees, listening to stories and just talking. There wasn't a single person in the settlement that didn't have a horrible tale of why they had ended up there. It was both sad to hear and a warning. If they didn't stop the Graygual, there would be many more stories, and fewer places to hide.

Rohnan had shadowed Shanti's every step, often cutting her off mid-sentence to say some poignant thing to the people they spoke with. Rohnan had a strange *Gift*, and a soft-handed way of working with it. He didn't seem like a warrior at all. Sure he might be excellent with his staff, with knives and bows, but fighting didn't come naturally to him. Neither did killing. Cayan felt Rohnan's joy every time he worked with Marc, going around the village trying to cure ailments and soothe aching joints.

The man was in the wrong line of work, but he would never pull himself away from Shanti. Not ever. Shanti's duty was Rohnan's, Cayan could see it. It was clear that she trusted and depended on his guidance. They were in this together.

What made Cayan laugh was her subtle transformation around Rohnan. She acted like a child or teenager at times. Like she'd gotten back a part of her past she thought had been lost and wanted to stay there. When Rohnan was around, her jokes were lighter and her mood was softer. She even acted more feminine. Or maybe, with someone to guard her back, she allowed herself to be who she really was. She'd once said that her people were much more sexual than his, and much more open about it, and now he saw the truth of that—her movements were more languid. Her hips swayed. She laughed deeper and took on a sensuous grace he could not tear his eyes away from.

"Are you listening?" Shanti asked in a warning tone. Her glare speared him from across the fire.

He tried to stifle a smile. "Of course."

She was still angry from earlier, but her desire to kill herself if taken was shortsighted—she had to see that. That was the reason she killed her people who were not strong enough to do it themselves after they'd been taken. Fear made her want to shut down, but with a strong force behind her, and the assurance she would not be killed, time would be enough to take her back. Cayan would demand the same of any of his men—he left no one behind. He would not treat her any differently.

If the worst happened, Sanders would most likely insist on being the one to physically save her. He wanted to even the score with his own rescues.

"Do you need a kick in the head?" she seethed across the leaping flame. The dancing light played across her dainty features and highlighted those large, wide-set eyes. She was such a beauty. An exotic, visually arresting beauty, as that Graygual had said all those months ago.

He felt a light touch on his shoulder and turned to find Rohnan bending beside him. "She is about to turn violent, Captain. You had best think those thoughts later. She would not appreciate them now."

Cayan couldn't help a startled laugh. "She's right, your *Gift* is unsettling."

Humor danced in Rohnan's eyes. "I love how much she hates it."

"Oh good, team up why don't you. I look forward to the witty banter that can only come of your friendship. Can we get to it, hmm? Burson is only lucid some of the time." Shanti stared at her brother.

"I am lucid all the time," Burson replied as he folded

his hands in his lap. His smile beamed. "You just like to cast some of my knowledge into the flames of madness."

"I'd love to cast you into the flames, yes." Shanti braced her elbows on her knees.

"You are being petulant again, Chosen," Rohnan said in a low voice. The taunting was evident, playing on her bad mood.

Shanti hunched, ignoring him.

Not bothering to hide his smile, Cayan looked up at Burson who said, "Yes, exciting things are in progress. So, where to begin?"

He looked at the dark sky before saying, "I think the first step to understanding our enemy is to understand how the Old Blood works. Just as there are different elements that create a person, there are different elements that make up the fabric of the Old Blood. Simply having the Old Blood is not enough to create someone such as yourself, Shanti. Or you, Cayan. It is, however, enough to pass down levels of power. You two are at the top of the power scale, as is this Inkna calling himself Chosen. But within that level of power, there are minute differences within each strand of your heritage. Cayan's power has raw force unlike any I have ever heard of. His blasts can bring a person to his knees. It is a low-level thrust of power and bluntly aims to demolish. His sub-level power, like we witnessed today, is much more powerful than Shanti's. I am guessing it takes sheer will just to contain it."

Burson put his finger into the air and waggled it back and forth. "Ah, but… Is he really the more potent? He cannot easily fight and use his *Gift* at the same time. He cannot use finesse. He has little direction and less control. This is not a failing, Cayan; do not let your face fall. I do not believe your power was made to be used alone.

"That is where young Shanti comes into play. She can weave her power in ways that cannot be learned. She understands the dynamics of her *Gift*, the very essence of it, and she can harness that to overcome someone with the same strength of power as herself. Had you two been on opposing sides, it would be a spectacular battle indeed. Who would win? Who would die? Or would it be a stalemate?"

"Except, we aren't on opposing sides," Shanti said with a fleeting glance at Cayan. "What about this powerfully-*Gifted* Inkna; have you heard any specifics about him?"

"Yes, the Inkna. The catalyst. Oh how tricky is that Xandre, hmm?" Burson smiled upwards. "He is trying to flush out the violet-eyed girl."

Rohnan leaned forward as he stared at Shanti. "It is trap, then. Why hadn't we thought of that?"

"This Inkna has a full dose of power, and he will try to get through the trials. Who's to say how the trials are setup. Power might be enough. We can't take that chance, regardless of what waits for us on the other side."

"His power will be enough to allow him to enter the trials," Burson said with a grave voice. "The trials were designed to measure power first. It is so rare to find someone with a full dose. Someone who recognizes their power *and* is trained accordingly. So rare. Only a handful in the whole of the land. Cayan would never have known his true potential had not Shanti realized it. He would've been overrun with Graygual, and died, without realizing he had so much more to fight with."

A chill went up Cayan's back. Burson was absolutely correct. Before Shanti, and before fighting the Inkna, he would've been irked at a comment like that. His men were tough and skilled. His army was organized. His allies were plenty. But he saw that wasn't enough. Not against mental warfare and the army Xandre had constructed.

Cayan blew out a breath at the gravity of the situation. He looked across the shimmering air at Shanti. Her gaze set on the base of the flame. She was shielding herself, so he couldn't read her emotions, but fear and uncertainty showed on her face. They had to intercept this Inkna, just in case his power was enough to gain the support of the Shadow People. Even if they succeeded, they'd still have the most powerful man in the land waiting for them.

This was a fool's journey. But what choice did they have?

"Xandre is not one to play by any rules," Burson said. "He has sent many through the trials, and had plenty of time to analyze those areas in which the accompanying party waits. The Shadow People will follow his rule, or will be annihilated. What a boon it would be to capture you at the same time."

"But I thought you said only those with a full dose of power can enter the trials?" Shanti asked with a furrowed brow.

"Yes, of course. But the trials begin after the Chosen declares him or herself. He declares, he steps through, and he never comes out. It is said that power is measured first, but beyond that, we have no way of knowing."

"And if the declared doesn't step through?" Rohnan asked.

"He is killed, of course. Not stepping through after a declaration is against the rules."

"So there will be two battles—one within the trials, and one by the supporters on the outside," Cayan said quietly.

Burson had said something to that effect before, but Cayan hadn't had a clear picture. There would be much killing on the sly. Poison now made perfect sense.

"This is not anything we had not already guessed," Rohnan murmured.

"We're missing a feast," Shanti said. Sorrow haunted her features. "I helped kill the animals, I'd really love to attend. If we could wrap this up…?"

"We have not discussed our opponent's weaknesses, yet." Burson smiled again. "Have you not wondered why the Inkna do not fight unless they have to?"

Cayan leaned forward. He had. He'd wondered often. They would be so much more of a threat if they used more than just their power in battles. Cayan expected someone like this Being Supreme, this hyper-intelligent dictator, to realize this. The fact that he hadn't made Cayan anxious. It hinted at knowledge Cayan didn't possess.

"Now we get to the other strands of the Old Blood," Burson said. He rubbed his hands together with a smile. "One of the things I studied intensely was lineage. It can be quite fascinating when you trace family lines, and traits, back generations. Xandre is constantly looking for powerful individuals. Always looking. Hunting. Mental power will be the key to a battle's victory, all other things being equal."

"Things are rarely equal," Shanti countered.

"Correct." Burson ticked the sky with his pointer finger. "But it starts with you."

Shanti's brows pulled down into a frown.

Burson continued, "Where did this high-powered Inkna come from? How long was he trained, and by whom? Whatever the answer to these questions, it will not equal the length at which Shanti has worked. Or Rohnan. Or any of your people. Nor will it be under the same threat of annihilation."

"Xandre trains with pain, though," Rohnan said softly. "He creates pressure with all his advanced forces."

Burson ticked the sky again. "Creates the pressure, yes. But where is the sense of duty to each other, the backbone to survive as a people?" Burson smiled. "Absent. They survive the pain, but only for themselves, not for each other. They have no loyalty to those who fight by their side. They have no bond. So they are lacking in that way. They were not brought up steeped in a rich tradition that was preserved in a tiny niche of the land, passed down for generations. They were forced into the training, hurt in the training, toughened by the training, but not nurtured. *That* creates a brittle, imbalanced warrior. Shanti is the myth reincarnate, but not because of her power—because of the environment that harvested that power."

"They have more second-class warriors than we do," Cayan said. "Many more. They might not be as good, but with supply in plenty, they are still more powerful as a whole."

Burson threaded his hands together. His smile did not diminish, though Cayan had no idea what could possibly be pleasing about this conversation. The situation was dismal.

"Yes and no," Burson continued. "Xandre can find other full-powered individuals in the *Gift*. And be sure that he is looking for them. He will find them, and train them, but he cannot create an environment such as Shanti came from. He has tried, I know this firsthand. I have passed through the tiny settlement he uses for his best. But it is not the same. It is not creating the same warrior he seeks. The best. The myth. And Xandre must have the best. He is bent on it."

Cayan's suspicion rose. "How do you know him so well?"

Shanti's eyes drifted toward Burson, awaiting the answer.

Burson smiled at Cayan. "Because like Rohnan, I allowed myself to be captured. I needed to see the enemy, firsthand. That is the only way one is to learn. Of course, I only got a few glimpses of the great man himself. He keeps his own company apart from his guards, which are around always. He came and he went, but you can tell a lot about a person by his movements, the environment he creates, and the men he puts in charge. Oh yes, quite a lot."

"Okay, he always wants the best," Shanti pushed.

"So he thinks he needs me."

"Correct," Burson stated. "He can't duplicate it, so he needs the product of it. He needs the master. He needs your experience, and your cultural conditioning. He needs you to breed, and train your children how you were trained. That is the only way to get more of his perfect warrior. Shanti, you are his version of the perfect specimen, hinted at when you beat his men the first time at age five, and cemented when you thwarted his rule a year ago. You are the elusive gem he covets. He will not have won until he not only has his empire, but you within it."

"I didn't think you could put me in a worse mood, Burson. You have proved me wrong." She gave Cayan that leveling look: equal parts confidence, intelligence, defiance, and vulnerability. He felt his insides heat and melt within that gaze.

"I'm sorry for returning to you," she said seriously. Her voice was sultry and soft, dripping with remorse. "I think you would've been safer waiting to see if I made it through."

"Don't—" Cayan wanted to lean through the fire and quell the hopelessness swimming in her eyes. He settled for pushing against her shield. When she didn't relent, he summoned more power and *punched*.

"Ow."

Only she could pull off the glassy-eyed scowl that

made his muscles tense for a vicious fight, while still looking helpless and forlorn. She dropped her shield, though, and let him soothe her mind with his own. Their power entwined. A pleasant hum fizzled in his stomach.

"I knew what I was getting into," he said softly. "Together we have twice the power—or more, if I can figure out how to work with what you found today. We have a better chance together than apart."

"A much better chance. We have fewer, but the greatness of the Old Blood is stacked in our favor," Burson continued. "There is another element of the Old Blood, one not so rare as mental power. It is enhanced physical prowess. One does not have to possess the *Gift* to harness the Old Blood's other attributes. Much of the top tier of the Graygual is built with individuals possessing this physical prowess. This person is faster, stronger, and more adaptable. They are naturally athletic, and think well on the move. Their bodies alone are a superpower." Burson's laughing eyes hit Cayan. "You have a great supply of that blood within your city, Cayan. You are breeding it without knowing it. Its strength festers within your walls. More than I have seen in a great many places. Look at you, for example. You are above the rest, even Shanti, in your strength, power and skill. I bet you barely had to try to be the best. Nothing was beyond your reach.

"You two have these warrior traits, in addition to your mental traits. The Inkna do not. They do not excel in fighting, even when they train for it. They are dismal, at best. And so, they put all their faith in their mental ability. They band together, they attempt to breed stronger powers, but they focus solely on their mind."

"Again, they have a huge army," Cayan persisted. "They don't have to fight. Not with an elite frontline to take or push the attack."

Burson gave that damned smile. "Wrong. The mental power works best with an intimate understanding of the body. You have to envision what it is you want to do, and your power will react to these demands. To heal with it, you need to understand the art of healing. To fight, it is best to physically understand how to fight. Shanti and Cayan, you are both very detailed in your attacks with your mental power—Shanti more so, because of the type of power she possess. But Cayan, you understand driving the attack, the end result you desire, and your power shows that beautifully.

"The Inkna are more general with their power: gouge the eyes; rake the throat. These are all painful, sure, but they are not as effective against someone who knows how to block an attack and counter with speed, agility, and experience. A fighter already has the conditioning that lends itself to mental warfare. With my *Gift*, I envision smothering the brain. I put a blanket over those I want to cut off from their power, or put up a shield—an invisible barrier I've envisioned—around those I want to protect. It is all visual."

Shanti sighed loudly. She dropped her hand from her chin. Her arm fell across her lap. "So, with the Inkna proclaiming himself Chosen, I can work with my power better, I can fight, but…"

"You don't have a huge army to protect you," Cayan finished.

"Right. I can find him, I can kill him, but the Elders will have their laugh when I try to return home, because Xandre's army will be waiting. Fascinating, Burson, I am so glad we've had this chat. It's really shed light on things. Now, since you've thoroughly ruined my night, let's get to you. Who are you? Where do you come from and how come you know so much?"

"And while we're at it, what is Wanderer?" Rohnan chimed in.

Burson laughed up at the sky. "And now we get to the meat of it."

"Lovely." Shanti leaned back and looked to the side at the looming trees dancing in the flickering light.

"The Wanderer is the beginning. Like a prophet, in some cultures. Some might call her a doomsayer, but to many, she is the bringer of hope. In a time of great darkness, comes the shining light. I was one of many to study the coming of this person. I grew up in a small village south of Chesna, Xandre's home town. We were among the first to fall under his rule. For a while he brought prosperity and growth to us, and many others. Wealth and power were granted to many. Our young joined his armies, and our old cheered them on. But he is an excellent manipulator, and soon it became apparent that his goals and interests weren't in our best interest. We were just a means to greater power. When he had that power, and we were no longer useful, he turned his attentions from us. That was when the famine struck. Disease followed. The livelihood of our village crumbled without the brightest and strongest to hold us up. Xandre had taken those away.

"My *Gift*, my real *Gift*, started in full force when Xandre first came speaking of wealth and power. It took a while to realize it, but I could see glimpses of what was to come. Of choices and decisions that should be made in order to bend my path to a predictable future. At the time, I knew not to trust Xandre. Not to join his growing empire. I knew that my duty lay in finding, guiding, and helping the Wanderer. So I went to our old house of records and sorted through everything I could find on the myth of the Wanderer. I'd grown up thinking she was a children's tale about a beautiful young princess who granted wishes to good little girls and boys. But when I found some scrolls, mostly forgotten like many old things, a new shape took form. Of a broken warrior. Of a doubting savior. I made notes, took down all that was relevant, and began to travel the land, finding all the information I could.

"I've met many. A great many. And through my exploits, I've found those who knew about the coming of the Wanderer. I have joined groups of people watching the signs, noticing the unrest, and wondering if I would be the lucky one to guide the Wanderer through the darkness so that she may show us the light. And look—here I am."

"Yes, look. Here you are. So Xandre knows you have the *Seer Gift*, but didn't guard you himself?" Shanti asked.

Burson shook his head. "Oh no, he thinks my *Gift* is restricted to deadening mental power. Very few know of my *Seer* abilities. If they did, I would be hunted like you."

"You are hunted like me."

Burson tilted his head in contemplation. "Quite right. Yes, you are right. Well then, I guess I've landed where I was meant to be."

"Where are you guiding the Wanderer to?" Cayan asked. "What is your plan?"

"My plan unravels as does this journey," Burson answered. "As choices are put before us, I must direct you in the best path. My *Gift* shows me that path as it is presented. I believe this is why I have been chosen to guide."

"And this Wanderer, she…" Shanti let her voice trail.

"Why, she gathers her army." Burson laughed. "Xandre creates enemies by the masses. And like moths, the masses will drift toward the flame. The Wanderer must make her journey across the land to the great sea and beyond. For she will unite them with her suffering, and lead them with her love."

CHAPTER 20

SHANTI GAVE BURSON AN UNBLINKING stare. His smile curled his lips in glee, as if some great present were dropped on his lap. She asked, "So if the Wanderer is supposed to create an army out of the people, what is the Chosen?"

Burson met her stare. "The term Chosen is only a stage in the overall journey. The Wanderer needs to learn the required elements, and accomplish the necessary milestones, to grow into the Chosen. Viewing her as just the Chosen is like viewing a map with just the major routes. It is a distant, general view. Look closer, and you can see all the many roads and paths, the active towns of today, and the ghost towns of the past. The trials will make the Chosen. Don't you see? To get into the trials, you need a certain level of power. But to get *out* of the trials, you will be Chosen."

Shanti shook her head and stared at the fire. Her eyes stung with frustrated, suppressed tears. They'd gone from discussing her obvious demise, because surviving the trials would mean landing into Xandre's hands, to then talking about a list of requirements to become the thing her people thought she was born into. All this knowledge, and Burson hadn't told them a single thing that would help. She would still need to go to the Shadow Lands, and survive to make it back out. After that…

"I think I've got it." Shanti moved to get up. Cayan stood with her and moved to her side immediately. He threaded his fingers through hers, and for once, she welcomed it. "We'll keep on this path and hope for the best."

"We'll fight, we'll win, and we'll find a way home," Cayan said in a fierce voice. He tilted up her chin until she looked into his eyes. "We have power, we have skill, and we have a man who can direct us with a unique *Gift*. You've beaten impossible odds just to be here. You'll keep beating those odds all the way to victory."

"I didn't beat the odds, I nearly succumbed to them; or don't you remember how you met me?" she said softly. Hopelessness washed over her.

"And I was there to pick you up. I will continue to let you do all the hard work, and then pick you up when you are overpowered." He wiped a tear from her cheek as he smiled down at her. "We have a hard journey, but so does Xandre. He just doesn't know it yet."

Shanti couldn't help but smile at the conviction in Cayan's voice, at the soft warmth coming through his touch. She nodded and heaved a sigh. "Well, then." She broke away from the large security blanket and looked at Rohnan. He was waiting with an expectant expression. "Wine?"

"Yes. I'm in terrible mood."

"You're in *a* terrible mood. I swear, I got all the intelligence." Shanti started toward him.

"I think that line only works when two people have same parents."

Shanti laughed. It had been a shitty meeting, added on to a shitty journey, on the way to a shitty future. But at least she had family to cut down the misery of it. It could be worse.

TWO DAYS LATER SHANTI LOOKED at the map wondering why she'd ever thought something so stupid as *it could be worse*. That was just an open invitation for things to get worse. And they had.

Supply carriers had returned to the wooded village with news. The Hunter had gathered a small force near the port city of Clintos. While there were other ports they could leave from to travel to the Shadow Lands, at this time of year the seas were wild, and Clintos was the closest, safest leaving point. Worse still, all travelers and vessels had to be approved before leaving port. Even if Shanti were to sneak by the Graygual keeping guard around the city, the ship would be inspected before leaving.

"But how would they know who we are?" Marc asked as he stood to the side with the Honor Guard and Ruisa. Daniels, Cayan, Burson and Rohnan examined the map with Shanti, trying to plan out the next steps. They planned to head out, and had a route in mind, when the news came of what lay waiting for them. Shanti had assumed the Hunter would try to attack when they left the wood, since there were only a few safe ways out. The Hunter must've known he'd be anticipated.

"That Hunter has seen us," Sanders answered Marc with a surely expression. "He's going to know what we look like."

"You can take us with you—we'd have a bigger army," Tomous said. He stood to one side, watching the discussion. It was no secret that he wanted to go with them, and he wasn't the only one. Knowing that someone was openly challenging the Graygual's rule gave everyone hope, and those who could fight wanted a piece of the action. Shanti understood how they felt—she'd want to go, too. But this wasn't the time for a battle, it was time for sneaking and secrecy. If they got out of the Shadow Lands in one piece, and then passed Xandre, things would be different.

"We've talked about that," Shanti said to Tomous.

Cayan shifted as a warning pulsed from his mind. Rohnan smiled, feeling it—he thought Cayan being possessive was as hilarious as it was absurd. Shanti had to agree, and if she'd been in any sort of mood for company after Burson's talk, she would've ignored Cayan's scowls and joined Tomous for a night or two. Unfortunately, certain death had a way of diminishing her sex drive.

"What about sneaking onto a ship?" Marc asked in a quiet voice.

"Most roads leading into the port are open but he'll have them all covered soon, especially if the rumors about his abilities are true," Yeasmine said as she approached. Her graying hair was tied back in a bun. Shanti could read anxiety and determination in her mind, but her face was completely blank. "You'll need to choose the most open road and force your way into the city."

"No Captain is going to welcome us onto his ship with a line of Graygual chasing behind," Shanti reasoned. "Even if we managed to get in unnoticed, with the ships being checked, we wouldn't make it far. We're going to have to choose another port."

"The other ports won't take someone to the Shadow Lands at this time of year. Not even one of the craziest captains," a ruddy-faced, middle-aged woman said. She was Tara, their chief trader, doing the most traveling, and learning about the goings-on "outside", as they called everything beyond this wood. It was she who brought the news of the Hunter. "Only those who make their money trading brave the seas. Or, lately, those wanting to see the Chosen make it through the trials."

An uncomfortable shiver went up Shanti's back. "Has he entered yet?"

The woman shrugged. "So far, I've heard that three people have gone in directly before him, and none have come out. It seems as though the Chosen sent them first. He's going in soon."

"He sent in his people to die?" Rachie asked. He hunched down and backed up behind Xavier when the Captain glanced his way.

The women grinned. "It's all unknown with the trials, isn't it? The Chosen is going to walk into a place no one has ever survived. Makes a man nervous. So to stall, he sent in a few of his own men to see what would happen. One was moderately powerful, I've heard, but he was the last. He hasn't come out."

"And he's next…" Shanti said in a hoarse voice. She didn't like the sound of entering these trials any more than that Inkna. She wouldn't send someone to die in her place, but she would definitely stall for a while.

"Think so. Heard from a trader just back." The woman took a bite of bread. With a full mouth, she finished with, "Any day."

"If we can fool a captain into taking us, we can get through. The Hunter can't inspect every ship," Marc persisted with a red face. "He's waiting with the army. Burson can disguise minds, so if we get in the town, we can hide S'am—you know, because of her eyes—and then when someone checks us, we're just a bunch of stinky, dirty men on a glory expedition to see the Chosen."

"But we'd still cause a stir with the battle getting into the city," Daniels said. "Disappearing after that would be impossible. The town might be full with tourists, but it isn't that big, and is stuffed with Graygual. Those aren't good odds."

"We can get you in with our trading supplies," Yeasmine said in a steady, clear voice. "And our Captain can take you. He would only have room for fifteen or so with the supplies, but once in the city, the others—the more harmless looking among you—can charter another ship."

Anxiety was starting to eat away at the older woman, Shanti could feel it. Yeasmine held her head high, though, with a straight back. An older man moved beside her and put his hand in hers. "We knew this wood would not be a permanent solution when we came here," he said. "The lands are restless. We do not know of this Wanderer, but news has reached us of a woman who rescued two captives out from under the

Hunter's nose. Word has spread. This violet-eyed woman and her Ghost are our best hope, and we are ready to do our part."

"And I will be your guide," the woman said as she ripped off another piece of bread with her teeth.

"Just lost your job, Burson," Sanders said in his customary growl.

THEY LOST ANOTHER DAY IN order to construct an entirely new plan involving hollow barrels, covered wagons, and items to trade with the Shadow Lands. A select group would lead the larger than normal trading party in through a gate of the port city with some of Tara's network, and directly to the ship where a Captain named Jooston the SeaFarer would take them aboard, deal with the inspection, and set sail.

Jooston was hailed as the best sea captain in the land, facing and beating more storms than anyone out of legend. He was crazy, wild, and hated the Graygual with a passion, though no one had ever heard exactly why. He was the perfect choice.

The plan sounded so easy. So effortless. Unfortunately, in Shanti's experience, nothing ever went to plan.

Shanti sat with Cayan and Sanders, tucked into the back of a cart with wood carvings and a few baskets of fresh, wild roots and vegetables only found within the woods. The cart behind them held five barrels, currently without lids, which would hold four boys and Ruisa when they came to the inspection. Currently, the boys and the girl dressed as a boy were riding, since they could pass for hired guards—extremely cheap hired guards, given their age, which fit Tara's known lack of funds. Xavier would get to ride through the gate, since he was too big to fit into one of the barrels. Rohnan and Burson were in the next cart, chatting about their various studies of the Wanderer versus the Chosen, and there was one more cart at the back holding Tepson, Etherlan and Tobias. Each cart had a tarp over it that made it look more like a flattened wagon, hiding who was inside. This gave the illusion of higher priced goods, which Tara assured them she traveled with no more than twice a year—the spoils of those that ventured through the woods. The backs of the wagons were open for air while there were very few travelers on the road. Daniels also got to ride, as he looked more refined than the others.

The hope was that, even if the Hunter himself was at the gate, he wouldn't see Shanti or her crew to be able to recognize them.

"My legs are falling asleep," Sanders said in his gruff voice as he rocked to one side and straightened a leg. He accidentally kicked Shanti trying to find room to stretch it out, and then again on purpose when she didn't allow him more space.

"You aren't the only one sitting like a child for hours at a time." Shanti moved until he could get his leg straight, then pushed back against it so she wasn't pressed against Cayan's side.

"You're younger, more agile and you're a woman. You bend." Sanders punched his thigh. "Ah! The needles are pricking me!"

"I'm more agile because I stretch." Shanti reached back and wiggled his foot.

Sanders huffed out a laugh. He wiggled his foot. "Better. How far—what's he doing?"

Shanti glanced to the rear as Cayan turned around to see Burson riding up the line of wagons on his horse, a cockeyed smile on his face.

"He's smiling," Sanders growled. "No sense ever comes out of him when he smiles."

"Smartest thing you've said all day," Shanti mumbled.

Burson drew even with the back of their cart and hunched down so he could peer in the back. "Hello."

"Burson, that isn't the best place to be traveling. We're getting close to Clintos," Shanti remarked.

"Yes, yes. I will not be discovered, though. I thought a nice ride through the countryside might clear my head. It was a small risk, but worth it, I think. I did wonder, you see." Burson did his customary glance at the sky that Shanti had come to recognize as either thinking about his Wanderer texts or his *Seeing Gift* in some way.

"Is this where we ask what he wondered?" Sanders drawled. "Because I'd just as soon let him wander around on that horse and talk to himself."

Shanti couldn't help a smirk. "Be good, or we'll put you back with him and Rohnan."

"The mind reader and the madman—hopefully the Captain doesn't hate me that much."

"What did you wonder?" Cayan asked, still looking out at the older man.

"Well," Burson straightened up until Shanti could only see his chest. "It seemed as though the journey was leading to a dead end. This is the reason I needed some air, of course. I could not fathom why the All Mighty would lead us to a closed door. We are on the right journey—I am sure of it. But I could not see how we would not die after the Shadow Lands. I wondered if the next milestone, the most important milestone, wouldn't be reached. Which, currently, seems likely."

"Comforting," Sanders snarled. "Just a ray of damn sunshine."

"You mean passing the trials?" Cayan asked Burson.

"Yes, of course," Burson replied. "So I wanted to ponder that great mystery and see if we weren't missing something."

"And what did you *See*?" Shanti asked, trying to see the man's face.

"Xandre is an exacting man," Burson said in a wispy voice. "Everything must be in his control before he engages. He must know all the pieces and how they work before he makes a move. Shanti taught him this valuable lesson when he was young and new to his self-made position. That had been a big setback for him. It took him a couple years to recover. He is cautious now. And rightly so, with an enemy such as the violet-eyed girl."

"How does this relate to our situation?" Cayan asked.

Shanti could see Burson's elbow move. She bet he'd just ticked the sky with his index finger in that weird way he did. "We will soon introduce a new element. A new, incredibly destructive weapon. One that Xandre does not know how to combat, does not even know exists. He will be set back, again. Hit in the blindside, once again. And he will have something new to covet—one that he has not studied—one that will inspire fear in Xandre. The unknown makes him wary."

"Your *Gift*," Shanti said, meeting Cayan's eyes.

"But when does he see it?" Cayan asked. Wariness crept into his gaze.

Shanti shook her head slowly and looked out at

Burson again. "Are we about to run into trouble, Burson? Is that why you couldn't wait to tell us this?"

"What are you doing outside the cart?" Tara's voice boomed down the line. "We're in sight of the gates, you fool. Get inside! Boys, get into your barrels. Everyone close up your tarps."

"Great timing, as ever," Sanders said as Burson fell back. "Deliver a message like that, leave us hanging, and then drift away. That guy never fails to amaze me."

"The question is, if we *do* run into trouble, do I show my *Gift* now, or try to wait until after the trials?" Cayan asked softly. "When is the right time?"

Shanti shook her head again in response. She didn't know, but she had a feeling that answer would be crucial.

CHAPTER 21

WITH THEIR TARP CLOSED AND their *Gifts* shielded, Shanti and Cayan could do nothing but listen to the clomping of hooves and the creak of the cart as they made their way along the road. Tara made outbursts and inspired raucous laughter from the few up front with her, one of which was Tomous. It sounded completely natural. Tara hadn't had the chance to prove it, but she seemed tranquil under pressure. She was a lucky find.

"What's all this?" Tara asked in suspicion, using the common trader language as Shanti's cart slowed.

Shanti looked at Cayan, who had a throwing knife in his hand. Sanders held a dagger over his knees, staring straight ahead without expression. These men were ready.

"Inspection," came a gruff voice.

"Since when?" Tara asked in outrage. Leather groaned before the soft thud of boots hit the dirt. "I was here not two weeks ago. I got a buyer."

"Listen, doll, this ain't a tax or a shakedown. See

them guys in the black shirts? Yeah, them's Graygual and Inkna. Just looking for passengers."

"Passengers?" Tara started laughing. "Well, have your look. But don't you be getting sticky fingers pawing through my stuff. And don't get the rugs dirty, neither!"

"Lady, where do you hail from?" came a cultured voice sounding completely out of place with the language. Obviously an officer of some sort.

"Tomous, follow that beady-eyed sod, will ya? I don't trust him with my stuff," Tara's voice boomed. "I come from all over. I'm a trader for hire. Or haven't you heard of that?"

"Enlighten me," came the cultured voice, a little closer.

"Be glad to. Lately, folks have been a bit under the heel. Seems a bunch of dirty low-lives have come through and turned small towns upside down. Folks are afraid to leave their homes. They're afraid to travel the roads, and it *ain't* because of thieves, neither. They're afraid of organized army-types..."

Sanders gently shifted forward and lightly shook his head. He was probably worried about the thinly veiled contempt in Tara's voice. He probably thought she would push the Graygual into action. And if it had been one of the low-lives in question she would have. But she knew what she was doing—she knew the sort of man that had stopped her. Officers thought the tactics and heavy-handedness of the lower ranks were disgusting. An officer might take a beauty from a town and force her to be his concubine, but she would be treated well in her new life. The officers thought any woman should be proud to bear his children, and as such, didn't think of it as forcing. To them, that was different to taking a woman in the streets against her will. Tara was playing the part of disgruntled trader perfectly. She was making money off the Graygual tactics in this lie, but she didn't much like why. Shanti nearly laughed.

A shadow fell over the tarp right before the fabric rustled. A wad of material shook before being pulled back. A ruddy face appeared with blue sky behind him. Cayan held up his knife to throw as Sanders leaned forward, ready to launch himself over Shanti and at the man. The man's eyes widened slightly, but he made the motions of peering through the cart, anyway. When he was done, he tugged the tarp closed again. They heard, "Vegetables and bread. A couple days from going off."

"It's food, ain't it?" Tara yelled defensively. "It'll keep people from going hungry."

The man grunted as he moved away. The shadow of Tomous moved away behind him. Sanders settled back. Cayan lowered his knife.

They waited another ten minutes before the same cultured voice said, "That bodyguard's a little young, isn't he?"

"Young and handsome, just like I like 'em. He can go for hours." Tara laughed.

"And cheap," the gruff man called from down the line.

"Well, hell. Do I look like I'm swimming in gold coins?" Tara shot back.

"I should report you for trying to sell poisoned goods," the gruff man said as his voice neared. Footsteps passed their cart. "That wine smells rancid."

"Hey, I don't produce it, I just sell it. If people want it, then they want it."

"Whatever," the gruff man replied.

"Move on," the officer called.

"Waste of time," Tara grumbled. They heard the leather of her saddle creak. "I'd have fresher goods if I didn't have to worry about stuff like this."

"Ten minutes ain't going to make a whole pile of difference with them goods," the gruff man said.

The cart groaned as the procession started moving. "Just stick to what you're good at—standing there like a lump," Tara badgered.

Shanti allowed a soft sigh to escape her lips. She let go of her knife and wiped her sweaty palm on her pants.

"Wait," called the cultured voice. The breath caught in Shanti's throat as the officer followed up with, "Stop! Let me see that horse."

"That horse is going for market," Tara said as the progression ground to a halt again. Shanti picked up her knife.

"Where did you get that horse?" the officer asked.

"Which one? That black one?" Tara was referring to Cayan's horse. "Why, you want to buy it? Beauty, ain't he? I'll give ya a good price."

"No. The brown stallion. You, son, bring that horse here."

Shanti squeezed her eyes shut. *Please be a normal horse, you bloody bastard. Please be timid.*

"I haven't seen the equal to Shanti's horse," Sanders said in a low whisper. "Hell, any of those Graygual horses. Cayan's comes close, I'd recognize the blood line of Cayan's horse if one just showed up out of the blue."

Cayan nodded. It was a finely bred animal, and his city had bought it from the Duke to secure the blood lines. It made sense that people who knew horses would recognize finely bred animals. Unfortunately, this officer was one such man. Just their luck.

"Bring him here, I said," the officer called again.

"I'm trying, but he's..." that strange horse-growl cut Xavier off. Sanders and Cayan both looked at Shanti.

"Get ready. Everyone who meets that horse remembers him," Shanti uttered in defeat.

The horse whinnied. Hooves stomped. Xavier let out a sound of surprise before the officer yelled, "Grab that horse! Grab those horses!"

Another whinny followed in front of them. The cart started rocking and shaking. It jerked forward and then back, as if the more timid horses pulling it were rearing.

"I can't use my power!" someone shouted.

"Apprehend them!" the officer yelled.

"That's our cue!" Sanders jabbed the tarp with his sword and slashed. Cayan punched through the back and spilled out onto the dirt as Sanders leapt out over the side. Shanti followed Cayan as the muffle on her *Gift* disappeared. The cart jerked forward as she jumped. Cayan caught her arm and steadied her, giving her one moment to take in the scene.

Her horse and the other two stolen Graygual horses were galloping at the guards' horses. Shanti's horse got there first and reared, battering the other horses with its hooves. His fellow warhorses were just as wild, biting and bucking and kicking, following the Bloody Bastard's lead. Shanti didn't have time to marvel. The Graygual were on their feet with swords drawn, running at Tara and Tomous.

"Tara, Tomous, run ahead and warn the ship's captain that we're coming," Cayan ordered.

"Do we kill these men, sir?" Sanders asked as he dove onto a running officer. His compact body of muscle knocked the taller but lankier man to the dirt. Sanders kicked away the officer's sword and rolled him over amid a cloud of dust.

Cayan glanced at Shanti.

"Kill them quickly, we must flee!" came Burson's voice. He was running toward Shanti. "Unhook the horses from the carts. We must take those."

Tara took off at a gallop as an arrow sailed past her back.

"Daniels!" Cayan yelled. He pointed to two archers. Daniels was already on it. He loosed an arrow. The shaft dug into the middle of a black-clad chest. Another arrow stuck into the neck of the Graygual beside him. Xavier had reacted as well.

Sanders pulled his knife across the neck of the Graygual before snatching the man's sword and hopping up. Cayan ran forward, sword out, as a Graygual approached Sanders' back. Cayan slashed down and opened a red gash along the man's arm. The Graygual spun, without surprise or pain in his expression. He didn't have time to raise his sword before Cayan stabbed him through the chest then yanked out his blade. In a single motion he chopped at the man's wrist. The Graygual's hand and sword dropped onto the road.

Sanders snatched that sword too as he started running toward his horse. Rohnan unhooked the mounts from Shanti's cart before running to his own animal. Reaching it, he jumped on. His staff spun as he kicked the horse into action, chasing two Graygual on foot who were trying to get to the loose horses of the Honor Guard. The boys were still spilling out of their cart amid rolling barrels.

"Do I use my *Gift*, Burson?" Shanti yelled as she ran toward a tame horse newly freed from the cart. Before she reached it, her horse thundered up and stopped at her side. Without another thought, she jumped up onto her animal—he was wild and unruly, but he was hers.

"No! No powers," Burson barked. He looked behind him wildly. "Not yet. Hurry! We must go!"

Cayan swung his leg over the back of his horse as the boys mounted theirs. Rohnan turned his animal toward the front of the progression. The ends of his staff dripped crimson.

The sound of steel rang out. Etherlan feinted and blocked a Graygual's downward swing. Before he could counter, the Graygual arched back. Blood gurgled out of his mouth as Tobias pulled his sword from the man's back.

"Let's go!" Cayan called, urging his shining, black horse forward.

"Where to, Burson?" Shanti asked.

"We need to reach the ship before the Graygual," Burson said, coaxing his horse into a rapid stride. "When I cut off the Inkna, I felt others reach this direction. They are monitoring each other. They know we are here."

Everyone pulled their horses together, and as one urged the animals faster and faster until they were galloping toward the bustling city. The remaining traders stayed behind to deal with the carts.

The weeds and wildflowers on the sides of the road gave way to small houses and tended bushes. Structures closed in on them and people started to litter the streets. Shops and fish markets crouched beside the road as they neared the city center.

“Keep going!” Burson yelled.

The horses clattered through the streets. People scurried or dived out of the way, shocked and shaken, yelling at their backs. Burson did not slow and neither did anyone else. They wound through the streets and forced through crowds. Burson had clearly been to the city before and knew his way. Or maybe his *Gift* was leading.

The shops came to an end and turned into stalls run by traders or fishermen’s wives. A wide expanse of blue opened up before them. The sun glittered on the stretch of sea leading to forever. Masts rose, tall and stark, in the sleepy harbor. A ship was making its way out of the sheltered harbor toward the wide open sea.

The lane led down to the docks. Traders and fisherman moved to and from ships.

“There!” Marc pointed at a large, weather-beaten ship at the beginning of the docks. Tomous stood in front, staring in their direction. Tara was already on the ship gesturing wildly to a skinny man wearing dirty overalls over a splotched brown shirt with the legs rolled up to his calves. His feet were bare, as were those of his crew running around him.

"Captain!" Alarm colored Tobias' voice.

Shanti glanced at Tobias and saw that coming down a parallel lane ran twenty horses carrying Graygual and a few Inkna. Hooves behind them had everyone turning in their saddles to see another group running directly behind them. The Hunter's men were closing in.

"We're too late!" someone yelled. It sounded like Tepson. "We'll never make it!"

CHAPTER 22

"NEVER TOO LATE TO KILL the enemy!" Sanders yelled as he urged his horse faster.

Shanti and Cayan led the pack, galloping down the slope to the harbor. People looked up at the thunder of hooves converging on the muddy beach before the docks. Many started running to one side or the other, as metal glinted in the late afternoon sun when fighters drew swords and prepared to fight. Rising above the clamor rang a few distinct words, "Take the girl and the old man alive. Kill the others."

It wasn't a battle call. There was no cry of testosterone-filled men rising up to lead their Captain to victory. These were simply instructions. These men were bred to fight and kill. That is all they knew.

A cold trickle of fear dribbled down Shanti's spine. Not for herself; battle ran in her blood. She was hot with it. Ready to take up her sword and defend what was hers—her life and her freedom. But the men around her weren't born in the fires of the underworld. Their lives weren't shaped by the threat of annihilation. They weren't prepared for what Xandre had to throw at them.

"Settle me right at the mouth of the docks, Cayan," Shanti yelled above the din as the gravel and dirt path turned into trodden grasses and mud. "Make them funnel down the slope to Rohnan and me. I need Burson behind me to keep the Inkna powerless, but otherwise, get your people onto that ship."

"No way, Captain!" Sanders yelled. "I'm in this fight. There is no way a woman is saving me again. It's not natural!"

"The best of us will be at the tip of the funnel," Cayan said in a voice that brooked no argument. "Everyone else will get the ship ready to depart."

"We're outnumbered. We can't take them all," Daniels called as they came upon the now-cleared beach. All activity had stopped. Those who didn't get down the docks and away in time hunkered on their boats or the boats of those they knew, trying to hide or stay out of the way of the Graygual they must've recognized, and those running before them.

"Right or wrong, it's time they felt your *Gift*, Cayan," Shanti said as she pulled her horse to a trot and then jumped off. She staggered to a stop, and then turned back and slapped the animal. It whinnied at her, bobbing its head.

"Get gone—you'll just be in the way and then killed!" Shanti yelled. She gave its mind a *wrench*. It growled, but relented, galloping after the other horses down the beach.

The Honor Guard ran to Shanti. Pale and panting, they held their swords and awaited instructions. Even Marc had a shine to his eyes, terrified though he was. He'd fight and die right beside her if she said the words.

And he would die, along with all the other boys.

"Go get that ship ready," Shanti barked, shoving Marc onto the dock. "This is no place for you."

"I can help!" Xavier said in a fierce growl.

"Yes, you can." Shanti punched him in the gut and then shoved him, wheezing, after Marc. "Get the ship ready. If I survive this, we'll need to make a hasty getaway."

"You'll survive, S'am!" Leilius said with utter conviction as he ran onto the docks. "See you in a while."

"We *will* survive," Cayan said in a low tone. He stood next to her, facing the charging horses with a solid frame and flexed muscles. His blue eyes shone with the fierce light of confidence and victory. His *Gift* surged up and wrapped around him before connecting with hers and igniting the power running through her blood.

"Fuck yes, we will!" Sanders growled. He stood with his legs bent. A sword adorned his right hand, a knife clutched in the other.

Etherlan and Tepson waited behind him. Tobias

was up on the dock with his bow out.

Rohnan stepped up beside Shanti with his staff at his side. His green eyes were clear and his face tranquil. He looked over at her and winked. "Today, we kill Graygual."

"Today, we avenge our people," she responded. Her adrenaline spiked. Her blood surged. "Today, we do our people proud."

Shanti turned her face slowly to watch the incoming horses. The Graygual would try to run them down, to stampede over the fighters stupid enough to get off their horses.

"Oh Hunter, how you do underestimate my ability." Shanti grabbed the first line of horses' minds and *twisted*. The animals screamed, eyes rolled. Most bucked, punching the sky with their hooves.

Men held on as the horses behind them rammed into those pulled up short. Two horses fell. Men tumbled off as horses crashed down into the mud. One head burst like a melon as a hoof landed on his temple with incredible force. The other screamed as a horse landed in the center of his back, breaking his spine.

More men fell as Shanti increased the power. "They are well-trained animals," she said as more equine screams pierced the day."

Chaos covered the slope as animals baulked and ran. Men fell or hastily clambered off, hitting the ground with two feet and scrambling to get out of the way of the wild, maddened horses.

"Prepare," Cayan commanded.

Thumping sounded behind them. Tomous jumped into the defense, sword drawn, eyebrows low over his eyes. Tara stopped right next to Tobias, an arrow nocked and ready.

"Loose!" Cayan ordered.

The sound of bowstrings sang. Two men fell, but the tide of black was running down the slope, swords out, faces a blank mask. Cold-blooded killers would meet hot-blooded vengeance.

Shanti stepped forward with her sword drawn. She sought out the minds of the Inkna, tugging on Cayan's power and feeling his *Gift's* strength fortifying her own. She found those soft and vulnerable minds, useless in the face of Burson's *Gift*, which was powerful enough to reach from the ship where he stood and watched. With one surge of power, she wasted no time and *stabbed* into their meaty brains. The Inkna barely had time to scream before their minds turned blank.

The Hunter hadn't brought enough. He had planned for Shanti, alone. Thank the Elders they had kept Cayan's *Gift* a secret.

Shanti found the intelligent and cunning mind of the Hunter, standing way behind his thrust of men, before a wave of black descended upon her. A sword slashed toward her middle, the stroke expert and precise. She blocked, shifted her weight, and struck. Her blade slid between his ribs. She pulled it back and turned her body to the side as shining metal cut down. The blade barely missed her arm. She kicked to the left, catching a man that was running toward Cayan in the solar plexus before twisting to get her sword into the guts of the man in front of her. She used his body as a shield against the next while snatching a knife out of her leg strap, tossing it up, and throwing. The business end blossomed red in the neck of a man running for the docks.

"*Chosen, incoming!*"

Shanti glanced up and saw a large but agile man preparing a sword strike to her right. Rohnan twirled away to another attack, throwing a knife to catch someone trying to run by. Shanti grabbed another knife, stepped within his arm's reach, rendering his sword stroke ineffective, and stabbing him in the eye. She jabbed his inner elbow to render his sword arm useless as he died, and then plunged her knife into an enemy neck before pivoting and throwing at someone running at Etherlan.

"We don't have much more time," Shanti yelled at Cayan. "And our combined power won't kill all these. They're too spread out and far away. You need to access that sub-level of power!"

"I don't know how!"

"You must!" Rohnan yelled as a throwing knife skimmed off his arm, ripping through fabric and opening up a gash. "Or we will all die!"

MARC STOOD ON THE DECK of the ship with his heart in his mouth. Most of the others had been given jobs to speed up their getaway. Even though it would make the Captain of this ship a marked man for life, he still planned to take them across the sea, but Marc had been too panicked, and shaking too badly, to help. He gripped the worn wood railing beside Burson as he watched the battle.

"Why don't they use their power?" he asked desperately.

"Shanti is a master at her craft, but she is not the almighty," Burson said in a strangely solemn voice. "She must work with Cayan to access his awesome power. It all depends upon this battle. We will live or die depending on him allowing her the access she needs."

"Why wouldn't he?" Marc asked in a whining voice.

"It takes great courage to expose our vulnerability to another, especially if our whole existence has been based on confidence. Not many would let down their guard within a battle setting—or at all. That kind of trust is a slow-built thing. It cannot be rushed, and this is the worst time to call upon it. Two guarded individuals must rely on opening themselves to the other after no time at all. It is an almost impossible feat."

"God, you talk too much," Marc said as he bounced from foot to foot. He wanted to help. He wanted to grab his sword and run down the docks and launch himself at the enemy. Because S'am and everyone needed it. The enemy was swarming them all. There was just too many of them.

"Why did S'am bring us?" Marc begged. "They should've brought someone who could help."

"You will play an important part, yet."

"I think you got the wrong set of guys," Marc said as Xavier came jogging up to the banister.

"Holy—I've never seen the Captain really fight. He's… holy shit," Xavier breathed.

Marc took his eyes off S'am's liquid, graceful, yet extremely deadly movements and looked to the large man next to her. Marc's eyes widened. The Captain was strength and power, but he moved with such synchronicity it made the mind boggle.

Marc watched as the Captain blocked a sword strike with an almost lazy movement. He spun with unnatural speed and stabbed down through the shoulder of an enemy. He kicked the knee of an oncoming attacker, bending the joint backwards before shifting his balance and slashing down for the kill strike. And he was on to the next. And the next. The man was fast, and lethal, but also elegant in his fighting, such that it was art.

"I won't ever be that good," Xavier said in a hush.

"Not many could," Burson said. Marc could hear panic creeping into the older man's voice. "He is one of a kind. But it won't be enough. There are still too many."

The tide of black pushed the few back toward the docks. Tobias ran out of arrows and took out his sword to join the fray. He was immediately met with two of the enemy.

Marc reached for his sword. He'd be damned if he just stood by while they died.

"C'mon, Xavier—we're not as good, but we're better than nothing." Marc trotted to the side of the ship where the ropes were pulled away and the deck hands waited for the command to embark.

"Wait for me!" Marc heard. Sounded like Rachie.

A sword swiped toward the Captain's head as Marc ran down the dock. Marc screamed, but the Captain had ducked just in time, stabbing his sword into his opponent. Two more took the dead man's place. And up on the slope, sitting on a perfect specimen of a horse, sat the Hunter, looking down on the battle. Marc couldn't make out his features, but he knew that disgusting man had no expression at all. He was watching and waiting for his time to strike and claim his prize.

"Hurry!" Marc shouted. His feet pounded the dock.

Xavier was right behind him. More feet sounded on wood.

They'd be too late. The Captain and everyone were at the water's edge, right in front of the dock, trying to keep people off. Trying to keep Marc and everyone safe.

"No!" Marc cried as a sword glanced off S'am's leg. She staggered, righted herself, and then tripped on a lifeless body at her feet. She fell into the Captain, who stabbed his sword through someone's gut and turned to catch her before she fell into the mud. Black shirts descended on them.

CHAPTER 23

"RUN, CAYAN. GO KILL THE Inkna-Chosen. It's me they want," Shanti said through gritted teeth as Cayan grabbed her.

He looked up with terrified eyes as a sword arched through the air, right for her back. She didn't even have time to scream. She looked up into the handsome face of the Captain and leader of the Westwood Lands, preferring those crystal blue eyes as her last image over the disgusting visage of Graygual scum. But the killing blow never came.

"Given up, Shoo-lan?" Sanders growled as he stabbed a Graygual with four slashes across his breast. "One more and we're even."

Shanti straightened up and tried to turn, to get back to the battle they were losing, but Cayan held her fast. He stared down into her face as his men rushed by him to keep the Graygual back.

"What are you doing, Cayan?" Shanti demanded, trying to break free.

"We have to use the *Gift*!" he said, his gaze delving

into hers. His hands clutched her shoulders. His face hovered inches away.

"I've been trying! I can't get at that power. And I can't concentrate long enough to get at the Hunter. Let me go!"

"We need to do whatever we can."

"I can't kill this many, Cayan!" Shanti screamed. "If I try, I'll only kill a couple while just hurting the others, and deplete myself and you in the process. Then the boys won't even be able to get away. We have to hold out so the others have a—" Shanti looked up at the movement on the dock. Her heart sank. Marc was sprinting toward them with a terrified but determined expression, holding a sword. Xavier was right behind with Rachie and Gracas behind him. Leilius was not last—Ruisa was, though she knew so little about fighting.

"No," Shanti said in a defeated sigh.

"Now, *mesasha*! Access my power *now*!" Cayan yelled, shaking her.

Desperate, horrified, Shanti looked up into Cayan's eyes. Pleading. Knowing she was the reason everyone would die. She would not only be killing Cayan and his men, but boys who weren't even men yet. Boys she'd deserted and who now couldn't fight well enough to save their lives.

Cayan grabbed her face with surprisingly delicate

hands as someone screamed—it sounded like Jaime. Cayan's gaze locked with hers. "I'm ready."

She focused on those eyes. She clutched his chest. Taking a deep breath and letting the world around her haze, knowing she had to lose the world for a moment as the only way to save those boys' lives, she let her mind merge tighter with Cayan's. His emotions, anxiety, fear, determination, tenderness, flew by her in a flash. She sank into him, to that intimate place, and let herself open to him in turn.

His power rushed into her as hers sank into his. Their power rolled and boiled, mated and now flowered. Brewing then surging. Brewing. Surging.

The spice turned to heat, but this time, not arousal. This time, her rage fueled the fire. Her vengeance. And most of all, the deep, aching sorrow that made up the very base of her being: her loss, her memories, and the people she loved that she hoped to see again.

All this she offered up to Cayan while trying to sink toward that well within him. To access the recesses he didn't share with others, holding his own loss, and his insecurity. His own sorrow, and the aching loneliness. Their moment of sharing created a level, even, balance of their mated powers.

Shanti ripped off the cover to the deep vat of power within Cayan.

Power gushed through his body, filling him up then

immediately spilling over into her. It raged through them, blistering in its heat and power. It moved along the newly balanced plateau they had created and then crouched, waiting to be directed and released.

Shanti sheathed her sword, slipped her hand into Cayan's so that contact reminded her to keep this balance lest that power tip and crush one of them, before turning to the battle. Etherlan limped. Blood dripped down his right arm. But still he fought, using his left. Sanders was growling and grappling, head butting, biting, stabbing and jabbing his fingers in eyes, anything he could to get his opponent down. The boys were slower, cumbersome and jerky in their movements, but they fought with everything they had, barely escaping blows and jabs by pure luck in some cases.

No time to lose, barely seeing the others fighting people away, Shanti felt with her *Gift* for the Hunter. Such a weak, feeble bit of power she possessed in comparison to what she was holding at bay with her and Cayan's strange but intimate truce. She almost laughed with the paltry quality of it, high on power as she was.

She found him, coming closer. Dead center to her position, though she couldn't tell how far away. Not with the seething, foaming power lapping at her senses.

She turned toward the ship and met eyes with Burson, standing barely ten paces behind her. With a voice she barely recognized within a body blistering with power, she said, "Protect our own."

A smile lit up his face as he looked toward the sky. She felt the minds of the boys, and then the rest of them, wink out. And then, thinking of her lost, hoping for a union with the few, she squeezed Cayan's hand. Together, they *RELEASED*.

A bone-shaking rumble filled her ears as a torrent of power rolled from her and Cayan's bodies. Like a tsunami, it first swelled, and then surged before them, crushing minds with a subsonic might so intense, the Graygual faces screwed up in fear and pain as they dropped their swords and clutched at their hearts. One by one they fell, gasping and panting, clawing at their chest.

"Go!" Cayan yelled at his men while still holding her hand. "Get to the ship."

"What about you?" Sanders asked as he bent to a man on the ground with blood down the side of his face and staring eyes. Jaime.

Shanti felt a pang of sadness well up. She hadn't been in time. She hadn't saved him. She hadn't saved them all.

"We're right behind you," she heard Cayan say.

The last of the power streamed from her and Cayan's bodies. Still more Graygual bodies fell as the roar tore through the battlefield.

"C'mon, *mesasha*. We have to go," Cayan said in a

soft voice.

"Let's go, Chosen. We have to go," repeated Rohnan's urging.

Shanti turned on wooden feet, the picture of Jaime replaced with that of Romie. Then the crowded landscape of her memory filled with blood and screaming—images from when she was a child, to those a year or so ago, to right now.

Would it never end? Would death by her hand of those she loved ever end?

"Now is not the time, Chosen. We will mourn later," Rohnan said in a hard voice. *"We must go, Chosen. You did not get them all."*

Shanti blinked past the memories clamoring for her attention and forced her mind into the present. She pushed away the sorrow for Jaime and focused instead on the thanks that the others had made it.

Still holding Cayan's hand, she turned with him and ran up the docks, skirting by Daniels who was active with his bow. Their feet thumped off the wood planks as they made it to the ship. She jumped the small gap between the ship and the dock and jogged to the edge.

The battlefield was littered with bodies in black. Those in the front were not moving at all. Those toward the back, way up the slope, flopped back and forth, in obvious pain, but not dead.

One man pushed himself to his knees. His head

hung for a moment. Even from the distance, Shanti could see his body moving as if he struggled with breath. His head lifted. His face pointed in their direction.

The Hunter.

She knew without being able to see that it was him.

The salt sea air bathed Shanti's face as she stared at the man. She made a promise of his death as surely as he made a promise of her capture. She'd beaten him again. Escaped yet again. He would not take that lightly.

She turned away and looked out over the ocean. The ship was drifting into the harbor as the sails lowered. The calm breeze licked her sweat-stained face and for a brief moment, she was reminded of home, of setting out on their old and creaky fishing boat, looking up at the sky and letting the sun warm her face.

"That was close," Rohnan said as he walked up beside her. Fatigue dragged at his movements.

"Yes, too close, but...that's always been our life."

"Yes."

"Do you think we will see them again, Rohnan?" Shanti asked with a voice half-pleading, and half-hopeful. *"The ones we saved?"*

He sighed as he stared out over the water. *"I hope so, Chosen. I hope so."*

THEY GAVE JAIME A SEA burial, offering his body and soul to the Gods of the Sea. To the ship's crew, who believed in the Gods of the Sea, he was going home. To Shanti and Rohnan, he died an honorable death in battle, and they said a blessing to speed his journey up to the Elders for their care.

The coming week or so would be harsh, fraught with storms, raging seas, and seasickness for those born landlocked. For Shanti and Rohnan, it would bring nightmares and constant fear. Their entire journey had always been to get to the Shadow Lands and secure the help of their distant kin. They'd beaten impossible odds already, getting farther than either thought they would, and all their toil would soon be put to the test. Burson had a plethora of choices ahead of them, but no answers. It was too early to tell.

AS THE VESSEL SPED ACROSS the waters, only a few days into the journey, Shanti stood at the rail, looking out into the stinging, salty air. Cayan's presence moved to her side before leaning on the railing and looking out with her.

"How are the men?" she asked, not bothering to look away from the horizon.

"Most have gotten used to the sway, but Leilius and Xavier are still throwing up. Sanders checks on them often, losing his lunch every time he does."

"They'll get used to it."

Cayan's shoulder brushed Shanti's, sending sparks of electricity into her body.

They'd gotten extremely intimate within a few heartbeats. She'd already known plenty of his secrets from their first mind-share, but now he knew the vulnerabilities she never shared. Delving so deeply into each other, even with a battle raging around them, was like a window into the most secret of places. Now he knew that she wanted to be a mother someday. Most embarrassing of all, he knew that she desperately missed the quiet moments by a fire in her lover's arms, watching the stars.

It hurt, admitting to those things. Only a fool would assume she could finish her duty alive, which meant she could never live the normal life she had always wanted. She feared seeing the pity in the eyes of others, knowing that her lot in life was death and sorrow, and not much else.

Like the gentleman he was, though, he hadn't said a word about it. He'd made one quick reference to their need to train, but other than that, he hadn't mentioned the new knowledge.

She sighed as he shared the quiet moment staring ahead at their probable death, way across the open waters. They had another handful of days before they'd see land.

"Has Burson mentioned anything to you about what we can expect?" Cayan asked.

"No. He hasn't smiled much, either, which means his *Gift* is silent. It's a sad day when you wish Burson would start smiling like a madman again."

Cayan huffed out a laugh. "It is, at that. And if the Inkna-Chosen is in the trials, do you plan to go in?"

"I have to." Goosebumps spread across Shanti's skin. "There is no other option."

"And you have to go alone?"

"Yes."

Cayan hung his head. "I feel like we're headed right into Hell, and there isn't a thing I can do to prevent it. In my gut I know we shouldn't separate. I *know* it, Shanti. There's a reason I need you to access the well of power, just as there's a reason you appeared on my doorstep. Our feet are being guided toward one another. It doesn't make sense to separate at the most perilous moment."

Shanti straightened and threw up her hands. They'd only been at sea a few days, and already they'd had this argument half a dozen times. "Cayan, I don't know what to tell you. If I'm the Chosen, I'll see you at the end. If I'm not, well…"

Cayan straightened up, too, stubbornness lining his face. "Not good enough."

"What do you want me to do? Beg them to change the rules?"

"Not beg, demand."

Shanti rolled her eyes. "You are the leader of a small nation, Cayan. Your desires mean nothing to the Shadow People. This is how it's done. When we arrive, I'll go into the trials, and you will secure the surrounding area. If I make it out, I'll be relying on you to have everything safe within the city. Burson agrees. Daniels agrees. Rohnan, who has been assigned the duty of protecting me from childhood, agrees. Why can't you get this through your thick head?"

Cayan stared down at her for one tense beat, his eyes on fire, his body looming over hers. The muscles in his arms flexed. Judging by the rage and desire both pulsing through his mind, he was fighting an impulse to both throw her overboard, and kiss her. It seemed he hadn't yet decided which action he'd rather choose.

"Act on *either* of your thoughts, Cayan, and one of us is going swimming. I've survived stormy waters. Have you?"

His blue eyes flashed. With a rush of movement, he turned and stalked away.

Shanti let out the breath she didn't know she was holding and sagged against the ship. She turned her gaze back toward the sea. If she could, she'd take them all with her. She did not want to walk into those trials alone. But what choice did she have? This was her duty. She could not back out now.

Made in the USA
Middletown, DE
26 September 2021